The Bridge of Beyond

SIMONE SCHWARZ-BART

Translated from the French by Barbara Bray

Introduction by Bridget Jones
University of the West Indies

HEINEMANN

Heinemann International Literature and Textbooks
a division of Heinemann Educational Books Ltd
Halley Court, Jordan Hill, Oxford OX2 8EJ

Heinemann Educational Books Inc
361 Hanover Street, Portsmouth, New Hampshire, 03801, USA

Heinemann Educational Books (Nigeria) Ltd
PMB 5205, Ibadan
Heinemann Kenya Ltd
Kijabe Street, PO Box 45314, Nairobi
Heinemann Educational Boleswa
PO Box 10103, Village Post Office, Gaborone, Botswana

LONDON   EDINBURGH   MELBOURNE   SYDNEY
AUCKLAND   SINGAPORE   MADRID   PARIS
HARARE   ATHENS   BOLOGNA   TOKYO

British Library Cataloguing in Publication Data

Schwarz-Bart, Simone
  The Bridge of Beyond.—(Caribbean writers
  series; 27)
  I. Title   II. Pluie et vent sur Télumée miracle.
  English   III Series
  843[F]   PQ2679.C43

ISBN 0–435–98770–4

Set in 10pt Garamond
Printed in Great Britain by
Cox & Wyman Ltd, Reading, Berkshire

92 93 94 95 10 9 8 7 6 5

FOR YOU

Belle sans terre ferme
Sans parquet sans souliers sans draps
PAUL ÉLUARD, *Les Yeux fertiles*

Beautiful without solid earth
Without floor without shoes without sheets

Introduction

Aimé Césaire pledged himself to the unheard people of his native land, Martinique, vowing that he would be the voice for 'the sufferings that have no mouth'.[1] This is a generous ideal shared by many Caribbean writers, but none finds it simple to put into practice. The writer is separated by education from people who belong to an oral culture in Creole, and whose view of the world has been cramped by poverty or illiteracy and bounded by mountain walls or island shores. This is why so many novels trace how a child loses a first, innocent vision of Caribbean experience in order to become conscious of it in terms of a metropolitan language and view of life. Joseph Zobel's *Black Shack Alley* (CWS 21) is an obvious example. However, to build bridges of understanding with the humblest and most deprived people in a society is a vital function for the writer.

In *The Bridge of Beyond* Simone Schwarz-Bart has responded to this challenge. She takes a character who could merely be seen and taken for granted, an old woman offering peanuts for sale by a country church. Her novel makes that woman exist for us as a unique and irreplaceable person. For a writer who is herself highly sophisticated and much travelled, it is an achievement to have thought herself into the experience of an old peasant woman who has spent her life in a remote district of Guadeloupe, and to have found a style in which to tell the story from inside, as a first-person narrative. In Caribbean fiction we so often hear the voices of the emancipated young men, exiles and intellectuals. It has taken a woman author to give a hearing to the voice of the mothers and grandmothers.

The Bridge of Beyond is the title given to the English edition of a novel which first appeared in French in 1972 as *Pluie et vent sur Télumée Miracle*. A more literal translation would read: 'Rain and Wind on Miracle-Woman Télumée'. This identifies the book clearly as a tribute to an exceptional woman who withstands the adverse elements. It is useful to see the novel's origin in this way, as a positive act of paying homage. It commemorates Fanotte, a real person from Goyave, Simone Schwarz-Bart's village in Guadeloupe, who died in 1968. In such circumstances we expect an affectionately nostalgic portrait and a concern to bring out the positive values of the past. The attitudes and situations also reflect the earlier part of this century, not contemporary ideological debates.

Ideas

Simone Schwarz-Bart has chosen very deliberately to focus on what is distinctive about a woman's experience. It is altogether appropriate that France's most important magazine for women, *Elle*, should have awarded this book its literary prize. The heroine belongs to a dynasty of Lougandor women (family relationships have been clarified by an outline genealogical table, p.vi). From Minerva, her great-grandmother, freed from slavery (abolition finally came in 1848 for the French colonies), down to her adopted daughter, Sonore, we have a span of five generations of women harshly dealt with by life. Yet their sufferings only strengthen them, and their abundant faith in life is never lost. Even the best of their menfolk seem vulnerable in comparison, and most prove downright inadequate. In an accurate reflection of the sociology of the West Indian family, Schwarz-Bart shows fathers too often proving temporary, and failing in their role as providers and guides. It is the mothers, and in many cases the grandmothers, who are the mainstay of the family unit. The essential idea of *The Bridge of Beyond* is contained in the relationship between Telumee and her grandmother Toussine, whose skills and moral values she inherits in a triumphant example of continuity.

The English title, *The Bridge of Beyond*, emphasizes a significant aspect of Schwarz-Bart's image of woman, that is as a link with the unseen world and source of spiritual values.[2] Telumee is led across the bridge, symbolising a first stage towards inheriting Toussine's powers. The last stage occurs when she in turn goes to live with Ma Cia, Toussine's old friend, who is not only skilled in healing arts,

The Family Tree of the Lougandor Women

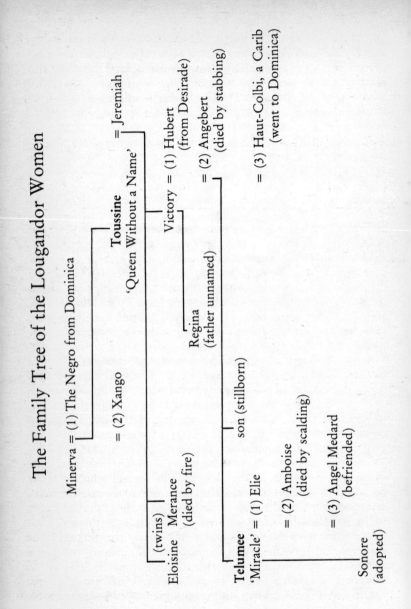

Minerva = (1) The Negro from Dominica

= (2) Xango

Toussine = Jeremiah
'Queen Without a Name'

(twins)
Eloisine   Merance
         (died by fire)

Victory = (1) Hubert
         (from Desirade)

     = (2) Angebert
         (died by stabbing)

Regina
(father unnamed)

     = (3) Haut-Colbi, a Carib
         (went to Dominica)

son (stillborn)

Telumee = (1) Elie
'Miracle'

     = (2) Amboise
         (died by scalding)

     = (3) Angel Medard
         (befriended)

Sonore
(adopted)

VI

but 'closer to the dead than to the living', a witch in traditional Creole terms. Telumee becomes a wise woman almost despite herself, when the community affirms its faith in her gifts. Spiritual wisdom and physical solace are combined in this role, akin to that of a village priestess, and illustrated when Toussine comforts battered Telumee or Sonore is healed. No male figure has such powers.

If their calm sense of a continuum between seen and unseen, living and dead, lends spiritual poise to these women, their strength is also shown in the economic sphere. Domestic skills in cooking, preserving and fine laundering are featured, and also the peasant woman as equal partner in cultivating the land. In hard times Telumee resorts to paid domestic work, and almost loses her self-respect labouring in the cane fields. Thus, although Schwarz-Bart does not show women moving outside traditional occupations, she asserts their importance as independent providers, when no man supports the family.

At the heart of this book is grandmother's rocking chair, where an old woman sits to braid a little girl's thick black hair, sings old songs and tells stories. She is an image of loving and giving, but her stories preach self-confidence in a woman's ability to shape her own destiny.

Schwarz-Bart composes a stirring hymn to the survival power of women, although her first concern is the specific example of the black woman of the Caribbean. She is writing about the uprooted Africans who have emerged from slavery to reconstruct village communities, but who are still living precariously, threatened constantly in their self-confidence by social discrimination, and economically by the plantation system.

Slavery is still vibrating in the landscape, present in the memories of older folk, and in all the proverbs and sayings which ruefully comment that the Negro's place is 'in the midst of the cane prickles', with the reality of the whip and the grave at the end. The legacy of humiliation makes more striking the pride of the unbowed Lougandor women. Throughout the book we share in the experiences of Telumee and her community, gaining an intense impression of its solidity and richness. The cane-field is held in reserve as a desperate resort, late in the book. The white Desaragne household is made to seem almost a dream interlude, among people who dissolve like starch into a transparent glaze. In this way the author makes her impact through an implied contrast, needing no major scenes of racial confrontation.

Despite her very controlled effects of contrast, Schwarz-Bart makes her position clear. Anyone who doubts this should reread the episode of the strike, when Amboise is scalded to death. This moment of sudden horror brings to a point a series of hints which delineate a plantation system still dehumanizing and repressive. It is worth noting that the whole movement of the book parallels the path of the maroons, the rebel slaves who sought freedom in the densely wooded uplands. The characters find the worthwhile things of life remote from the plains and towns where French dominance imposes assimilation.

Another aspect of Negritude is more emphatically presented. Schwarz-Bart celebrates lyrically the beauty of her black characters, their glowing skin often 'blue-black'. A sustained example is the description of Victory, which also includes an insidious clause: 'No one . . . noticed her beauty, for her skin was very dark' (p.17), to remind us how often physical appearance can become a morbid obsession in the Caribbean.[3]

If part of her portrait of a potentially viable black community is contained in the economic stress on independent peasant farmers and fishermen, Schwarz-Bart also takes great care to show cultural autonomy. Her eye for cultural retentions is trained and acute, and we shall return to the central question of the Creole proverb. Traditional customs are not only shown on key ceremonial occasions such as marriages, setting up house or wakes, but also forming part of the texture of life in an oral culture where so much social exchange is stylised by conscious performance. Among a wealth of examples we find the episode of fish-poaching, the use made of Christmas songs, the questioning of Telumee about Belle-Feuille, the house-moving. There is no explicit 'African' consciousness which would strike a false note in Telumee's character, but the reader is constantly made aware of a style of behaviour and response to life which owe nothing to approved French models. As usual Grandmother sums up, rejecting fine white béchamel sauce in favour of breadfruit roasted over a wood fire.

Attitudes to the supernatural are shown which transcend

European rationality. Fond-Zombi is a carefully chosen name, it means a valley bottom peopled by spirits or ghosts. The reader is led into participating in Telumee's belief system, as when she accepts the metamorphosis of Ma Cia into a black dog. We find in this novel the same sense of complicity between man and nature which radiates through Jacques Roumain's *Masters of the Dew*. (CWS12) Both novels try to express the values inherited by the black population of the Caribbean countryside.

Characters

It is tempting to look at the characters in *The Bridge of Beyond* in two separate groups, women and men, so dominant is the impression of outstanding women. However, studying *how* this impression is created will lead us closer to understanding Schwarz-Bart's achievement.

The fullest portrait is of course that of Telumee, presented as a self-portrait. She tells her own story. Her 'tone of voice' conveys an attitude to the experiences narrated, and reveals her personality more fully but indirectly. For example, much of the tender relationship with Amboise is expressed in the description of how they cultivated their garden together, while the numbing shock of his death is suggested by the absence of personal comment. Moreover, the author aims to give us a sense of Telumee's life unfolding, from childhood, through the joys and pain of adulthood, to a calm waiting on death. Earlier in the book we find details to emphasize the child's perspective: the feeling of awe that Grandmother and Ma Cia inspired, the shelter of wide skirts, Telumee crouching under the counter in Old Abel's shop listening to the grown-ups' talk. To begin with a child's view also helps Schwarz-Bart establish the feeling of rightness and inevitability about life in Fond-Zombi. As the book ends, there is more tendency to be sententious, and a kind of detachment which suggests the close of a life. Telumee's reminiscences constitute the whole book. Time flows unevenly; sometimes lingering over the texture of a moment, the colour and shapes of happy days with Elie, for example, or a quick sketch will heighten pace, before another event is embalmed in the proverbial wisdom which almost removes all sense of human urgency. Little by little, the narrative fills in that outline figure of an old woman, who stands in her garden at the beginning of the book. By the close she has become an individual whose serene will for happiness seems precious and important because we now know her through and through.

The portrait of Telumee's grandmother, Toussine, is next in importance. The author suggests so strong a bond of love and continuity between them that the two figures almost fuse into one, hinting at reincarnation (as in African belief). A concept of time as cyclical rather than linear underlies the recurring patterns in these two lives. To take obvious examples, Telumee in turn suffers bereavement by fire and the loss of a girl-child. Thus the description of the Grandmother, which can be a more detailed third-person account, also influences how we imagine Telumee. The title, Queen Without a Name, which is ceremonially bestowed, continues to be used in the narrative, keeping alive the aura of mystery with which Toussine is first introduced. (Children fathered by spirits have no name.) Tiny details, like the pink nightdress ironed ready for the entrance into the other world, anchor the portrait into observed domestic reality. Often these touches identify a Creole reality, like the madras scarf of faded yellow check cloth. Toussine's relationship with Ma Cia offers a beautiful example of the term commère, a supportive bond between women, as of mother and godmother, even though the word is never pronounced.

Ma Cia, who extends the spiritual side of the portrait of Grandmother, figures in half-magical episodes which build bridges between this novel and the world of the folktale. Witch, obeah woman, flying soucougnan: we are asked to suspend disbelief in her powers, and show respect, like Telumee.

By contrast, Telumee's own mother, Victory, is shown without reference to a spiritual dimension. Her ecstasy she finds in love, or when love forsakes her, in rum. Yet her daughter reflects the community's tolerant generosity towards her, and tells sympathetically of her labours as laundress and her search for true love. Victory plays no role in Telumee's deeper life. Schwarz-Bart seems to be demonstrating a West African proverb, also found in the Caribbean: 'If your mother doesn't nurse you, grandmother will.'

Like Victory, the male characters tend to be the focus for a self-contained section or two of the narrative, without ever becoming woven into that strong central strand of Lougandor tradition. Each man incarnates an aspect of love, sometimes too close to a stereotyped quick sketch of wise paternity or lust. The portrayal of Elie is the most extensive, and remains remarkably free from bitterness. Despite his cruel betrayal of Telumee, the reader is asked to see him as a victim, less spectacularly martyred than Amboise, but permanently warped by the unemployment gripping the district during drought.

The white characters are left insubstantial, irritating but remote, to show how far they remain from contact with the hidden truth of Telumee and her people. Here too we detect an unexpected tolerance. Telumee can believe that Madame Desaragne is sincere in regretting the barrier of incomprehension between them.

Schwarz-Bart avoids giving a sentimental picture of a warm peasant community. She stresses a few enduring family relationships in the midst of a group eroded by hard times and lack of self-confidence. Moments such as the singing to remake battered Telumee's link with the web of village life, thus come across with a special poignancy. The sense of a community is more often achieved through the recourse to Creole sayings, which imply a collective response to experience, and link Telumee to a distinctive group of people.

Aspects of the Text

Imagery

This is a dense text, which repays more than one careful reading. Part of the meaning is conveyed through a network of images and symbols, often drawn from nature but used and reused until they enhance the significance as well as decorating the surface.[4] Particularly important is the imagery based on water, the archetypal female element, which develops and diversifies Grandmother's saying that 'All rivers go down to the sea.'

The reader can enjoy collecting the clusters of images, and decoding the patterns into which Schwarz-Bart has grouped them. A simple example would be the floral images for the women: upstanding congo cane and 'red canna' link the Lougandor, whereas the treacherous Letitia is a water-lily in stagnant water.

The contrast between the grace and radiance of a happy woman which the flower images imply, and the sharp wounding cane in the plantation fields hardly needs stressing.

In creating these symbolic patterns, the author is drawing on a poetic tradition already well-established in the Caribbean. The realities of history and the landscape have shaped a stock of images, first used with special brilliance by Aimé Césaire, and enriched by novelists like Edouard Glissant. Since sugar grows most profitably on well-irrigated level lands, plantation slavery is associated with the coastal plains, while the forested uplands served as refuge for the maroons, and then for the independent peasant farmers who left the estates on abolition.[5] Wood and the forest readily come to signify positive values of freedom and independence, as we can see in Schwarz-Bart's choice of the trade of sawyer for Telumee's men. Moreover, fire, the enemy of wood, repeatedly destroys life and hope, and is unmistakably linked, through the scorched cane-fields on the way to Belle-Feuille, with the white master.

There are many other memorable images, such as the two-sided drum, which are sustained and enriched through the book. One which might prove puzzling is Telumee as a crystal glass. The metaphorical link suggests a fragile transparent beauty, a cupped female shape, but it is tempting to see here also a delicate allusion to André Schwarz-Bart's *The Last of the Just* (especially Part VII, Chapter V). Jewish legend also provides examples of the reversibility of man and dog, used here in suggesting the abjection of Telumee among the cane-cutters, and the inhuman perversity of Angel Medard.

These major image groups by no means exhaust the resonances of this text. Indeed, another woman writer and critic from Guadeloupe, Maryse Condé, suggests the possibility of seeing the whole book allegorically, with the Lougandor women representing Mother Earth/Guadeloupe.[6] However, the use of symbolic nature imagery is a universal feature of poetic expression, rarely absent from any literary work set in a peasant community. What is distinctive here is the Caribbean region and the Creole language.

Creole

Schwarz-Bart has attempted to render the consciousness of a Creole speaker not by creolized dialogue or footnotes, but by sustaining the strangeness of an unfamiliar world-view. The metaphors based on Caribbean reality aid the process, but run the risk of seeming too pretty and artificial, since country folk are usually sparing of words. It is the use of Creole sayings and expressions which authenticates the vision and strengthens the narrative texture.[7] The opening of Part Two, Chapter 4 is an example of the interpenetration of proverbial wisdom and individual experience.

Each time the book is read, more Creole sayings seem to emerge from the text. Just as Grandmother tells a folktale to reinforce the lesson: 'The horse mustn't ride you, you must ride it', so Schwarz-Bart seems to adopt the same role, articulating her whole novel as the demonstration of a number of potent Creole sayings, especially those dealing with women and with resisting adversity. Her autobiographical narrator slips fluently into story-telling forms; passing on the dreadful exploits of the White of Whites, dramatising the death of Angebert, or retelling the biography of Amboise. At least seven typical sayings are woven into this last account, which is designed to illustrate the Negro 'beaten for a hundred years' but with courage for a thousand. In this way we have much less of an introspective personal view of Telumee's experience, despite the autobiographical form. Instead these proverbial reflections sum up the collective responses of a community to experience, a solidarity which has aided survival.

Some metaphors, as we have seen, originate in proverbs. In addition, the absolute form of sayings about 'Life', 'The heart of a Negro', etc. is used to flavour many of Telumee's remarks, and characters such as Toussine and Ma Cia converse typically in the impersonal oracular form of the proverb and the riddle.[8] These stylistic traits maintain a distance from the more realistic personal narrative we might expect to emerge from written French conventions.

For more insight into Creole proverbs, it is useful to consult one of the existing collections,[9] or better still, a native speaker with a good repertoire of traditional lore. Often going back to the early years of plantation society, the proverbs transmit some of the African heritage of the slaves, while incorporating a stoical perception of a vicious racial hierarchy. A proverb's function is often to console a victim of fate by a formula which takes hold consciously of the dilemma and shares it. This helps account for the fatalism of many Negro proverbs and tales. But for every expression of self-doubt there will be a countering affirmation of endurance. We can quote as typical a well-known saying which sums up Schwarz-Bart's message. *Tetees pas janmain trop loud pou lestomaque* (However heavy a woman's breasts, her chest is always strong enough to carry them), graphically evoking the burden of sustaining life and yet the strength to stand tall and proud.

Translation

This is an unusually good translation in view of the complex problems posed by the style of the novel. At times, the English version seems to improve on the original, since Barbara Bray, a very experienced literary translator, favours a plainer and more direct text which checks the tendency to whimsical rambling. She often breaks up sentences into terser units, and goes for economy without always pursuing finer shades of meaning. She is sensitive to the proverbial turns of phrase, and to Schwarz-Bart's use of significant proper names. However, her solution to the very difficult problem of labelling local flowers and fruit, and rendering the eloquent names of people and places is not really a solution at all. Either names are left in the original, justifiable with place names, but less so with fish or plants, or approximations are attempted. Schwarz-Bart has often been specific as to the exact variety of a vegetable, so that such short cuts do not do her full justice. With a little more research regional equivalents could have substituted for more of the terms. Trinidadian English would for example have allowed the retention of *balisier* (heliconia or wild banana) not the use of *canna*. It would have been difficult to decide which variant of Caribbean English to use, but an opportunity to recreate Telumee's Creole world has been neglected. The proverbs in particular are clumsy in Standard English, but have lively equivalents in most of the Creoles of the region.

* * *

Finally, it may be useful to consider some of the adverse comments made about this book as a stimulus to critical evaluation. Several reviewers have reacted against Toussine and Telumee as characters who are too good to be true, too saintly and forgiving and full of wisdom to be plausible as real people, least of all in a harsh post-slavery world. Simone Schwarz-Bart has also been taxed with lack of militancy, and accused of sharing the passivity of her women characters who accept and even glorify ill-treatment. The text has been found too rambling and lacking in dramatic pace and tension to retain the reader's interest, or too prettily 'exotic'.

These comments merit discussion, but the main intention of the book seems well achieved: to recreate the qualities of a distinctive peasant culture, surviving through the strength and wisdom of its women. The novel has much warmth in its portraits, a poised and intricate structuring reinforcing its lyrical surface, and the Creole elements support the testimony to an independent culture and view of life. Tape-recorded interviews in Creole could have rendered the experience of 'Telumee' with great authenticity. It is the writer's special gift to recreate that material in a pleasing and significant pattern.

Simone Schwarz-Bart

Simone Schwarz-Bart was born in Charente-Maritime in 1938 and her family returned to Guadeloupe when she was three. Her mother was a teacher in a village school. In *The Bridge of Beyond* she takes a real locality, La Ramée, and adapts several local place names. It is a small town with a hilly hinterland, situated on the edge of the north-eastern mountains, and belonging to an area of settlement dating back to the *ancien régime* but now relatively undeveloped. During Simone's childhood, her father was away, fighting with the Free French forces. The war years were very difficult in the French West Indies, as the Vichy regime controlled the islands through the French fleet, and the Allied blockade created serious shortages of food. After the war she left to study in France, and met and married a young Jewish writer, André Schwarz-Bart. The couple have two sons, and have travelled widely, living for a while in Africa (Senegal) and Switzerland. They have now settled in Goyave, a small but old-established community between hills and sea in Guadeloupe, where Simone lived as a child.

Simone and André Schwarz-Bart

Simone Schwarz-Bart first met her husband when he was finishing work on his prize-winning novel, *The Last of the Just* (published 1959). Out of this encounter between a black woman and a Jewish man has grown a collaboration which is both a literary and a personal partnership. Since their joint novel, *Un plat de porc aux bananes vertes* (1967), the couple have pursued parallel literary careers which suggest a shared creativity. Like other famous literary couples, such as Sartre and Simone de Beauvoir, or Aragon and Elsa Triolet, they seem certain to discuss and criticize each other's work, and to hold in common some important values.

André Schwarz-Bart's *The Last of the Just* is one of the major works which find a literary form adequate to deal with the horror of the destiny of the Jews under Hitler. He uses a Talmudic legend to frame and intensify the story of Ernie Levy, an exemplary victim of the Nazis. First his lineage is traced, and then his life stage by stage, from playground tormenting to final extermination at Auschwitz. Later works by Schwarz-Bart direct attention to another major historical tragedy, Negro slavery, with the same painfully acute insight. African people, like the Jews, were sold into bondage and dispersed, and came by cruel necessity to learn the essentials of survival. Naked in the yard of a forced labour camp or on the deck of a slave ship, a person survives only by strength of spirit and will. Possessions and places become unimportant. Such a racial heritage teaches the meaning of compassion and faith, and the significance of the lore and simple rituals which keep alive bonds of kinship and cultural identity.

The jointly-produced Schwarz-Bart novel, *Un plat de porc aux bananes vertes*, presents the experience of an old woman from Martinique, who is ending her days in an institution for the aged in Paris.[10] Her physical world is almost a prison; she is confined with eccentric and sometimes racist old folk under the control of impersonal nuns. She writes down her thoughts in seven note-books, and gradually comforts herself recalling childhood days, especially her grandmother (a chilling portrait of alienation through slavery) and the rebel drummer Raymoninque. Though the evocation of childhood in the hills behind Saint-Pierre does not occupy much space, it is very clearly realised, and we are made to feel the almost sacramental significance of the traditional dish which provides the novel's title.

The Guadeloupean mulatto heroine, Solitude, who fought against the French, and was excuted in 1802, the day after her baby was born, was intended to form the focus of a cycle of novels, *Plat de porc* being the prelude. André Schwarz-Bart tells her story in a fictional biography (published in 1972). With great attention to historical authenticity, he recreates the time of the slave trade in Africa to portray Solitude's mother, and then the violent upheavals in Guadeloupe during the Revolution. The novel celebrates the courage of the maroon bands, but also explores the ambiguities of Solitude, set apart from both races. She becomes a strange, almost unearthly figure, reflecting popular legend as well as attested fact. (In Guadeloupe, a mulatto class never fully developed after the massacres of the revolutionary years.)

Simone Schwarz-Bart has followed *The Bridge of Beyond* with *Ti-Jean Jean L'horizon* (1979), using the hero of the Creole folktale cycles (cf. Derek Walcott's play, *Ti-Jean and his Brothers*). Aiming to arouse a sense of mystery and wonder, this epic binds together both shores of the Atlantic, and the kingdoms of the living and the dead. It is a quest for the lost sun, which begins from Fond-Zombi, across the Bridge of Beyond, though it does not use the characters of the earlier, more realistic work. Another poignant love-story is told, and blended into Creole and African myths. Again the story is beautifully composed, and almost too beautifully told.

This quick look at other novels by the Schwarz-Bart couple helps us to see their informed interest in the history and life of the Caribbean people least often found in official records. It also highlights their concern with the craft of the writer, since their observation and research, enriched by first-hand study in West Africa, is embodied in imaginative works not treatises. Their sustaining legends and fables build on traditional forms of oral literature, but confront implicitly the problems of today. *The*

Bridge of Beyond provides an admirable example, rooted in the land of Guadeloupe, of woman's courage and self-reliance, an image of independent survival with great importance for the future.

BRIDGET JONES
Department of French
University of the West Indies
Jamaica

NOTE: Study questions for students are provided on page 174.

NOTES

1 *Return to My Native Land*, Présence africaine bilingual edition, 1968, p.42.
2 Compare Maureen Warner-Lewis' tribute to Miss Queenie, 'The Nkuyu: Spirit Messengers of the Kumina', *Savacou*, No.13 (1977).
3 Explored to the point of neurosis in the novels of Michèle Lacrosil, a Guadeloupean woman writer of an earlier generation. Merle Hodge contrasts her with Schwarz-Bart in 'Social Conscience or Exoticism? Two Novels from Guadeloupe', *Revista Interamericana*, Vol.IV, No. 3 (Fall 1974).
4 Beverley Ormerod, 'L'aïeule: figure dominante chez S. Schwarz-Bart', (*Présence francophone* No.20, Spring 1980), has a particularly good discussion of imagery.
5 Neatly illustrated in Lasserre's geography of Guadeloupe, Vol.II, Plate LVII (Bordeaux, 1961).
6 Maryse Condé, *La parole des femmes* (Paris: L'Harmattan, 1979).
7 For a detailed analysis by the Creole linguist Jean Bernabé, see 'Contribution à l'étude de la diglossie littéraire', *Textes Etudes et Documents*, No.2 (1979). Published by G.E.R.E.C., Centre Universitaire Antilles-Guyane.
8 Note the work of Velma Pollard on figurative language in Jamaican Creole (based on recordings made by Erna Brodber for an oral history project on Jamaica 1914-1948).
9 B.David, J-P.Jardel, *Proverbes créoles de la Martinique* (Martinique: C.E.R.A.G., n.d.). 'Zagaya', *Proverbes créoles en Guadeloupe* (Madrid, 1965)
10 On this novel see Beverley Ormerod, *Essays in French Literature*, No.8 (Nov.1971)

PART ONE

My People

1

A man's country may be cramped or vast according to the size of his heart. I've never found my country too small, though that isn't to say my heart is great. And if I could choose it's here in Guadeloupe that I'd be born again, suffer and die. Yet not long back my ancestors were slaves on this volcanic, hurricane-swept, mosquito-ridden, nasty-minded island. But I didn't come into the world to weigh the world's woe. I prefer to dream, on and on, standing in my garden, just like any other old woman of my age, till death comes and takes me as I dream, me and all my joy.

When I was a child my mother, Victory, often talked to me about my grandmother Toussine. She spoke of her with fervour and veneration: Toussine, she'd say, was a woman who helped you hold your head up, and people with this gift are rare. My mother's reverence for Toussine was such I came to regard her as some mythical being not of this world, so that for me she was legendary even while still alive.

I got into the habit of calling her, as men called her, Queen Without a Name. But her maiden name had been Toussine Lougandor.

* * *

Her mother was Minerva, a fortunate woman freed by the abolition of slavery from a master notorious for cruelty and caprice. After the abolition Minerva wandered in search of a refuge far from the plantation and its vagaries, and she came to rest at L'Abandonnée. Some runaway slaves came there afterwards, and a village grew up. The wanderers seeking refuge were countless, and many would not settle anywhere permanently for fear the old days might return. One Negro from Dominica vanished as soon as he learned he had

2

sired a child, and those in L'Abandonnée whom Minerva had scorned now laughed at her swollen belly. But when dark-skinned Xango took on the shame of my great-grandmother Minerva, the laughter stopped dead, and those who had been amusing themselves at others' misfortunes choked on their own bile. Little Toussine came into the world, and Xango loved her as if she were his own. As the child grew, shooting up as gracefully as a sugar cane, she became the light of his eyes, the blood in his veins, the air in his lungs. Thus through the love and respect lavished on her by Xango, Minerva, now long dead, could walk without shame along the main street of the hamlet, head high, back arched, arms akimbo, and foul breath turned from her to blow over better pastures. And so life began for young Toussine, as delicately as dawn on a clear day.

They lived in a hamlet swept alternately by winds from the land and winds from the sea. A steep road ran along by cliffs and wastelands, leading, it seemed, to nothing human. And that was why it was called the deserted village, L'Abandonnée. At certain times everyone there would be filled with dread, like travellers lost in a strange land. Still young and strong, always dressed in a worker's overall, Minerva had a glossy, light mahogany skin and black eyes brimming over with kindness. She had an unshakable faith in life. When things went wrong she would say that nothing, no one, would ever wear out the soul God had chosen out for her and put in her body. All the year round she fertilized vanilla, picked coffee, hoed the banana groves, and weeded the rows of sweet potatoes. And her daughter Toussine was no more given to dreaming than she. Almost as soon as she woke the child would make herself useful sweeping, gathering fruit, peeling vegetables. In the afternoon she would go to the forest to collect leaves for the rabbits, and sometimes the whim would take her to kneel in the shade of the mahoganies and look for the flat brightly coloured seeds that are made into necklaces. When she came back with a huge pile of greenstuff on her head, Xango delighted to see her with leaves hanging down over her face, and would fling both arms in the air and shout: 'Hate me, so long as you love Toussine. Pinch me till you draw blood, but don't touch so much as the hem of her robe.' And he would laugh and cry just to look at the radiant, frank-faced child whose features were said to be like those of the Negro from Dominica, whom he would have liked to meet once,

3

just to see. But as yet she was not in full bloom. It was when she was fifteen that she stood out from all the other girls with the unexpected grace of a red canna growing on a mountain, so that the old folk said she in herself was the youth of L'Abandonnée.

There was also in L'Abandonnée at that time a young fisherman called Jeremiah who filled one's soul with the same radiance. But he paid no attention to girls, to whom his friends used to say, laughing, 'When Jeremiah falls in love it will be with a mermaid.' But this didn't make him any less handsome, and the girls' hearts shriveled up with vexation. He was nineteen and already the best fisherman in Caret cove. Where on earth did he get those hauls of vivaneaux, tazars, and blue balarous? Nowhere but from beneath his boat, the *Headwind*, in which he used to go off forever, from morn till night and night till morn; all he lived for was hearing the sound of the waves in his ears and feeling the tradewinds caressing his face. Such was Jeremiah when Toussine was for everyone a red canna growing on a high mountain.

On windless days when the sea was dead calm Jeremiah would go into the forest to cut the lianas he made into lobster pots. One afternoon when he left the beach for this purpose, Toussine appeared in his path, right in the middle of a wood. She was wearing one of her mother's old dresses that came down to her ankles, and with her heap of greenstuff coming down over her eyes and hiding her face, she looked as if she didn't know where she was going. The young man asked her, 'Is this L'Abandonnée's latest fashion in donkeys?' She threw down her burden looked at him, and said in surprise, almost in tears: 'A girl just goes to collect greenstuff from the forest, and here I am, insulted.' With that, she burst out laughing and scampered off into the shadow. It was then Jeremiah was caught in the finest lobster pot he ever saw. When he got back from his excursion his friends noticed he looked absentminded, but they did not ask any questions. Real fishermen, those who have taken the sea for their native country, often have that lost look. So his friends just thought dry land didn't agree with Jeremiah, and that his natural element was the water. But they sang a different tune in the days that followed, when they saw Jeremiah neglecting the *Headwind*, deserting her and leaving her high and dry on the beach. Consulting among themselves, they came to the conclusion he must be under the spell of the Guiablesse, the most wicked of

4

spirits, the woman with the cloven hoof who feeds exclusively on your desire to live, and whose charms drive you sooner or later to suicide. They asked him if he hadn't met someone that ill-fated day when he went up into the forest. Eventually Jeremiah confessed: 'The only Guiablesse I met that day', he said, 'is called Toussine – Xango's Toussine.' Then they said, chuckling, 'Oh, so that's it! Now we see. But it's not such a problem as you might think; if you want our opinion there are no prince's daughters in L'Abandonnée that we know of. Fortunately we're only a pack of Negroes all in the same boat, without any fathers and mothers before God. Here everyone is everyone's else's equal, and none of our women can boast of having three eyes or two tourmalines sleeping in the hollow of her thighs. True, you'll say *she* isn't like all the others, the women you see everywhere, like lizards, protected by the very insipidity of their flesh. We answer: Jeremiah, you say well, as usual. For we too have eyes, and when Toussine brushes against our pupils our sight is refreshed. All these words to say just one thing, friend: Beautiful as she is, the girl is like you, and when you appear with her in the street you will be a good match for her. One more thing. When you go to tell her parents of your intentions, remember we don't have any cannibals here, and Xango and Minerva won't eat you.

Then they left Jeremiah to himself, so that he could make his decision like a man.

Thank God for my friends, thought Jeremiah the day he went to see Toussine's parents, dressed as usual and carrying a fine catch of pink crabs. As soon as they opened the door he told them he loved Toussine, and they asked him right in, without even consulting the young lady. Their behaviour gave the impression they knew all about Jeremiah, what he did in life on land and sea, and that he was in a position to take a wife, have children, and bring up a family. It was the beginning of one of those warm Guadeloupe afternoons, lit up at the end by the arrival of Toussine with a tray spread with an embroidered cloth, with vermouth for the men and sapodilla syrup for the weaker sex. When Jeremiah left, Minerva told him the door of the cottage would be open to him day and night from now on, and he knew he could consider the vermouth and the invitation as marking definite victory: for in the case of such a choice morsel as Toussine it isn't usual for people to fall on

5

someone's neck the first time of asking, as if they were trying to get rid of a beast that had something wrong with it. That evening, to celebrate this triumph, Jeremiah and his friends decided to go night fishing, and they brought back so much fish their expedition was long remembered in L'Abandonnée. But they had enjoyed catching those coulirous too much to sell them on the beach, so they gave them away, and that too remained in everyone's memory. At noon that day the men, with glasses of rum in their hands, threw out their chests with satisfaction, tapped them three times, and exulted: 'In spite of all, the race of men is not dead.' The women shook their heads and whispered, 'What one does a thousand undo.' 'But in the meanwhile', said one of them, as if reluctantly, 'it does spread a little hope'. And the sated tongues went full tilt, while inside Jeremiah's head the sound of the waves had started up again.

Jeremiah came every afternoon. He was treated not as a suitor but rather as if he were Toussine's brother, the son Minerva and Xango had never had. No acid had eaten into the young man's soul, and my poor great-grandmother couldn't take her eyes off him. Gay by temperament, she was doubly gay to see this scrap of her own country, the man sent by St. Anthony in person especially for her daughter. In the overflowing of her joy she would sometimes tease her. 'I hope you're fond of fish, Miss Toussine. Come along, you lucky girl, and I'll teach you to make a court-bouillon that'll make Jeremiah lick the fingers of both hands, polite as he is.'

Then she would hold out her wide yellow skirt and sing to her daughter:

> 'I want a fisherman for a husband
> To catch me fine sea bream
>
> I don't know if you know
> But I want a fisherman
>
> O oar before, he pleases me
> O oar behind, I die.'

But Toussine scarcely listened. Since Jeremiah had taken to spending his afternoons with her his image danced continually in her mind's eye, and she spent the whole day admiring the one she loved, unsuspected, as she thought, by all the world. She looked at his figure and saw it was slim and supple. She looked at his fingers and saw they were nimble and slender, like coconut leaves in the wind. She gazed into his eyes, and her body was filled with a great peace. But what she liked best of all about the man St. Anthony had sent her was the satiny, iridescent skin like the juicy flesh of certain mauve coco plums, so delicious under one's teeth. Minerva with her song about the fisherman knew very well how her daughter passed her time, but she still sang and danced just for the pleasure of seeing Toussine go on dreaming.

Here, as everywhere else, reality was not made up entirely of laughing and singing, dancing and dreaming: for one ray of sun on one cottage there was a whole village still in the shade. All through the preparations for the wedding, L'Abandonnée remained full of the same surliness, the same typical human desire to bring the level of the world down a peg, the same heavy malice weighing down on the chambers of the heart. The breeze blowing over Minerva's cottage embittered the women, made them more unaccountable than ever, fierce, fanciful, always ready with some new shrewishness. 'What I say is, Toussine's more for ornament than for use. Beauty's got no market value. The main thing is not getting married, but sticking together year in year out', said one. 'They're laughing now, but after laughter come tears, and three months from now Minerva's happy band will find itself with six eyes to cry with', said another. The most savage of all were those living with a man on a temporary basis. They grudged in advance the scrap of gold that was going to gleam on her finger, they wondered if she really possessed some unique and exceptional quality, some virtue or merit so great it elicited marriage. And to console themselves and soothe a deep-seated resentment, they would come right up to Minerva's cottage at dusk and mutter, with a kind of savage frenzy, incantations like:

7

Married today
Divorced tomorrow
But Mrs just the same.

Minerva knew these women had nothing in their lives but a few planks balanced on four stones and a procession of men over their bellies. For these lost Negresses, marriage was the greatest and perhaps the only dignity. But when she couldn't stand hearing them any longer, Minerva would plant her hands on her hips and shout: 'I'm not the only one with a daughter, my fine windbags, and I wish yours the same you wish my Toussine. For, under the sun, the saying has never gone unfulfilled. All they that take the sword shall perish with the sword.' Then she would go inside and shut the doors and let the mad bitches yelp.

On the day of the wedding all the village paths were swept and decorated as for the local feast day. Xango and Minerva's cottage was surrounded by huts of woven coconut palm. The one reserved for the bridal couple was a great bouquet of hibiscus, mignonette, and orange blossom – the scent was intoxicating. Rows of tables stretched as far as the eye could see, and you were offered whatever drink you were thirsty for, whatever meat would tickle your palate. There was meat of pig, sheep, and cattle, and even poultry served in the liquor it was cooked in. Blood pudding rose up in shining coils; tiered cakes were weighed down with lacy frosting; every kind of water ice melted before your eyes – custard-apple, water-lemon, coconut. But for the Negroes of L'Abandonnée all this was nothing without some music, and when they saw the three bands, one for quadrilles and mazurkas, one for the fashionable beguine, and the traditional combination of drum, wind instruments, and horn, then they knew they'd really have something worth talking about at least once in their lives. And this assuaged the hearts swollen with jealousy. For three days everyone left behind hills and plateaus, troubles and indignities of every kind, to relax, dance, and salute the bridal couple, going to and fro before them in the flower-decked tent, congratulating Toussine on her luck and Jeremiah on his best of luck. It was impossible to count how many mouths uttered the word luck, for that was the theme they decided to adopt for telling their descendants, in later years, of the wedding of Toussine and Jeremiah.

* * *

The years flowed over it all, and Toussine was still the same dragonfly with shimmering blue wings, Jeremiah still the same glossy-coated sea dog. He continued to go out alone, never bringing back an empty boat, however niggardly the sea. Scandalmongers said he used witchcraft and had a spirit go out fishing in his stead when no one else was about. But in fact his only secret was his enormous patience. When the fish would not bite at all, he dived for lambis. If there were no lambis, he put out long rods with hooks or live crabs to tempt the octopi. He knew the sea as the hunter knows the forest. When the wind had gone and the boat was hauled up on the shore, he would make for his little cottage, pour the money he'd earned into his wife's lap, and have a snack as he waited for the sun to abate. Then the two of them would go to tend their garden. While he dug, she would mark out the rows; while he burned weeds, she would sow. And the sudden dusk of the islands would come down over them, and Jeremiah would take advantage of the deepening dark to have a little hors d'oeuvre of his wife's body, there on the ground, murmuring all sorts of foolishness to her, as on the very first day. 'I still don't know what it is I like best about you – one day it's your eyes, the next your woodland laugh, another your hair, and the day after the lightness of your step; another, the beauty spot on your temple, and then the day after that the grains of rice I glimpse when you smile at me.' And to this air on the mandolin, Toussine, trembling with delight, would reply with a cool, rough little air on the flute: 'My dear, anyone just seeing you in the street would give you the host without asking you to go to confession, but you're a dangerous man, and you'd have buried me long ago if people ever died of happiness.' Then they would go indoors and Jeremiah would address the evening, casting a last look over the fields: 'How can one help loving a garden?'

Their prosperity began with a grass path shaded by coconut palms and kept up as beautifully as if it led to a castle. In fact it led to a little wooden house with two rooms, a thatched roof, and a floor supported on four large cornerstones. There was a hut for cooking in, three blackened stones for a hearth, and a covered tank so that Toussine could do her washing without having to go and

9

gossip with the neighbours by the river. As the women did their washing they would pick quarrels to give zest to the work, comparing their respective fates and filling their hearts with bitterness and rancour. Meanwhile Toussine's linen would be boiling away in a pan in the back yard, and she took advantage of every minute to make her house more attractive. Right in front of the door she'd planted a huge bed of Indian poppies, which flowered all year round. To the right there was an orange tree with hummingbirds and to the left clumps of Congo cane from which she used to cut pieces to give to her daughters, Eloisine and Meranee, for their tea. She would go to and fro amid all this in a sort of permanent joy and richness, as if Indian poppies, Congo canes, hummingbirds, and orange trees were enough to fill a woman's heart with complete satisfaction. And because of the richness and joy she felt in return for so little, people envied and hated her. She could withdraw at will into the recesses of her own soul, but she was reserved, not disillusioned. And because she bloomed like that, in solitude, she was also accused of being an aristocrat stuck-up. Late every Sunday evening she would walk through the village on Jeremiah's arm to look at the place and the people and the animals just before they disappeared in the darkness. She was happy, herself part of all that spectacle, that close and familiar universe. She came to be the thorn in some people's flesh, the delight of others, and because she had a distant manner they thought she put on aristocratic airs.

After the grass path came a veranda, which surrounded the little house, giving constant cool and shade if you moved the bench according to the time of day. Then there were the two windows back and front, real windows with slatted shutters, so that you could close the door and shut yourself safely away from spirits and still breathe in the scents of evening. But the true sign of their prosperity was the bed they inherited from Minerva and Xango. It was a vast thing of locust wood with tall head posts and three mattresses, which took up the entire bedroom. Toussine used to put vetiver roots under the mattresses, and citronella leaves, so that whenever anyone lay down there were all sorts of delicious scents: the children said it was a magic bed. It was a great object of curiosity in that poor village, where everyone else still slept on old clothes laid down on the floor at night, carefully folded up in the morning,

10

and spread in the sun to get rid of the fleas. People would come and weigh up the grass path, the real windows with slatted shutters, the bed with its oval-panelled headboard lording it beyond the open door, and the red-bordered counterpane, which seemed an additional insult. And some of the women would say with a touch of bitterness, 'Who do they take themselves for, these wealthy Negroes? Toussine and Jeremiah, with their two-roomed house, their wooden veranda, their slatted shutters, and their bed with three mattresses and red borders – do they think all these things make them white?'

Later on Toussine also had a satin scarf, a broad necklace of gold and silver alloy, garnet earrings, and high-vamped slippers she wore twice a year, on Ash Wednesday and Christmas Day. And as the wave showed no sign of flagging, the time came when the other Negroes were no longer surprised, and talked about other things, other people, other pains and other wonders. They had got used to the prosperity as they had got used to their own poverty. The subject of Toussine and wealthy Negroes was a thing of the past; it had all become quite ordinary.

Woe to him who laughs once and gets into the habit, for the wickedness of life is limitless: if it gives you your heart's desire with one hand, it is only to trample on you with both feet and let loose on you that madwoman bad luck, who seizes and rends you and scatters your flesh to the crows.

Eloisine and Meranee, twins, were ten years old when luck forsook their mother Toussine. A school had just opened in the village, and a teacher came twice a week to teach the children their letters in exchange for a few pennyworth of foodstuff. One evening as they were learning their alphabet, Meranee said her sister had all the light and told her to move the lamp to the middle of the table. And so just one little word gave bad luck an opening. 'Have it all, then!' said Eloisine, giving the light an angry shove. It was over in an instant: the china lamp was in pieces and the burning oil was spreading all over Meranee's legs and shoulders and hair. A living torch flew out into the darkness, and the evening breeze howled around it, fanning the flames. Toussine caught up a blanket and ran

11

after the child, shouting to her to stand still, but she rushed madly hither and thither, leaving a luminous track behind her like a falling star. In the end she collapsed, and Toussine wrapped her in the blanket, picked her up, and went back toward the house, which was still burning. Jeremiah comforted Eloisine, and they all sat in the middle of their beautiful path, on the damp grass of evening, watching their sweat, their life, their joy, go up in flames. A big crowd had gathered: the Negroes stood there fascinated, dazzled by the magnitude of the disaster. They stared at the flames lighting up the sky, shifting from foot to foot, in two minds – they felt an impulse to pity, and yet saw the catastrophe as poetic justice. It made them forget their own fate and compare the cruelty of this misfortune with the ordinariness of their own. At any rate, it's one thing that won't happen to us, they said.

Meranee's suffering was terrible. Her body was one great wound attracting more and more flies as it decayed. Toussine, her eyes empty of all expression, fanned them away, put on soothing oil, and grew hoarse calling on death, which, being no doubt occupied elsewhere, refused to come. If anyone offered to replace Toussine at the bedside for a while, she would say, smiling gently: 'Don't worry about me. However heavy a woman's breasts, her chest is always strong enough to carry them.' She spent seventeen days and seventeen nights cajoling death, and then, ill luck having gone elsewhere, Meranee expired. Life went on as before, but without one vestige of heart left, like a flea feasting on your last drop of blood, delighting in leaving you senseless and sore, cursing heaven and earth and the womb that conceived you.

Against sorrow and the vanity of things, there is and will always be human fantasy. It was thanks to the fantasy of a white man that Toussine and Jeremiah found a roof. He was a Creole called Colbert Lanony, who in the old days just after the abolition of slavery had fallen in love with a strange and fascinating young Negress. Cast out by his own people, he had sought refuge in a desolate and inaccessible wasteland far from the eyes that looked askance at his love. Nothing remained of all that now but some fine blocks of stone mouldering away in the wilderness, colonnades,

12

worm-eaten ceilings, and tiles bearing witness still to the past and to an outlawed white man's fancy for a Negress. To those who were surprised to find a house like that in such a place, the local people got into the habit of saying, 'It's L'Abandonnée', and the name later came to be used for the hamlet itself. Only one room on the first floor was habitable, a sort of closet, where the window openings were covered with sheets of cardboard. When it rained the water trickled through a hole in the roof into a bucket, and at night the ground floor was the resort of toads, frogs, and bats. But none of this seemed to bother Toussine, who had gone to live there like a body without a soul, indifferent to such details. As was the custom, she was visited there the first nine evenings by all the people of the village, who came to pay their respects to the dead and to keep the living company. Toussine did not weep or complain, but sat upright on a bench in a corner as if every breath of air were poison. People did not want to desert a ship like Toussine, but the sight of her was so unbearable they cut the ceremony short, just coming in, greeting her, and leaving, full of pitying kindness, thinking she was lost forever.

The leaf that falls into the pond does not rot the same day, and Toussine's sorrow only grew worse with time, fulfiling all the gloomy predictions. At first Jeremiah still went to sea three times a week, but then only twice, then once, then not at all. The house looked as deserted as ever, as if there were no one living there. Toussine never left the room with the cardboard windows, and Jeremiah collected their food from the woods around – purslane, scurvy grass, pink makanga bananas. Before, the women going to market used to take a path that led by the ruined house; it was a shortcut to the main road and Basse-Terre, where they sold their wares. But now they were afraid, and they made a big detour through the forest rather than go near the pig-headed Toussine, who didn't speak, wouldn't even answer, but just sat staring into space, a bag of bones as good as dead. Every so often, when the conversation came around to her and Jeremiah and little Eloisine, a man would shin up a tree, peer towards the house, and report that it was still the same; nothing had changed, nothing had moved.

Three years went by before people began to talk about them again. As usual, a man climbed a tree and looked towards the ruins; but this time he didn't say anything, and showed no sign of coming

13

down. When questioned he only signed for someone else to come up and look. It was the second man who announced that Toussine, the little stranded boat, the woman thought to be lost forever, had come out of her cardboard tower and was taking a little walk outside in the sun.

Glad as they were at this news, the Negroes still waited, hesitating to rejoice outright until the kid was safely caught and tethered and they were sure they hadn't sharpened their knives for nothing. And as they looked, this is what they saw: Toussine was cutting down the weeds around the ruined house. She shivered a moment, went in, then came out again almost at once and began to cut down brushwood and scrub with the furious energy of a woman with something urgent to do and not a minute to lose.

From that day on the place began to be a little less desolate and the market women went back to using the shortcut to Basse-Terre. Toussine had taken her family into prison with her, and now she brought them back to life again. First Eloisine was seen in the village again, as slight and brittle as a straw. Next poor Jeremiah came down to the beach, filled his eyes with the sea and stood staring, fascinated, then went back smiling up the hill as in the days when the song of the waves sounded in his head. It could be seen plainly written across his brow that he would go back to sea again. Toussine put curtains up at the windows, and planted Indian poppies around the ruin, Angola peas, root vegetables, and clumps of Congo cane for Eloisine. And then one day she planted the pip of a hummingbird orange. But the Negroes did not rejoice yet. They still watched and waited, from a distance. They thought of the old Toussine, in rags, and compared her with the Toussine of today – not a woman, for what is a woman? Nothing at all, they said, whereas Toussine was a bit of the world, a whole country, a plume of a Negress, the ship, sail, and wind, for she had not made a habit of sorrow. Then Toussine's belly swelled and burst and the child was called Victory. And then the Negroes did rejoice. On the day of the christening they came to Toussine and said:

'In the days of your silks and jewels we called you Queen Toussine. We were not far wrong, for you are truly a queen. But now, with your Victory, you may boast that you have put us in a quandary. We have tried and tried to think of a name for you, but in vain, for there isn't one that will do. And so from now on we shall call you "Queen Without a Name!"'

And they ate, drank, and were merry, and from that day forth my grandmother was called the Queen Without a Name.

Queen Without a Name went on living in L'Abandonnée with her two daughters, Eloisine and my mother, Victory, until my grandfather died. Then, when her daughters came to have the wombs of women, she left them to steer the course of their lives under their own sail. She wanted to go away from the house where her fisher husband had loved and cherished her and kept her safe in her affliction, when her hair was unkempt and her dress in rags. She longed for solitude, so she had a little hut built in a place called Fond-Zombi, which was said to be very wild. An old childhood friend of hers, a famous witch called Ma Cia, lived nearby, and Toussine hoped she would put her in touch with Jeremiah. So Toussine lived in the woods, and came very seldom to L'Abandonnée.

2

Mama Victory was a laundress, wearing out her wrists on the flat stones in the rivers, and her linen emerged like new from under the heavy waxed irons. Every Friday she would go down the old path of the market women to the main road, where a horse-drawn cart had left a huge bundle of washing for her to collect. She would hoist it onto her head, climb up to L'Abandonnée, and as soon as she got there start washing the clothes, singing as she worked. All the time she was washing, drying, starching, and ironing she would go on singing. For whole afternoons she would work away at a table set up under a mango tree, singing like a happy magpie. As they passed by on their way to the road her neighbours would often call: 'You're so slight you'll work your innards out, heaving those heavy irons.' Then her eyes would smile shyly and she would answer: 'A small ax cuts down a big tree, and we'll manage, please God.' My sister Regina and I, frisking about under her feet, would hear her say to herself afterwards: 'Suffering brings scorn. Better to be envied than pitied. Sing, Victory, sing!' And she would go on with her song.

We lived outside the village on a kind of plateau overhanging the first houses. Our mother was not the sort of woman to unpack her heart everywhere: she looked on human speech as a loaded gun, and, to use her own expression, talking often felt to her like an issue of blood. She would sing, say a few words about the dead, those imprinted on her eyes as a child, and that was all. Our thirst for the present remained unsatisfied. So in the afternoon, when the air grew like limpid water, my sister Regina and I would take ourselves off to the broad terrace surrounding Monsieur Tertullien's pit, where all the local cocks fought on Sundays. Monsieur Tertullien also kept a small bar, and people used to gather on his veranda with glasses of rum and absinthe, laughing and squabbling and speaking ill of those they thought could not stand up for themselves. One day as were there picking up tittle-tattle as usual, we heard them talking about our mother. Victory had no status and no ornament in this world – not so much as a pair of earrings, only a couple of bastards. So why did she avoid them all as if they were a pack of lepers? The words seemed to bury themselves in the depths of the earth, like a lost seed with no hope of sprouting: everyone scratched idly and cracked the joints of their fingers, tired even before they had opened their mouths. Then, with visible reluctance, the oldest inhabitant opened his lips and said very slowly: 'Why won't you people ever admit it? Everyone lives at a certain height above the ground – it's in the blood. The Lougandors have always liked to fly high, grow wings, raise themselves up. And', he concluded decisively, 'Victory still hasn't even reached her true height.' And then, noticing we were there, the oldest inhabitant coughed and smiled shyly at us, and the conversation shifted to other things. Back home, when we tried to question our mother, we got the same mysterious answer we always got:

'They can say whatever they like. Some people can't sleep easy unless they've spoken ill of someone else. But I am what I am, just at my right height, and I don't go begging in the streets to fill your bellies.'

Mama was a woman who carried her head high on a slender neck. Her eyes, always half shut, seemed to be asleep, dreaming in the shade of their thick lashes. But if you looked into her eyes well, you saw her determination to stay serene however harshly the winds might blow, and to see everything from the point of view of that head held high. No one in L'Abandonnée noticed her beauty, for her skin was very dark; it was only after my father set eyes on her that everyone else did the same. When she sat in the sun the black lacquer of her skin had glints the colour of rosewood, like those you see in old rocking chairs. When she moved, the blood rose near the surface and mingled in the blackness, and glints the colour of wine appeared in her cheeks. When she was in the shade she at once coloured the air surrounding her, as if her presence created a smoky halo. When she laughed her flesh grew rounded, taut, and

17

transparent, and a few green veins appeared on the backs of her hands. When she was sad she seemed to be consumed like a wood fire; she went the colour of a scorched vine, and as her emotion increased it would turn her almost grey. But it was very rare for her to be seen like this, the colour of cold embers, for she was never sad in public, or even in front of her children.

When she found herself pregnant for the third time she stopped singing by way of a reproach, and sadly told my elder sister: 'After you, Regina, I agreed to have Angebert in my house, but it was only because I needed bread. And as you see, I've reaped body for body, first Telumee and now this one, and still there's no bread on my table.' This confession seemed to relieve her, and, her anger gone, there came into her eyes a kind of old familiar resolution, and her lips parted in a peaceful smile. But one day when she was spreading the clothes out to bleach, she slipped on a stone, and though they carried her home and fanned her and rubbed her with camphorated rum, the child was born prematurely and died. It was a boy, fully formed, and Mama was always very proud of him. Sometimes she would pause in her ironing, run her fingers lightly over her stomach, and say: 'People see me in the street, but who can know this belly has carried a man, a man to laugh and cry and become Pope if he felt like it? Who can know that, eh?'

My father would listen attentively and watch for the quarters of the moon, hoping a similar moon would bring him a child exactly the same, a similar moon hung in the sky like the other. 'And when the time comes, what's done will be done', he would say quietly.

Angebert was a man who was naturally serious, but who made no effort either at laughter or gravity. He did not see life as a jungle through which one had to make one's way by every means available. In fact, he didn't really know where he was. Maybe it was a jungle, he would sometimes admit to a friend, but he didn't bother about that: 'Loot, break, steal – but count me out.' He was rather a small man whose aim was to go through life as inconspicuously as possible. He went about quite calmly, happy in the idea that his small concerns were getting on beautifully because no one noticed he was there. Alert to everything, he didn't need long confabulations with his friends to know what was going on around him. 'But who could imagine I see things this way?' he said to himself. And my father's face brimmed over with placidity.

He was from Pointe-à-Pitre, and like many others he had halted at the foot of the mountain because in those days L'Abandonnée seemed like the back of beyond. Looking into the houses as he went through the village, he had noticed, he thought, several cane-bottomed chairs that needed mending. So on the off-chance he said he was a chair mender, but he waited many long months after that and was never sent one chair to repair. He lived in the woods as peaceful as could be, setting traps for crayfish in the river, picking breadfruit, and digging up wild vegetables that he ate with a bit of salt and a drop of oil. One evening he felt like hearing people laugh, so he dressed and set off for Monsieur Tertullien's little shop, which was always full of men and women quarreling, playing at dice, drinking, and scoffing at life and death. The veranda was too small to hold everyone, so by the side of the road, in the shadows, little groups chatted together and others temporarily alone puffed thoughtfully at their pipes. Angebert didn't care for drinking, but he was careful not to condemn drinkers too sweepingly in his thoughts. Anyone may fall, he said: the pig dies, and he who kills the pig dies too – it's just a question of when. He had come to hear people laugh, but it wasn't the moment, perhaps because it was so long since the cane cutting was over. He was just about to go back to his solitude when Victory arrived with my elder sister Regina. My poor mother was quite drunk and staggered at every step. She was waving her arms about and talking to some invisible interlocutor. Suddenly, stopping opposite the little bar packed with people, she said to her ghost: 'As I told you, it's here I'm holding the dance – I'm the bride, and the one I'm marrying is Hubert. When I was up at the top of the coconut palm, I could see all heaven. My parents were at the right hand of God, and God looked at me and said quite simply, "Go back and get married, Victory, for the dance is about to begin with Hubert."'

According to what I was told more than twenty years after the event, Hubert was a Negro from Désirade who had stayed for several days in the ruins of the white man's house, and then disappeared none knew where. When he vanished Victory immediately abandoned her irons and her songs and wandered about for

19

six months, exalted with rum. A neighbour looked after my sister Regina, but one day the little girl saw her mother stagger by on the road, and from that moment she followed her everywhere she went.

On the evening we're speaking of, Angebert took Victory by the arm and brought her back as fast as he could to the ruin at L'Abandonnée. He put her to bed, she fell asleep at once, and he ate his supper in silence under the astonished gaze of Regina. That was how my parents came together.

He understood about Hubert, the Negro from Désirade, and waited calmly for Victory's grief to end, without ever raising a hand to her, even when he found her weaving about the streets drunk. It wasn't his line to beat people, he said, and anyway he didn't think not drinking and preferring to look at things clearly made him any better than anyone else. But a little icy mist crept further and further around his heart each time he had to put Victory to bed senseless and overcome with rum. Then he would be seized by a feeling of emptiness, nothingness, and would toss vainly on his pallet trying to find a place to lie that would not give way beneath him. This feeling of non-existence stayed with him, and later, when I was a very little girl, he would sometimes stroke my woolly braids and say uneasily, 'It's me, Angebert. Do you know who I am?'

Father set pots in the hollows of the streams and sold the crayfish he caught to the townspeople, or to Monsieur Tertullien, who in return provided us with salt and salted cod. From time to time a man called Germain would drag his baleful body to our lonely retreat. We used to give him a hot meal, and if he was in a good mood he would go and fetch us some wood or some wild roots that he used to throw into the pig bucket to cook. He was a notorious crayfish thief, and Father was always saying to him:

'Be sure you don't steal from me, Germain, or you'll pay for it. There are so many other pots in the river, all you have to do is act as if you didn't see mine. Thieve from the others if you like, on your nocturnal jaunts, but take care not to pinch even one of my crayfish, because they're my family's bread. I'm serious, so be careful.'

Germain, his eyes shining, would say nothing, and he carried on as ever, exploiting other people's hard work. Every night, torch in hand, he visited all the rivers and emptied one pot after the other, except those belonging to his friend Angebert. Everyone knew who it was who sneaked and stole and took advantage of the other Negroes' sweat, and more than once the culprit got himself thrashed. These punishments, though richly deserved, humiliated him deeply. He would hide in the bushes, jump out on his victim unawares, and slake his resentment as seemed to him appropriate. One day a man whose pots he had poached cursed him thus: 'Runaway slave, conscienceless robber, you'll come to such a bad end even the devil will laugh at you. You're like a dog tied to a rope that wants to be free, but you won't get far, your attempt won't get you any further than jail. For the attempt is one thing, but then come weariness and collapse.' Eyes shut, head thrown back, the veins standing out on his neck, the man cursed Germain in front of the whole population of the village, attracted by the row. The unhappy prophecy did not enter into earth or sky or the trunks of the trees, nor did it mingle with the falling dusk; it stayed there weighing on the heart, and there was a feeling that something terrible was impending somewhere. From that day Germain was a different man. Every evening he would come to Angebert and say mournfully: 'My life is torn apart, torn from end to end, and the stuff cannot be mended. Someone tosses a word in the air without thinking, and madness strikes, and men kill and are killed.' Father would take his arm and they would go together in silence, with bowed heads, to the bar, where they would down a glass of tafia in one gulp. Fortified by the rum, the two friends would sigh, look at the other customers, and join in a game of lotto. And the wind rose, sweeping before it the months, the seasons, and the dreams and lamentations of men. Then came the end of the harvest, when there was no work to be found and it was time to be smart. The Negroes' savings had melted away more rapidly than ever that year. They were reduced to eating roots from the forest; some were relying on the crayfish they caught to see them through till the sugar cane was ready. All the pots were watched over, camouflaged, hidden in inaccessible places upstream, and emptied before Germain even got wind of their mysteries. He prowled around L'Abandonnée like a wild beast in a cage, going up and down the street alone, breast bare, or lying down in the middle of the road

21

and shouting to the drivers of the ox carts: 'Run me over! Run me over! What race do I belong to? I belong to the road, so don't pick me up – run me over, I tell you!' And everyone stopped their ears, and shut their eyes so as not to see him who wanted to anticipate fate. Our house was quite bare now, and Mama shook the bottle of oil over our dinner of roots in vain. My father had set all his pots and was letting his catch mount up in the hope of selling it to the townspeople on Sunday morning. But that Saturday at the first light of dawn he found his recently set pots empty, and empty too the stores filled up the day before with crayfish with their long blue tails. When he got back home he found the thieving Germain, who smiled piteously and said, 'Watch out for yourself today, Angebert. I'm going to kill you.' My father had been stricken by what had happened; his gaze wandered and he was running with yellow sweat, like bile. But Germain's attack on him was so strange and unwarranted he couldn't help laughing. 'Be off', he said at last, very gently. 'Get out of my sight at once – the blood's suffocating me.' Germain went immediately, looking grave and astonished, and my father spent the whole day sitting on his little wooden bench, his head in his hands, silent. In the evening he got up, fed the animals, put on clean clothes, and walked calmly to the bar in the village. Regina, Mama, and I followed at a distance, so as not to undermine him with our women's fears. Germain was leaning on the counter, and my father got hold of him by the scruff of the neck, gave him a kick, and shouted, 'Why did you do it, eh?' They both went out and began to fight in the semidarkness, in a patch of scrub adjoining the bar. Suddenly my father's voice was heard: 'Oh Germain, you've stabbed me!' And then a rattle. Everyone ran out of the bar to find my father lying in a pool of blood and Germain standing beside his victim, a penknife all slimy in his hand Germain at once threw the knife into a thicket of acacias on the edge of the field. Someone lit a torch and Monsieur Tertullien went down on his knees among the acacias looking for the weapon that had just killed Angebert. A crowd was gathering now, everyone giving his own account of the murder. One man emerged from the rest and struck Germain a blow right in the chest. This first blow acted as a signal: people spat in Germain's face, plucked at his flesh, tore off all his clothes to see, so they said, what a murderer looked like. I gave him a good punch myself. One woman dipped her hands in my father's blood and smeared it all over Germain's face, arms, and naked torso, shouting shrilly: 'Murderer, you're stained and defiled for ever by this blood! Smell it – enjoy the smell!' Insults and blows rained down, and I could no longer recognize the man I knew in the naked form covering his genitals with his hands and repeating ceaselessly, his eyes closed: 'I stabbed Angebert, and you can kill me. Go on – you've every right. But I swear it's not my fault. No, not my fault.' His lamentations only increased the hatred; already Germain was of a different species from the people of L'Abandonnée. The murder had taken place before their eyes, and they had not prevented it. Everyone had always known deep down that Germain was bound to kill someone sooner or later: he was born to it. Yet no one had moved when the two men went out of the bar. This thought only made them crueller, and they would probably have killed Germain if the police, summoned by no one knew whom, had not ridden up. Germain went slowly away behind them, a rope around his neck, stumbling through the darkness. After that two men picked up the body, and through the shadows a voice was heard saying: 'I forgive Germain, because his will was no longer his own. Human wickedness is great, and can turn a man into anything, even a murderer – yes, I'm not joking, even a murderer.'

Messengers were already plunging through the night to report Angebert's death. The procession moved off toward the ruins of L'Abandonnée, where the wake was to be held. Unweeping, her eyes half shut, Mama walked along in the starlight, one shoulder higher than the other, dragging her feet, limping almost, as under a burden heavier than herself.

When, in the long hot blue days, the madness of the West Indies starts to swirl around in the air above the villages, bluffs, and plateaus, men are seized with dread at the thought of the fate hovering over them, preparing to swoop on one another like a bird of prey, and while they are incapable of offering the slightest resistance. It was on Germain's shoulder that the bird alighted, and it put the knife in his hand, and aimed it at my father's heart. Angebert had led a reserved and silent existence, effacing himself

23

so completely that no one ever knew who it was who had died that day. Sometimes I wonder about him, ask myself what anyone so kind and gentle was doing in this world at all. But all that is gone, and in front of me the road rushes ahead, turns, and is lost in the dark.

PART TWO

The Story of My Life

1

Two years after Angebert's death a stranger, a man called Haut-Colbi, came to the village and altered the course of my destiny. He was a Carib very well set up, but he moved as if his natural element was water – it was as though he was swimming, he was so smooth and supple. His eyes rested on you like a silk scarf, and his coaxing mouth, his cascading laugh, and his dark, violet-shadowed skin fascinated any woman he happened to pass in the street. He came from Côte-sous-le-vent, the lee shore.

Despite her two bastards, my mother was not a fallen woman. She went through life with the same expectation, the same lightness she had when no man's hand had yet touched her. The years had merely drawn her open a little, and now she was a vanilla pod that has burst in the sun and at last gives forth all its perfume. One morning she set out on an errand, singing as usual and with her usual grace. Then she saw Haut-Colbi and the song ceased. It is said they stood for an hour gazing at each other, in the middle of the street and in full view of all, transfixed by the astonishment that grips the human heart when for the first time dream coincides with reality. They soon set up house together, thus transforming my fate. Haut-Colbi was only passing through L'Abandonnée, our hamlet, by chance, but he saw my mother and stayed.

The fact is that a mere nothing, a thought, a whim, a particle of dust can change the course of a life. If Haut-Colbi had not stopped in the village my little story would have been very different. For my mother found her god that day, and that god was a great connoisseur of feminine flesh, or at least that was his reputation. The first thing my mother did was send me away, remove my little ten-year-old flesh to save herself the trouble, a few years later, of trampling on the womb that betrayed her. So she decided to pack me off to my grandmother at Fond-Zombi, a long way away from her Carib.

She was criticized greatly for this, and generally accused of spitting on her own womb—for whom and for what? For a coaxing mouth from Côte-sous-le-vent. But she had known life for a long time, my amorous mother with her two bastards for earrings; and she knew that almost always you have to tear out your entrails and fill your belly with straw if you want to enjoy a little walk in the sun.

Queen Without a Name had not been too pleased with the way her daughter was steering her boat on the waters of life. But when Haut-Colbi came to live in our tower she began to think Victory wasn't such a bad sailor after all. To those who criticized her daughter's conduct she would say in a soft, amused voice: 'My friends, life is not all meat soup, and for a long time yet men will know the same moon and the same sun and suffer the same pangs of love.' In fact, she was overjoyed at the mere idea of having my innocence cast a halo around her white hair, and when she came to fetch me she went away from L'Abandonnée blessing my mother.

It was the first time I'd been away from home, but I wasn't at all upset. On the contrary, I felt a kind of excitement, going along the white chalky road bordered with filaos with a grandmother whose earthly existence I'd thought was over. We walked in silence, slowly, my grandmother so as to save her breath and I so as not to break the spell. Towards the middle of the day we left the little white road to its struggle against the sun, and turned off into a beaten track all red and cracked with drought. Then we came to a floating bridge over a strange river where huge locust trees grew along the banks, plunging everything into an eternal blue semidarkness. My grandmother, bending over her small charge, breathed contentment: 'Keep it up, my little poppet, we're at the Bridge of Beyond.' And taking me by one hand and holding on with the other to the rusty cable, she led me slowly across that deathtrap of disintegrating planks with the river boiling below. And suddenly we were on the other bank, Beyond: the landscape of Fond-Zombi

27

unfolded before my eyes, a fantastic plain with bluff after bluff, field after field stretching into the distance, up to the gash in the sky that was the mountain itself, Balata Bel Bois. Little houses could be seen scattered about, either huddled together around a common yard or closed in on their own solitude, given over to themselves, to the mystery of the forest, to spirits, and to the grace of God.

Queen Without a Name's cabin was the last in the village; it marked the end of the world of human beings and looked as if it were leaning against the mountain. Queen Without a Name opened the door and ushered me into the one little room. As soon as I crossed the threshold I felt as if I were in a fortress, safe from everything known and unknown, under the protection of my grandmother's great full skirt. We had left L'Abandonnée in the early morning and now the evening mist was about to descend. Grandmother lit a lamp that hung from the main beam of the ceiling, turned down the wick to save oil, gave me a furtive kiss as if by chance, and took me by the hand to introduce me to her pig, her three rabbits, her hens, and the path that led to the river. Then, as the mist had fallen, we went back indoors.

In the cabin there was an iron bedstead covered with the poor man's sheet – four flour bags with the print still showing despite much washing. The bed alone took up half the available space. The other half contained a table, two chairs, and a rocker of plain unvarnished wood. Grandmother opened a can and took out two manioc cookies. Then, to wash all that dryness down, we sipped water out of the earthenware jar that occupied a place of honour in the middle of the table. By the faint light of the lamp I plucked up courage to look at Grandmother, to look her in the face for the first time directly and without disguise. Queen Without a Name was dressed in 'mammy' style with a head scarf. It was drawn tight over her brow and fell down her back in three narrow, nonchalant points. She had an almost triangular face, a finely drawn mouth, a short, straight, regular nose, and black eyes that were faded like a garment too often exposed to sun and rain. She was tall and gaunt though almost unbent; her feet and hands were particularly thin. She sat up proud and straight in her rocker looking me over thoroughly as I examined her. Under that distant, calm, happy look of hers, the room seemed suddenly immense, and I sensed there were others there for whom Queen Without a Name was examining me, then kissing me with little sighs of contentment. We were not merely two living beings in a cabin in the middle of the night, but, it seemed to me, something different, something much more, though I did not know what. Finally she whispered dreamily, as much to herself as to me: 'I thought my luck was dead, but today I see I was born a lucky Negress and shall die one.'

Such was my first evening in Fond-Zombi, and the night was dreamless, for I had already dreamed in broad daylight.

Grandmother was past the age for bending over the white man's earth, binding canes, weeding and hoeing, withstanding the wind, and pickling her body in the sun as she had done all her life. It was her turn to be an elder; the level of her life had fallen; it was now a thin trickle flowing slowly among the rocks, just a little stirring every day, a little effort and a little reward. She had her garden, her pig, her rabbits, and her hens. She made manioc cookies on a tin sheet, coconut cakes and barley sugar, and crystallized sweet potatoes, sorrel, and 'forbidden fruit', which she took every morning to Old Abel, whose shop was next to our house. I helped her as best I could: I fetched water, ran after the pig and the hens, ran after the hairy-shelled land crabs, so delicious salted, ran after weeds with the 'little bands' of other children in the canefields belonging to the factory, ran with my little load of fertilizer, ran all the time with something on my head – the drum of water, the weed basket, the box of fertilizer that burned my eyes at every gust of wind or trickled down my face in the rain, while I dug my toes into the ground, especially on the slopes, so as not to drop the box and my day's pay with it.

Sometimes there would be the sound of singing somewhere; a painful music would invade my breast, and a cloud seemed to come between sky and earth, covering the green of the trees, the yellow of the roads, and the black of human skins with a thin layer of grey dust. It happened mostly by the river on Sunday morning while Queen Without a Name was doing her washing: the women around about would start to laugh, laugh in a particular way, just with their mouths and teeth, as if they were coughing. As the linen flew the women hissed with venomous words, life turned to water and mockery, and all Fond-Zombi seemed to splash and writhe and swirl in the dirty water amid spurts of diaphanous foam. One of them, a lady by the name of Vitaline Brindosier, old, round, and fat, with snow-white hair and eyes full of innocence, had a special talent for upsetting people. When souls were heavy and everything proclaimed the futility of the black man's existence, Madame Brindosier would flap her arms triumphantly, like wings, and declare that life was a torn garment, an old rag beyond all mending. Then, beside herself with delight, laughing, waving her fine round arms, she would add in a bittersweet voice: 'Yes, we Negroes of Guadeloupe really are flat on our bellies!' And then the other women would join in with that strange laugh of the mouth and teeth, a kind of little cough, and suddenly darkness would descend on me and I would wonder if I hadn't been put on earth by mistake. Then I would hear Queen Without a Name whispering into my ear: 'Come away, Telumee, as fast as you can. They're only big whales left high and dry by the sea, and if the little fish listen to them, why, they'll lose their fins!' With the washing heaped on our heads and my grandmother leaning on my shoulder, we would leave the river and go slowly back to her little cabin. Sometimes she would stop, perspiring, by the side of the road, and look at me with amusement. 'Telumee, my little crystal glass', she would say thoughtfully, 'there are three paths that are bad for a man to take: to see the beauty of the world and call it ugly, to get up early to do what is impossible, and to let oneself get carried away by dreams – for whoever dreams becomes the victim of his own dream'. Then she would set off again, already murmuring a song, some beguine from the old days to which she would give a special inflection, a sort of veiled irony, the object of which was to convey to me that certain words were null and void, all very well to listen to but better forgotten. Then I'd shut my eyes and grip Grandmother's hand, and tell myself it had to exist, some way of dealing with the life Negroes bear so as not to feel it pressing down on one's shoulders day after day, hour after hour, second after second.

When we got home we would spread the linen out on the nearby bushes and that would be the end of the day. It was the moment when the breeze rose and climbed gently up the hill, filled with all the scents it had picked up on the way. Grandmother settled herself in her rocker in the doorway, drew me beside her, up against her skirts, and, sighing with pleasure at every movement of her fingers, peacefully set about doing my braids. In her hands the metal comb scratched nothing but the air. She moistened each lock with a drop of carapate oil to make it smooth and shiny, and, deft as a seamstress, separated strands, arranged them in little bunches and then in stiff plaits that she pinned up all over my head. And, only stopping to scratch her neck or shoulderblade or an ear that irritated her, she would give a delicate rendering of slow mazurkas, waltzes, and beguines, as sweet as syrup, for, with her, happiness expressed itself in melancholy. She sang 'Yaya', 'Ti-Rose Congo', 'Agoulou', 'Trouble Brought on Yourself', and many other splendid things from the old days, many of the lovely forgotten things that no longer charm the ear of the living. She knew old slave songs, too, and I used to wonder why, as she murmured those, Grandmother handled my hair even more gently than before, as if they turned her fingers liquid with pity. When she sang ordinary songs, Queen Without a Name's voice was like her face, where the cheekbones were the only two patches of light. But for the slave songs her pure voice detached itself from her old woman's face, soaring up into amplitude and depth, and reaching distant realms unknown to Fond-Zombi, so that I wondered if Queen Without a Name, too, had not come down on earth by mistake. I listened to the heartrending voice, to its mysterious appeal, and the waters of my mind began to be troubled, especially when Grandmother sang:

> Mama where is where is where is Idahe
> She is sold and sent away Idahe
> She is sold and sent away Idahe.

Then Grandmother would bend down and stroke my hair and say something kind about it, though she knew very well it was shorter and more tangled than it should be. And I always loved to hear her compliments, and as I leaned, sighing, against her stomach, she would put her hand under my chin, look into my eyes, and say, with an expression of astonishment:

'Telumee, little crystal glass, what have you got inside that body of yours to make an old Negress's heart dance like this?'

31

2

Life at Fond-Zombi was lived with doors and windows open: night had eyes, and the wind long ears, and no one could ever have enough of other people. As soon as I arrived in the village I knew who was aggressor and who was victim, who still held his soul high and who was on the road to ruin, who poached in waters belonging to his friend or brother, who was suffering, who was dying. But the more I learned the more it seemed that the main thing escaped me, slipped between my fingers like an eel.

Old Abel's shop was on the other side of the road, a few steps away from our cabin but toward the hamlet, not the mountain. When Queen Without a Name sent me there with cassavas, coconut ice, and bags of kilibibis or crystallized fruit in exchange for some oil or salt or a strip of dried fish, I used to hang around as long as I could in the hope of discovering the grown-ups' secret, the secret that enabled them to stay on their feet all day without collapsing. Using a plank for a counter, Old Abel dispensed oil and cod, kerosene, candles, salted meat, matches by the box or three at a time, aspirins singly or by the tube, cigarettes as required, and all the various sweet things Queen Without a Name made him to warm the cockles of his customers' hearts. There was a bar for the men on the other side of an open-work partition; the women stayed out on the veranda, straining to hear the shouts that rose from the inner room with the evening rum, lotto, dice, fatigue, and boredom. I was usually to be found under the plank that served as counter, while Old Abel's son, a boy of my own age, came and went on the other side, in the bar proper. As he served and cleared away he would every so often give me a long, incredulous glance, as if I were something in a dream. But I paid no attention to him – I was completely caught up with what was going on in the bar. Tongues wagged, fists were shaken for mysterious reasons, the dice went

32

rolling loudly over the tables, and my own thoughts seemed to roll over and over one another so that I couldn't sort them out. Sometimes a dim fear would come over me and my mind would seem to come apart, like a pearl necklace with a broken thread. Then I would say to myself, Lord, the incredible things one sees in this world.

Most of the time the bar rang with the din of dice, tokens, and dominoes being flung down on the table. The atmosphere was full of wrangling, mockery, and challenges that were hurled into the air and never came to earth. Once as I crouched under the counter I saw a frail young man called Ti Paille suddenly get to his feet, his eyes bulging with rage, and shout: 'No people deserves death, but I say the Negro deserves death for living as he does. Don't you agree it's death we deserve, brothers?' There was a silence, then another man got up and said he was going to kill Ti Paille just to teach him how to live. But Ti Paille answered that he wanted to die, that that was the very thing he longed for, and when, a little while later, he was carried out wounded in the head, he was smiling. This incident made a great impression on me. I was also very interested when the men started to talk about spirits, spells, a man who'd been seen the week before running about like a dog, and old Ma Cia, who flew about every night over the hills and valleys and cabins of Fond-Zombi, her ordinary human form insufficient for her. Grandmother had already spoken to me about this woman, her friend, who was closer to the dead than to the living, and she was always promising to take me to see her one afternoon. So I listened avidly to all that was said about her. One day Old Abel told the story of how Ma Cia had given him the scar he had on his arm, a scratch from the claws of the flying Negress. He was coming back from a night fishing when two huge birds started hovering over his head. One of them had breasts instead of wings, and Old Abel recognized Ma Cia by her transparent eyes and the breasts he'd seen one day as she was washing in the river. As soon as he recognized her, Ma Cia circled down and alighted on the branches of a nearby flame tree, which began to move around Old Abel, followed by all the other trees, their leaves rustling. Then, as Old Abel didn't give way, the trees withdrew and an enormous wave came down out of the sky, seething with foam, rocks, and sharks with their eyes full of tears. But Ma Cia was foiled again, for the water spout

33

disappeared up into the sky as swiftly as it had come. Then there appeared a horse the size of three horses one on top of the other. But Old Abel never flinched, and the horse galloped away. Before its final retreat, however, it lashed out with its hoofs, and it was then he got this gash.

And Old Abel, tracing the scar, which ran from wrist to elbow, with his fingernail, said in a low, expressionless voice: 'Oh, I was on the edge of a precipice, where to draw back was to die. But I wasn't afraid, and here I am with a tongue in my mouth still, with which to say—"Help me, my friends"'.

When I recounted all this to Grandmother, astonished that she should be friends with such a creature, she shrugged her shoulders and admitted, smiling: 'It's true Ma Cia is not satisfied with the human form God gave her, and has the power to change herself into any animal she likes. And who knows, perhaps she's this ant running over your neck and listening to all the nasty things you're saying about her.' 'But why should anyone turn into a bird or a crab or an ant, Grandmother? Isn't it really for the animals to turn into men?'

'It isn't for anyone else to judge Ma Cia. Man didn't invent misfortune, and before yaws came to eat the soles of our feet there were already flies in the world. Men take pleasure in winding their tongues around Ma Cia and tossing her about like the clothes we beat on the rocks to get the dirt out. It's true people are afraid to talk about her, and that it's dangerous to pronounce her name: But do they tell you what they do when they dislocate a bone, or have a muscle cramp, or can't get their breath?'

She concluded in a firm voice, smiling reassuringly: 'The truth is that Ma Cia is a good woman, but it's best not to get on the wrong side of her.'

Next morning Grandmother gave me a peculiar look, attended to her usual tasks, gave the animals a good feed, shut the door, wedged it carefully with a long stick, and said: 'We're going to see Ma Cia.' Turning toward the mountain, we took a little path overgrown with weeds. At first there were only ferns, then on either side of the path there appeared clumps of malaccas, tamarinds, and Chinese plum trees with their tempting fruit. But I never even thought of picking any – I was completely engrossed in following the long, silent strides of Queen Without a Name. Up above, the leaves of the tall trees touched, bent in the wind, hid the sky. The path came out into a clearing, a huge disc of red, sun-baked earth, in the middle of which stood a rickety little cabin. The thatch was almost green, the faded boards the same color as the mosses, rocks, and dead leaves in the neighbouring copses: it seemed to belong entirely to the spirits of the forest that rose up not far off against the hesitant light of dawn. Here and there, rags tied to branches, sticks driven into the ground, and shells arranged to form crosses protected the cabin from harm.

Queen Without a Name walked quickly up to the house, called out in a low, anxious voice, 'Does anybody live here?', and without waiting for an answer walked away to a nearby mango tree, where we sat down in silence on some fine flat river stones. At that moment, an ordinary-looking little old woman came out of the cabin. She was barefooted and wore a full Creole dress with a big white head scarf tied behind and falling down her back. As she glided swiftly toward us over the clay soil, I saw a subtle face that spoke of ecstasy, and involuntarily closed my eyes. With the hem of her dress the old woman wiped the sweat from Grandmother's brow and kissed her several times, apparently not noticing my presence.

'How's life, Toussine?' she said.

'I've had a dream, Cia, and I've brought the dream here to anoint your eyes.'

'What do you mean, a dream?' cried Ma Cia, pretending not to understand.

'A root of luck, then', said Grandmother, smiling, 'and I've brought it here for you to breathe its scent.'

Turning to me, Ma Cia noticed me at last, gave me a long look, and began to kiss me: a first kiss on the brow – for herself, she said, and the pleasure I gave her; a second one on the left cheek, because I was not one of those who danced when others pulled the strings; a third so that my right cheek wouldn't be jealous; and a last one because she could already see I was a fine little Negress. And she added, enveloping me in her lovely tranquil gaze: 'You will rise over the earth like a cathedral.'

35

The two old women began to talk under the big mango tree, while I stared avidly at Ma Cia trying to make out what made her different from other people. I scrutinized her curved fingernails grooved lengthwise like claws, her grey feet with their big prominent heels, the small bony body almost like a child's, and the weathered face, peeling in places. And the more I looked at her, the more she seemed just like everyone else, an ordinary little old woman from Fond-Zombi. But just the same, there was something about her, this friend of Queen Without a Name. And what was it? It was those eyes – huge, transparent, the sort of eyes people say can see everything, bear everything, because they never shut, even in sleep.

While I was studying and staring at her freely, she suddenly turned her transparent witch's eye on me and said:

'Child, why do you look at me like that? Do you want me to teach you to turn yourself into a dog or a crab or an ant? Do you want to stand aloof from human beings from now on, to keep them off with a barge pole?'

I would have liked to sustain that clear, serene, underlying laughing look, which seemed to contradict the seriousness of the words. But a great fear prevented me, and I hung my head in shame and stammered:

'You can see I'm not a cathedral, and if you're looking for a fine Negress she's not here.'

Grandmother frowned.

'Is that all you have to say to each other on this fine Sunday? What a waste of light!'

Then Grandmother was leaning close to her friend and telling her a dream. She was bathing in a river, and dozens of leeches were around her head. One of them attached itself to her forehead, and she thought, It's drawing off the bad blood. But mightn't it have been her life that the leech was sucking away? Mightn't it be a sign of approaching death? Grandmother ended with an uneasy smile.

'What do you mean, death?' cried Ma Cia briskly. 'The leech was just drawing off the bad blood, and that's the long and the short of it. When your hour comes you'll dream your teeth drop out, you'll see your body and your clothes floating along in the river, and you'll find yourself in a strange country with trees and flowers you've never seen before. Don't pay attention to any dream but

36

that. Meanwhile, my dear, I don't know whether it's a fancy of the dead or the living, but the smell of the stew I've got on the stove is going to my head – I can feel the meat melting in my mouth. So come along.'

We laughed and got up, and when we came back a little while later, each with a steaming bowl of stew, Queen Without a Name. said to herself, sighing.

'There you go, you wretch, listening to the sound of your own voice, nineteen to the dozen, and no more thought of the dead than fly in the air.'

And she sat down abruptly with a bitter laugh, and some gravy spilled out of the bowl and onto the ground.

'Oh', said Ma Cia. 'So the dead are served first now, are they?'

'You know Jeremiah always had a weakness for stewed pork', said Grandmother, smiling.

'And how is he?' asked Ma Cia gravely.

'He hasn't forgotten me', said Grandmother happily. 'He comes to see me every night without fail. And he hasn't changed, he's just the same as when he was alive.'

'But is he well?' said her friend.

'He's very well', answered Grandmother gravely.

We were steeped in day, the light came in waves through the shifting leaves, and we looked at one another astonished to be there, all three, right in the stream of life. Suddenly Ma Cia burst out laughing.

'Toussine, do you think we'd eat this nice stew so contentedly if we were still slaves?'

Her eyes grew sad and ironic. They suddenly seemed washed out by sun, rain, and tears, all the things they'd seen that had sunk right into her brain. I was surprised, and plucked up the courage to ask:

'Ma Cia, dear, what *is* a slave, what *is* a master?'

'If you want to see a slave', she said coldly, 'you've only to go down to the market at Pointe-à-Pitre and look at the poultry in the cages, tied up, and at the terror in their eyes. And if you want to know what a master is like, you've only to go to Galba, to the Desaragnes' house at Belle-Feuille. They're only descendants, but it will give you an idea.'

'But what do you expect her to see now, Ma Cia?' said Queen

Without a Name. 'She'll see nothing, nothing at all. They smile, people bow to them, in their weird porticoed house. But who would think, to see them all smiles, that their ancestor the White of Whites would take a Negro in his arms and squeeze him till his spleen burst?'

'But what did he do that for?' I said, terrified.

Ma Cia thought for a while.

'Long ago', she said, 'a nest of ants that bite peopled the earth, and called themselves men. That's all.'

Queen Without a Name leaned up against Ma Cia and tried to take away some of her bitterness.

'Who can blame a dog for being tied up?' she said. 'And if he's tied up, how can you prevent him being whipped?'

'If he's tied up he ought to resign himself', said Ma Cia, 'for he's bound to be whipped. For a long time now God has lived in the sky to set us free, and lived in the white men's house at Belle-Feuille to flog us.'

'That is a fine word', said Grandmother. 'And after that sadness here is another: to see the fire go out and the puppies playing in the embers.'

'With your permission, my friend, I'd say it is a piece of sadness, not a whole one. The whole sadness was the fire. But the fire is out, and it's a long time now since the White of Whites was in the ground, rotten meat that will not grow again. And even the embers will not last forever.'

Queen Without a Name, her eyes shining strange and feverish, gazed at me for a long while and said:

'No, even the embers will not last forever.'

The two old women fell silent, the afternoon slipped away, everything in heaven and earth was clear and tranquil. Queen Without a Name and her friend Cia sat propped up against each other, their faces peaceful and confident. In the silence I looked at them, and wondered where all the fires came from, all the sparks, that they kindled out of their old patched-up bodies.

Later, we went for a little walk in the woods to gather leaves and wild fruit, and Ma Cia suddenly seemed thoughtful. Grandmother

38

and I watched her all the time, observing the light and shadow in her face, and we saw that though we could not guess what was concealed behind her brow, it irked her to have us looking at her while she was thinking. Then Grandmother heaved a deep sigh that signified our visit was almost over, and Ma Cia, turning to me, child that I was, said, 'Be a fine little Negress, a real drum with two sides. Let life bang and thump, but keep the underside always intact.' Grandmother nodded, and we went back down the overgrown path, clinging to each other. The sky was already low and purple; it was the hour when you could sense the weary flight of the moths through the heavy air. As soon as we got home I walked soberly to the far side of the yard and hid in the lower branches of a clump of bamboo, invisible in my little cage of leaves. For the first time in my life I realized that slavery was not some foreign country, some distant region from which a few very old people came, like the two or three who still survived in Fond-Zombi. It had all happened here, in our hills and valleys, perhaps near this clump of bamboo, perhaps in the air I was breathing. And I thought of the laughter of certain men and women, and their little fits of coughing echoed in me, and a heart-rending music arose in my bosom. And I listened to the laughter again, and I pondered, and thought I heard certain things; and I parted the leaves to see the world outside, the fading outlines, the evening rising up like an exhalation wiping out everything, first the cabin, then the trees, the distant hills, and the slopes of the mountain. The summit still shone in the sky, though all the earth was plunged in darkness, under the uneasy, unreal trembling of the stars, which seemed to have been put there by mistake, like everything else.

3

One day Mama Victory paid us a flying visit, radiant, wild, somewhat dishevelled, and bearing about her the signs of love and all its pangs. She would smile without reason, or put a hand to her brow and enter into a state of meditation in which her eyes wandered over us without taking us in. Hurriedly, briefly, in words both evasive and ringing, she told us the latest news about my sister Regina, who was now living with her real father in Basse-Terre, sleeping in a bed, eating apples from France, wearing a dress with puff sleeves, and going to school. This last detail particularly delighted her, and she kept referring to it, saying that little spicy-headed Negress could already sign her name. 'Ah', she would say, 'talk of anyone you like, Regina has all the columns of the white folk in her head, she writes as fast as a horse can gallop, and smoke comes out of her fingers. She won't ever sign any paper without knowing all the whys and wherefores. Do you know anything more horrible or humiliating than when you're asked to sign something and you have to put a cross? You can't read or write, my dear Negresses! It's a shame one can't forget. And when it happens, the earth won't even open and swallow you up.'

As we listened to her, Grandmother and I were filled with an unnameable sadness, and our heads hung down as if under some invisible burden. But even now Mama Victory was throwing her arms around us, weeping, laughing, stammering indistinguishable words; and with a gesture of farewell she rushed out and hurried to meet her fate. Haut-Colbi was waiting for her at the landing stage in Pointe-à-Pitre, and that same evening, on the shrewd advice of a sorcerer, they both set sail for the island of Dominica, in the hope of escaping the fate pursuing the Zambo-Carib, a connoisseur of feminine flesh and no mistake. We never saw Victory again.

A few years later I saw my sister in a procession of married couples outside the church in La Ramée. Regina had become an elegant city lady. I took advantage of the crowd to go up to her unobtrusively, and as I bent forward to kiss her she held out a gloved hand and said awkwardly, 'Why, you must be Telumee!'

Queen Without a Name was talented, a real Negress with two hearts, and she had made up her mind that life was not going to lead her up the garden path. In her view a human back was the strongest, toughest, most flexible thing in the world, an unchanging reality stretching far beyond the eye's reach. On it descended all the ravages, all the furies, all the eddies of human misery. For a long time the human back had been so, and it would be so for a long time still. The main thing, after all the changes and chances, the traps and surprises – the main thing was just to get your breath back and go on; that was what God had put you in the world for. Nothing made her rejoice, or feel sorry for herself, or complain, and no one knew what she had boiling in her pot, meat soup or a stone fom the river. She had put up her cabin at the far end of Fond-Zombi, away from all the others, at the spot where the forest begins, where the trees come to meet the wind and carry it up to the heights. The people still couldn't make her out: for them she was a 'freak', a 'loonie', a 'temporelle', but all this only made her shake her head and smile, and she went on doing what God had created her for—living.

She was only waiting for me to pour forth the last floods of her tenderness, to revive the gleam in her wornout eyes. There we were in the woods, supporting each other, tackling life as best we could and as we pleased. But inside her big full skirt there was, I knew, something I myself would not suffer from—lack of love. She had found a little bamboo stick to serve as a prop to her old bones. And when she thought I wasn't there, she would sit sighing gently in her corner, saying aloud that she was at peace with life, for when everything was taken into account she and it were quits. She lived for me, she breathed through my mouth. When I was away she would get into a state of agitation that only ended with my return. One day when I came back from the river I showed her two little bumps on my chest, almost invisible to the naked eye but just perceptible there under the skin. Her face crinkled up with joy, and

41

off she ran along the road, her dress caught up above the knees, saying to all the women in the neighbourhood: 'Quick, come and look – Telumee's been stung by a wasp!' They all came running, singing, joking, proudly lifting their sagging bosoms, fêting in a thousand ways my little budding breasts, and saying teasingly: 'No matter how heavy your breasts you'll always be strong enough to support them. But the advent of my breasts had more serious consequences. Queen Without a Name no longer liked to see me go off for whole days planting out rows of bananas, picking coffee, or carrying buckets of fertilizer among the cane. Every day she warned me against the army of Negro boys that scoured the country. 'Don't mix with them, all they know is disrespect and no one can stop them following their own path. Leave them be, button up your lips in their presence, for they know everything, and they're bad lots already. They can only teach you vagrancy, theft, and insult. Don't you have anything to do with them, my little crystal glass. Just say good morning and good evening, listen to their tales and gossip if they must tell you them, but don't answer, whatever you do. Then you'll go on your way and stay as white as a tuft of cotton.' I didn't quite see how I was to follow Grandmother's advice. I wasn't the kind that hunts in packs, nor was I a lobster with cold blood and a cold stomach. I liked the company of the other children, those who worked among the canes, those who roved about and stole, those with fathers and mothers, and those without roof or bed who wandered through life like children of the devil. The boys played among themselves, and only came near us to tease, make us look small, pull our hair, and practice for their brilliant male future by gravely competing to see who could urinate the farthest. I preferred to be with the girls, especially two of them, Tavie and Letitia. We use to play with cashew nuts in a hole in the ground; we used to play pichine with little stones; we used to gossip about the women and their plans that came to nothing – about troubles, too, and spells, and all the things that happen in a house without a man. Tavie had a thin pointed face and dancing eyes. She was always on the lookout for a chink or an open door or a hole in a fence, and her favourite delight was to steal a hen and go and eat it alone in the woods, taking good care to bury the feathers. She was a particularly godforsaken little girl. Letitia used to go from house to house, picking up in each a piece of cod, a slice of breadfruit, some other fruit, or a scrap of meat, for the whole village was her mother. She was a bright little thing with a thick yet transparent skin that looked full of wine-coloured sap, like certain water flowers. She looked down at the world from a long neck that was usually supple, but which fright, anger, or triumph would suddenly stiffen like the neck of a wild goose. Like all little Negro girls, we affected the ways of grown-up women, waggling non-existent hips and breasts that were not there, strutting about, shouting at one another and waving our arms. We used to weigh up all the little boys, especially Elie, Old Abel's son, in whom my friend Letitia took a great interest. I myself had never paid any attention to him. But one day, as I was going along the path to the river with a bundle of dirty washing under my arm, young Elie suddenly emerged out of a clump of bushes overgrown with creepers. He was laughing to himself, and at his first glance I stood still, seized with a strange curiosity. A drum of water was perched unsteadily on his head, drenching him and splashing, every time he laughed, a skin that was like a chestnut after rain. A huge pair of khaki shorts flapped around his knees like a flared skirt – and, heavens, what knees! Great swollen calloused things that looked like the result of days of penance and yet were in fact just his own natural knees. His lips looked to me even more swollen than his knees, and as if all ready to insult me, but I forgot everything else, shorts, knees, and lips, as soon as I saw his eyes – great eyes lying there above his flat cheeks like two pools of fresh water.

After a long stare, his power of speech returned. He stood where he was and called out, still laughing with his lips:

'What are you doing here? Looking for the treasure your grandfather buried in the scrub?'

'What about you, know-it-all? Laughing for nothing!'

'Not for nothing', he said. 'It's seeing you makes me laugh.'

'What is there to laugh about in me? Is the part in my hair as crooked as a path the rats make, or is my dress inside out?'

'No, everything's in order, as neat as a well-kept chapel. I'm just laughing because you suddenly loomed up before me like an apparition. No offence, I hope?'

I answered that there was no offence, and went on towards the river, not suspecting my first star had just appeared in the east.

* * *

At about that time an elementary school opened in the little town of La Ramée. Its premises were an old stable, and the pupils sat or stood according to how many were present, their slates on their knees or held against their chests. One teacher was not really enough for all the children of the town itself and those from the nearby villages of Valbadiane, La Roncière, Dara, and Fond-Zombi. But those who dared attempt to learn their letters were few and far between. At first, people used to waylay the pupils on the road to school and ask them anxiously; 'How does it make your heads feel, little ones? Don't your brains feel too heavy? Don't they ever get so heavy inside you have to hang your heads?'

At daybreak we would scramble down the slopes, barefoot and carrying a lunch box done up in a cloth. At the end of the afternoon, home again, some sweaty and sleepy, others still lively under a sun veering gently to sink under the horizon. Elie and I had become friends. At noon we used to eat together under a huge flame tree that grew in a back yard not far from school. It was a cool spot, red with fallen flowers. It belonged to us, the other children only made passing visits. Elie helped himself to things from the shop, and with the aid of Old Abel's oil even the driest vegetables slipped down our throats like silk. When the meal was over, we chatted. In the atmosphere of La Ramée, and especially in the gloomy school building, there was something staid, severe, and pointless that made us uncomfortable, and to make up for the little sticks and the letters and the endless recitations, we always ended up talking about those fine creatures the men and women of Fond-Zombi. They lived there exposed to sun, rain, and wind, they might howl, they might die, they existed in complete uncertainty. But amid all the thunderbolts, one fine day, a single gleam was enough to start them off laughing again. But we pondered a lot about the personal life of the grown-ups. We knew how they made love, and we knew too how they tore at and clawed and trampled on one another afterwards, following an unchanging course that led from the chase to weariness and downfall. But it seemed to me the balance was in favor of the men, and that even in their fall there was still something of victory. They broke bones and wombs, then they left their own flesh and blood in misery as a crab leaves his pincers between your

44

fingers. At this point in my reflections Elie would always say gravely:

'Man has strength, woman has cunning, but however cunning she may be her womb is there to betray her. It is her ruin.'

These words troubled me, gripped my heart in a vise. I seemed to see a kind of smoke perpetually forming inside Elie, which would rise up one day and destroy him, and me with him. Dry-mouthed, I asked:

'Why are men like that? Tell me, Elie, tell me – does the devil live in Fond-Zombi? Oh, I wish I could know it by heart, the moment when you begin to lie to me.'

'Telumee, dear flame tree', Elie would say, stroking my hair, 'I am a man, and yet I understand nothing of all that, less than nothing. Imagine, even Old Abel sometimes seems to me a deserted child. Some nights he starts to shriek, in bed: "Did I really come from the womb of a human woman?" And then he leans over and takes me in his arms and whispers: "Alas, where can one go to cry out? It is always the same forest, always as dense as ever. And so, my son, put aside the branches as best you can, that's all."'

So saying, Elie would smile at me out of his beautiful eyes, large, bright, a little darker than his skin, a tear held back under the heavy lids with their tufted lashes, which all of a sudden he would lower as if falling asleep where he sat. And, still without looking at me, he would add:

'Telumee, if life is as my father says, I may one day lose my way in the forest. But don't forget – don't forget you're the only woman I shall ever love.'

Our talks under the tree were known to all Fond-Zombi, from the tiniest little green fruit to those already crumbling to dust. There were a thousand different versions of the business, everyone standing up for his own. In Fond-Zombi the night had eyes and the wind ears. Some had no need to see in order to speak, nor did others have to hear in order to know what was said. But Grandmother understood, and said I had inherited her luck, and how rare it was for a star to come out so early in a little Negress's sky. She looked at Elie through the same eyes as I did, heard him with my ears,

45

loved him with my heart. When I went into his shop, Old Abel's usual glum indifference would disappear. His eyes would come to life again, he seemed suddenly a man, and he would ask me a thousand little questions, just, he said, to sound out the future a little.

'Are you patient, little one?' he would ask, mischievously. 'If you're not, don't go aboard Elie's barge, or on any other for that matter, for above all a woman should be patient.'

'And what should a man be above all?'

'Above all', he would answer, 'a bit of a swaggerer. A man should have no fear either of living or dying.' Then he would take a mint drop out of the jar, quickly, and hold it out with a smile. 'May this little taste of mint make you forget my words – empty cartridges in a rusty gun.'

By common accord the Queen and Old Abel let us spend all Thursday, the weekly school holiday, together. If there'd been only Elie I'd have been a river, if there'd been only the Queen I'd have been Mount Balata, but Thursdays made me the whole of Guadeloupe. On Thursday we'd be up before the sun, and, in our own cabins, we'd watch through the chinks for daybreak. The crack of dawn saw water fetched, vegetables dug, the yard cleaned out; and at eight o'clock Elie would appear with a collection of big tins slung over his shoulder. Queen Without a Name nodded, and, as we set off, said: 'Don't be in a hurry to grow up, little Negroes. Frolic about, take your time – grown-ups don't live in paradise.' Then Elie would hunch his shoulders, and I would fall in step, an enormous heap of the town's dirty linen on my head. We took the path to the river, the one where he had appeared for the first time, the one where my star had risen. The river of Beyond had three branches. Instead of going to the ford that served Fond-Zombi in place of a fountain, we leaped from rock to rock until we reached a more isolated stretch of the river, where a waterfall tumbled into a deep basin called the Blue Pool. While Elie hunted crayfish, turning the stones one by one, I chose a good rock for my linen and began to pound and wring and larrup it as a torturer does his victim. Every so often Elie would let out a yell as a crayfish pinched his finger while he was putting it in the tin. The sun climbed slowly over the trees, and when, at about ten, it shone full on the river, I would splash myself with water, go back to my washing, splash myself again, and then, unable to resist any longer, jump fully dressed into the river. This happened every hour, until the whole pile of washing was done. Then Elie joined me and we'd dive together with all our clothes on, leaving our fears and youthful apprehensions deep at the bottom of the Blue Pool. Then we dried ourselves on a long flat rock, always the same one, exactly the right size to hold us, and as the words went back and forth I would be overcome by the thought that there was a small thing on earth, the same size as me, who loved me, and it was as if we had come out of the same womb at the same time. Elie would wonder if he'd get on well with his letters, because, if God willed, he wanted to become a customs clerk. He always drove before him the same dream, and I was a part of it.

'You'll see', he'd say, 'you'll see, later on, what a fine convertible we'll have, and we'll be dressed to match, I in a suit with a ruffle, you in a brocade dress with a cross-over collar. No one will recognize us. They'll say as we go by, "What beautiful young couple is this?" And we'll say, "One of us belongs to Queen Without a Name and the other to Old Abel – you know, the chap that keeps the shop?" And I'll give a toot on the horn and we'll whizz away laughing.'

I wouldn't say a word or utter a sigh, in case I gave voice to some evil influence that might prevent the dream from ever coming true. Elie's words made me proud, but I would have rather he'd kept them to himself, carefully sheltered from bad luck. And as I was silent, guarding hope, one of Queen Without a Name's stories came into my mind, the one about the little huntsman who goes into the forest and meets—'What did he meet, girl?' – he met the bird that could talk, and as he made to shoot it, shut his eyes, aimed, he heard a strange whistling sound:

> Little huntsman, don't kill me
> If you kill me I'll kill you too.

Grandmother said the little huntsman, frightened by the talking bird, lowered his gun and walked through the forest, taking pleasure in it for the first time. I trembled for the bird, which had nothing but its song, and lying there on my rock, feeling at my side Elie's damp and dreaming body, I too set off dreaming, flew away, took myself for the bird that couldn't be hit by any bullet because it invoked life with its song.

    Going down again to Fond-Zombi we felt as if we were still floating in the air, high above the wretched cabins and the abused, vague, fallow minds of the Negroes, and at the mercy of the wind, which lifted our bodies like kites. The breeze set us down in front of Queen Without a Name's house, by the smooth pink earthen steps. A wide band of setting sun swept in through the door on to the old woman, sitting scarcely raised above the ground on her tiny stool, in her everlasting gathered dress, rocking slowly back and forth, her eyes elsewhere. Elie would go and fetch wood for Old Abel, I'd spread my washing out for the night, and Queen Without a Name would set about cooking a crayfish sauce fit to make you go on your knees and give thanks. Already, here and there in the distance, a few lamps were already lit, though low, and the hens were starting to go up into the trees for the night. Elie would come running back, and Grandmother turned up the wick of her lamp so that we could see to shell our crayfish. Then she would seat herself carefully in her rocker, we would take our places at her feet on old flour bags on either side of her, and after a De Profundis for her dead – Jeremiah, Xango, Minerva, and her daughter Meranee – she would bring our Thursday to a close by telling us stories. Above our heads the land wind made the rusty corrugated iron roof creak and groan. But the voice of Queen Without a Name was glowing, distant, and her eyes crinkled in a faint smile as she opened before us a world in which trees cry out, fishes fly, birds catch the fowler, and the Negro is the child of God. She was conscious of her words, her phrases, and possessed the art of arranging them in images and sounds, in pure music, in exaltation. She was good at talking, and loved to do so for her two children, Elie and me. 'With a word a man can be stopped from destroying himself', she would say. The stories were ranged inside her like the pages of a book. She used to tell us five every Thursday, but the fifth, the last, was always the same: the story of the Man Who Tried to Live on Air.

*   *   *

'Children', she would begin, 'do you know something, a tiny little thing? The way a man's heart is set in his chest is the way he looks at life. If your heart is put in well, you see life as one ought to see it, in the same spirit as a man balancing on a ball – he's certain to fall, but he'll stick it out as long as possible. And now hear another thing: the goods of the earth remain the earth's, and man does not own even the skin he's wrapped in. All he owns are the feelings of his heart.'

At this point she would stop suddenly and ask:

'Is the court sleeping?'

'No, no, Queen, the court is listening', we'd hasten to reply.

'Well then, children, since you have hearts and ears well set, you must know that in the beginning was the earth, an earth all bedecked, with its trees and its mountains, its sun and its moon, its rivers, its stars. But to God it seemed bare, to God it seemed pointless, without the least ornament, and that is why he clad it in men. Then he withdrew again to heaven, in two minds whether to laugh or cry, and he said to himself, "What's done is done", and went to sleep. At that very instant the hearts of men leaped up, they lifted their heads and saw a rosy sky, and were happy. But before very long they were different, and many faces were no longer radiant. They became cowards, evildoers, corruptors. Some embodied their vice so perfectly they lost their human form and became avarice itself, malice itself, profiteering itself. Meanwhile the others continued the human line, wept, slaved, looked at a rosy sky and laughed. At that time, when the devil was still a little boy, there lived in Fond-Zombi a man called Wvabor Longlegs, a fine fellow the colour of burnt sienna, with long sinewy limbs and greenish hair that everyone envied. The more he saw of men the more perverse he found them, and the wickedness he saw in them prevented him from admiring anything whatever. Since men were not good, flowers were not beautiful and the music of the river was nothing but the croaking of toads. He owned land, and a fine stone house that could withstand cyclones, but on all that he looked with disgust. The only company that pleased him was that of his mare, which he'd named My Two Eyes. He loved the mare above all else, and would let her do anything: she sat in his rocking chair, pranced over his carpets, and ate out of a silver manger. One day, up early and full of yearning, he saw the sun appear on the horizon, and without knowing why he mounted My Two Eyes and rode away. Great pain was in him, he was wretched, and let the horse carry him where it willed. He rode from hill to hill, plain to plain, and nothing had power to cheer him. He saw regions never seen by human eye, pools covered with rare flowers, but he thought only of man and his wickedness, and nothing delighted him. He even ceased dismounting from his horse, and slept, ate, and thought on My Two Eyes' back. One day as he was riding about like this, he saw a woman with serene eyes, loved her, and tried to dismount. But it was too late. The mare started to whinny and kick, and bolted off with him far, far away from the woman, at a frantic gallop he couldn't stop. The animal had become his master.'

And stopping for the second time, Grandmother would say slowly, so as to make us feel the gravity of the question:

'Tell me, my little embers – is man an onion?'

'No, no', we'd answer, very knowledgeable in this field. 'Man isn't an onion that can be peeled, not at all.'

And she, satisfied, would go on briskly:

'Well, the Man who Tried to Live on Air, up on his mare, one day he was weary of wandering, and he longed for his estate, his house, the song of the rivers. But the horse still carried him away, further and further away. His face drawn, gloomier than death, the man groaned on from town to town, country to country, and then he disappeared. Where to? How? No one knows, but he was never seen again. But this evening, as I was taking in your washing, Telumee, I heard the sound of galloping behind the cabin, just under the clump of bamboo. I turned my head to look, but the beast aimed such a kick at me that I found myself back here, sitting in my rocker telling you this story.'

The light of the lamp faded, Grandmother merged into the darkness, and Elie said goodnight nervously, looked out at the dark road, and suddenly took to his heels and fled to Old Abel's shop. We hadn't stirred, Grandmother and I, and her voice grew strange in the shadows as she began to braid my hair. 'However tall trouble is, man must make himself taller still, even if it means making stilts.' I listened without understanding, and got on her knees, and she would rock me like a baby, at the close of those old far-off Thursdays. 'My little ember', she'd whisper, 'if you ever get on a horse, keep good hold of the reins so that it's not the horse that rides

50

you.' And as I clung to her, breathing in her nutmeg smell, Queen Without a Name would sigh, caress me, and go on, distinctly, as if to engrave the words on my mind: 'Behind one pain there is another. Sorrow is a wave without end. But the horse mustn't ride you, you must ride it.'

4

All rivers, even the most dazzling, those that catch the sun in their streams, all rivers go down to and are drowned in the sea. And life awaits man as the sea awaits the river. You can make meander after meander, twist, turn, seep into the earth – your meanders are your own affair. But life is there, patient, without beginning or end, waiting for you, like the ocean. We were a little apart from the world, little streams dammed up by school and protected from violent suns and torrential rains. We were safe there, learning to read and sign our names, to respect the flag of France our mother, to revere her greatness and majesty and the glory that went back to the beginning of time, when we were still monkeys with their tails cut off. And while school was leading us toward the light, up there on the hills of Fond-Zombi, the waters were intersecting, jostling, foaming, the rivers were changing their courses, overflowing, drying up, going down as best they could to be drowned in the sea. But however much care it took of us, and our frizzy little pigtailed heads, school could not stop our waters from gathering, and the time came when it opened its sluices and left us to the current. I was fourteen, with my two breasts, and beneath my flowered calico dress I was a woman. How often had Queen Without a Name told me that all rivers go down to and are drowned in the sea, how often had she told me? I pondered, I watched life wax and wane before my eyes, all the women lost before their time, broken, destroyed – and at their wakes the mourners tried, in vain, to think of the name, the true name they had deserved to bear. And so some looked on the sun while others disappeared into the night. And I pondered, calculated everything, wondering what loops, meanders, and gleams would be mine on my way to the ocean.

* * *

The time of the flame tree was well and truly over; we rode a great, continuous, shuddering wave; Fond-Zombi was astir as never before. We used to inundate the hamlet with our clatter. Shouts of laughter clashed and rose to the very tops of the trees; the air was a violin string, a pounded drum; gangs yelled to one another wildly. At all hours of the day, on the bridge, on the hill, on the road, under the lean-to roof of Old Abel's shop, there was some group of young idlers waving their arms about, discussing love at the tops of their voices, trumpeting their conquests, and quarreling, fighting, giggling about everything. They would walk up and down the valley, twitting those among them who'd found a job. With their women's bodies and children's eyes, my friends felt quite ready to get the better of existence: they intended to lead their lives full tilt, to overtake their mothers and aunts and godmothers. Warnings shot up on one hand, jeers on the other, and this whole new ovenful of hot bread rushed joyously to its fate in the ocean. Bellies grew round, wide skirts became the fashion. Flat bellies were mocked, were greeted with the song:

> No mother
> No father
> Bravo!
> A woman without two men
> Isn't worth a straw.

As they dragged their swollen legs about the streets, each carrying before her a little calabash of trouble, Queen Without a Name would throw up her arms and pray: 'I only hope the breeze goes on blowing on their poor balloons, I only hope it doesn't stop! So many pretty coconut flowers that will fade before their time. Hold fast, my girl, cling on, you must ripen, you must give forth your fruit.' I listened uneasily, looking at her gaunt cheeks and bony hands, at her eyes worn out with suns and rains and tears, with all the things she'd seen that had sunk into her retinas, slow to react of recent weeks, and sometimes sad and veiled with irony. Under the eternal three-cornered scarf a kind of light silvery nest had formed in the nape of her neck; it looked as if it would blow away at the slightest gust of wind. I should have loved to relieve her of her garden, her kilibibis and crystallized fruit, and her poor penny

53

barley sugars, and sit her in her rocker as was right at her age, to drink in through her ample nostrils the scents that wafted to her doorstep. That, that was what ought to await a poor she-ass of an old black Mama who had spent her life sweating and slaving. Since school I hadn't been idle. From sunrise to sunset I'd done nothing but tear about and drudge and wear my blood out. But only at odd jobs for which I was paid practically nothing: to bring in any money to speak of you had to go into the canefields, with their prickles, their wasps, their biting ants, and the foremen who were connoisseurs of feminine flesh. Grandmother herself ruled that out, saying my sixteen years were not going to provide them with their day's special. As for Elie, the very word cane drove him wild, filled him with incomprehensible fury. His dreams of being a great scholar were left far behind, the Customs had disappeared with school, and the convertible, the suit with the ruffle, and the brocade gowns with cross-over collars had all melted away into the same bitterness. All that survived were confused visions, a few pictures of snow and strange leafless trees in a book, a map of France, and some illustrations representing the seasons; the famous letters themselves, once the bearers of hope, they too were now fading into mere shades. Elie railed and swore by all the gods the cane would never get him, he was never going to buy a knife to go work on the land of the white men. He'd rather use it to cut his own hands off, he'd hack the air and cleave the wind but he wouldn't accept that fate. These words, uttered in the shop, entered the ear of a tall reddish-brown Negro called Amboise, a silent fellow, a philosopher, by trade a sawyer, who smiled and said: 'Here's what a Negro should do rather than go among the spikes of the canefields: cut off his right hand and make a present of it to the whites.' Next day Elie set off for the woods with Amboise, carrying a saw over his shoulder. By a mere word tossed into the air he had escaped doom.

From then on I only saw him on Sundays, for a few hours by the Blue Pool, where all the world's bustle died away. I used to tease him about his new trade. 'Do you want to die before your time, up there on the scaffolding in all that wet?' He would burst into his old laughter, the laughter of that first day on the path to the river. 'How are we to shelter our little carcasses later on if I don't saw planks?' And he'd laugh again, wheedle me, get around me

54

with a thousand words, imagine dresses for me, blue, red, and green, and end up by saying I was like a rainbow standing there before him. 'Oh stay, there where I can see you – don't disappear like that into the sky.' And he'd hold me so tight, to stop me from disappearing, that I could hardly breathe. One Sunday as I was sitting on a rock, in the cool, Elie sat down on another rock nearby and said:

'I think of the Blue Pool, like you, my little goatling, when the heat gets too much for me in the forest. You can run about when I'm not there, you can jump and dance – but you're mine, and your rope is tied around my waist. When you skip to the right, I go to the right. When you skip to the left, I go to the left.'

'Right. You've gone to the left. And then what?'

'Only you, leaping about far away from me – only you know that.'

'If I skip about, it's with my eyes fixed on your flesh and bones. You say my rope is tied around your waist. Don't pull on it, give me a little respite, a little time to breathe, that's all.'

We'd bathed together, and the sun was drinking the drops off us as we lay resting on a huge flat rock, burning hot, right in the middle of the river. The water slipped gently past it, and further on disappeared into a tunnel of mombins and giant ferns, which cast a restful but somewhat solemn shade. Turning toward Elie, I saw on his face the drawn expression he used to have under the flame tree when we were at school, when he spoke of his father, and the forest, life and its thousand and one paths, and his fears of getting lost. He dipped one hand into the clear water and said thoughtfully: 'You're right. Jump and frisk far away from me. What have I to offer you, and what good does it do me to see you as a fairy princess? One day our table will be set, our plates will be filled, and the next day we'll have salt water and three specks of oil staring at us. Only, Telumee, don't forget this: in my eyes nothing in the world is good enough for you, and if I have ten measly francs in my pocket and I see a dress that costs ten francs, I'll buy it for you, but it won't be good enough.'

I thought of lying there on the pebbles for Elie to stretch out at full length over me, but instead of that, lost Negress that I was, I took to my heels and ran away by the river while he called after me: 'But what did I say? What did I say?' But I kept running, and his voice got fainter and fainter, and soon all I could hear was the breeze among the cassias beside the path, and, somewhere, people laughing, people singing. I was back in Fond-Zombi.

Despite my wearing my fingers to the bone, cleaning the cabin where the women had their babies, looking after the animals owned in common, carrying the market women's loads to the main road, we still got barely a pound of fresh pork every Saturday and a cotton dress once a year. The tree of fortune didn't grow in Fond-Zombi. In spite of the grass that cut you, in spite of the red ants and centipedes, I'd willingly have broken my back among the canes and the pineapple rows. But every time I suggested it, this was all the encouragement I got from Queen Without a Name: 'My little sun, why would you want to serve up your sixteen years as a dainty morsel for a foreman? And all in exchange for what, for what wonderful reward? Just to be given a decent patch of ground to weed, a job that won't make you spit blood, where you won't cough your heart out among weeds taller than you are. And tell me this, too: where have you seen cane planted all the year round?' And if I thought of hiring myself out, behind the white man's chair, Queen Without a Name would say in a tone of deep reproach: 'Did I say you were in the way here? Did I?'

Seeing our hesitancy, our indecision, illness came and fell upon Queen Without a Name. From day to day she wasted away; little ailments came and perched on her old body, came and nested there like birds on a tree struck by lightning. On Ma Cia's advice I treated her with copious infusions and packs and wet cups. But proper pills were needed, too, and at every visit to the pharmacy our savings dwindled like a candle in a draft. Soon, however much we turned our purse upside down and shook it, not the smallest coin fell out. I'd have to go away, hire myself out by the month, sell my sweat in the usual regular manner. But where, in this out-of-the-way hole, was there a porticoed house with a gate and bougainvilleas? The biggest cabin in Fond-Zombi consisted of four rooms without the veranda. Grandmother and I went around all the neighbouring areas hoping to find a well-off house that might need a living-in servant. But our heads spun, and still not the slightest gleam appeared on the horizon. Then one day Queen Without a Name's face lit up and she said in a faintly reproachful voice: 'Why didn't I think of the Andreanors, and their big shop in Valbadiane?' But this beautiful vision was as short-lived as lightning. Grandmother, overcome with gloom, muttered: 'There are some very strange illnesses in this world. Man's blood turns to pus.'

I looked at her in astonishment, and she explained.

'The Andreanors are supposed to have leprosy in their blood, from father to son. I forgot it, thinking of Mamzelle Losea with her beautiful mulatto's hair and gentle sad eyes, who always puts a kind word in with the things she sells. The others, those you never see, the ones who hide their lions' faces out behind the shop – they went completely out of my head.'

We left the Andreanors to their fate, and tried to find some property where a root of the silver tree grew. Two white families lived thereabouts. One, at Bois Debout, was of poor whites as godforsaken as we were. The other family lived in style at Galba, behind a wrought-iron gate. These two descendants of the White of Whites, the one who used to burst a Negro's spleen just to relieve his own bad temper. They say a distant drum sounds best, but Queen Without a Name's mother had heard it with her own ears, the din of this drum, and she told Grandma, and Grandma herself had unclenched her teeth once to give passage to this echo from the old days. So it was as if I'd seen him with my own eyes, the White of Whites, who limped, who could lift a horse, whose hair gleamed like the midday sun, who'd squeeze a little Negro in his arms until he died. But a root of the silver tree grew in their yard, and however much I went over and over them in my mind, Minerva and the White of Whites and the Negroes' burst spleens, what was in store for me was the Desaragnes' house, Belle-Feuille. A river in flood sweeps away huge rocks, uproots trees, but the pebble which will cut your foot open – it leaves that there waiting for you. But nothing lasts forever, Grandmother told me, not even shaking off the dust of the whites; and, dressing herself carefully, with a scarf around her waist, a burning fever, and lusterless eyes, she set off for Galba and Belle-Feuille. How she approached Madame Desaragne, what she said to her, I'll never know.

I got a vague idea, later, one day when my employer said to me: 'You may be your grandmother's crystal glass, but you're not

57

anybody's crystal anything here.' And then I suspected, then I could well imagine, what she might have said to that white woman, Queen Without a Name.

A few weeks afterwards, Grandmother launched me into the sky, gently, carefully, like a kite one releases, tries, flies for the first time. She gave me her blessing for all the sunshine I'd brought into her little cabin. Then, rubbing me with a mixture of wormwood, citronella, and patchouli, she said:

'It happens, even to the flame tree, to tear the guts out of its belly and fill them with straw.'

So I in my turn set out for Belle-Feuille, my linen tied up in a big handkerchief, my sorrow folded double inside me. It was early morning, the dew still clung to the underside of the grass and the shiny leaves of the trees, the crowing of cocks rose high into the air – all foretold a bright day. Some women were already doing their washing under the Bridge of Beyond, the frail footbridge linking Fond-Zombi to the world, which I'd crossed for the first time, eternities ago, with Queen Without a Name. Just before La Ramée I turned off the path leading to school and on to a road that ran between nothing but canefields, without a cabin, without a tree in sight, without anything to arrest the eye. It was the time of year when the whites set fire to their land, and black stumps stretched out endlessly, with a bitter reek of nature smoked and cured. I drew nearer to Galba, torn between rage at having to go and the hope, in spite of everything, of finding a little respite there, a little shade, before I too was engulfed in the sun of the canes. I could hear, in the wind, over the scorched earth, the voice of Ma Cia: 'A Negro? A headless, homeless crab, that walks backwards.' Wandering thus in my head, I came to a long, silky green path all shiny with rich grass and shaded by clumps of white, pink, and red hisbiscus. Just behind me the road between the canes went on still, but already I felt as if I were in another world. It was like going right into the chancel of a church, the same cool, the same silence, the same remoteness. And as I walked along, involuntarily almost on tiptoe, there suddenly appeared a huge house with colonnades and bougainvilleas, a flight of steps leading up to the porch, two metal

58

arrows on the roof, and the amazing windows with glass and lace curtains that we used to talk about, Queen Without a Name and I. The whole front of the house was hung with scarlet flowers, deep and dazzling. Coming towards me from the porch where she had been sitting was the descendant of the White of Whites, a slightly built lady, rather old-maidish, with long grey and yellow hair, painted toenails, and sandals that she scuffed along like little paper boats pulled on strings across a pond. Two intensely blue eyes examined me – a gaze that struck me as cold, languid, and cavalier – while Madame Desaragne questioned me closely, as if she'd never set eyes on Grandmother.

'You're looking for a situation?'

'I want to hire myself out.'

'What can you do?'

'Anything.'

'Can you cook?'

'Yes.'

'I mean cook, not just drop a bit of breadfruit into a pan of hot water.'

'Yes, I know.'

'Good. But who taught you?'

'My grandmother's mother once worked for the Labardines.'

'Good. Can you iron?'

'Yes.'

'I mean iron, not just thump old rags into shape.'

'I know. Putting a gloss on poplin shirts with wing collars.'

'Right. But one thing must be clearly understood – this is a respectable house. Have you got a husband or anything?'

'No. I live alone with my grandmother.'

'Good. Loose living never got anyone anywhere, you know. If you show proper respect, get on with your work, and attend to your own troubles instead of dawdling around with your mouth open, you can stay. The job's there. But I warn you, you're only on trial.'

I left my bundle in what was to be my room, a little shack some distance from the house, by the stables, and started to wash a pile of dirty linen Madame Desaragne showed me, in a little sink with a brass tap.

Then Fond-Zombi was before my eyes and began to float up out of its slough – hill after hill, green after green, stretching wave upon wave to the mountain, Balata Bel Bois, where it melted into the clouds. And I realized a great wind might come and blow, and sweep away that godforsaken spot cabin by cabin, tree by tree, down to the last speck of earth, but it would always be reborn again in my memory, intact.

Noise, frenzy, bustle all died away at the end of that path. Everything had a place, a time, a precise reason; nothing was left to chance; the air itself distilled a sense of eternity. Every day unfolded as the mistress had decreed the day before. It was time divested of novelty or surprise, seeming to spin on its own axis. All day long each action smoothly succeeded another in its proper order. I was surrounded now with piercing, steely, distant eyes under whose gaze I didn't exist. My mistress's voice was rather curt, but what is a rather curt voice if you don't listen to it? And the master, and the master's son, and the foreman all chased other girls, not me, in the bedrooms, the kitchen, or the stable, according to their rank. My only concern was to keep out of the way, to nip this way and that, with one single thought in my heart: I must be like a pebble in a river just resting on the bottom. Let the water flow over me, clear or troubled, foaming, calm or turbulent – I was only a little stone.

At that time my work gave satisfaction, and I received many compliments on my béchamel sauce in the dining room full of solid mahogany furniture anchored heavily, immutably, to the floor. 'Don't praise her too much', said Madame to her husband. 'She won't take so much trouble next time, you watch.' But she was wrong: I wanted to spend my little respite here at Belle-Feuille in peace, I didn't want any trouble. Sometimes in the midst of this orderliness and bloodless serenity I would be overwhelmed by a sudden sadness; I was thirsty for a peal of laughter; Queen Without a Name's little lamp was calling to me, I missed it. On those days I would sing as I went about my work, and my heart would grow lighter, for behind one pain there is another – that was what Grandmother said. And through the darkness I would see Queen Without a Name's smile – 'The horse mustn't ride you, my girl, you must ride it' – and that smile would put heart into me, and I would sing as I worked, and when I sang I diluted my pain, chopped it in pieces, and it flowed into the song, and I rode my horse.

Once I got into the rhythm of Belle-Feuille, Madame Desaragne handed over the cooking and housekeeping entirely to me. We rarely had occasion to exchange even a few words. But every Tuesday afternoon she presided in person over the starching of the master's shirts. She would inform me, with a smile of wonder and delight: 'He's so sensitive, your master – too much starch and it cuts him, too little and the material is limp and sticks to him. So you see I have to watch and see you get it just right.' I was already used to these tricks, this humbug. I took the words and sat on them with all my sturdy weight – white man's words, that's all. As I listened I gradually added water to the mixture, running it through my fingers so that she could see and judge its strength for herself. This operation took place at the back of the house, on a veranda facing west. On the other side of the house the sun poured down in full force on the bougainvilleas, but on our side there was shade and a breeze. I mixed the starch and Madame wore a tranquil smile and an air of detachment. Then, without looking at me, she said dreamily, as if to herself: 'Tell me, girl – I'm very glad to see you so cheerful, singing and laughing and skipping about – but just the same, tell me: what do you really know?'

I went on mixing the starch carefully, on the alert, ready to dodge, to slip between the meshes of the trap she was weaving with her breath – I was a stone beneath the water, I said nothing.

'Ah', she continued, with the voice and expression of someone who looks at the sky and says it's going to be fine, 'ah, do you really know who you are, you Negroes here? You eat, you drink, you misbehave, and then you sleep – and that's it. But do you even know what you've escaped? You might be wild savages now, running through the bush, dancing naked, and eating people stewed in pots. But you're brought here, and how do you live? In squalor and vice and orgies. How often does your husband hit you? And all those women with their bellies on credit? Personally I'd rather die, but you people, you like it. Some taste! You wallow in the mire, and laugh'.

I glided in and out between the words as if I were swimming in the clearest water, feeling the cooling breeze on my neck, my arms, the back of my legs. And, thankful to be a little Negress that was irreducible, a real drum with two sides, as Ma Cia put it, I left one

61

side to her, the mistress, for her to amuse herself, for her to thump on, and I, underneath, I remained intact, nothing ever more so.

After a pause she resumed, but now with a shade of irritation:

'Look at you yourself – I talk to you and you don't even answer, you haven't got anything to say for yourself. Tell me now, honestly, do you think that's any way to behave? Good Lord, what's one to do with such people – might as well talk to a brick wall!'

Then I looked up, and, still stirring the starch around in the calabash, I gazed at Madame Desaragne from under my eyelids, seeing her whole, however, thin and transparent, with her eyes that had classified and arranged and thought of everything behind their lifeless pupils. And I said softly, with an air of surprise:

'Madame, they say some people love light and others love filth, and that's the way of the world. I know nothing about all that, I'm a little blue-black Negress, I wash and iron and make béchamel sauce, and that's all.'

Madame Desaragne gave a sigh of satisfaction, shook her yellow hair close to me, and said in a tone of faint but I think sincere regret:

'Oh, I shall never understand you people.'

Then she tested the starch to see if it was the right consistency and went away, her head thrown slightly back, swinging her long loose hair as if to say, 'Where's your hair, black girl, hanging down behind?' And she opened the big French window, turned around once more, and tossed her hair again. 'You can add the blue now, Telumee, and get on with the starching.' And she vanished lightly away, trailing her sandals behind her like little boats on the water.

I dipped the shirts carefully in the thick blue water, singing already, in the saddle already, riding my horse.

5

On Sunday, if there was a party, it was one long procession of open carriages, a day of bowing, kissing hands, curtseying, and the sound of fingernails on Baccarat glasses, punctuated with wistful talk about the old days, when everything was in its proper place, including the black man. The guests seemed to be on the lookout for the slightest defect in the service. If a dish wasn't set down as quietly as it ought to be, or if a plate or glass wasn't offered from the right side, they saw it as confirmation of their opinion about Negroes. They'd comment noisily and laugh and tap you condescendingly on the arm. 'Nothing to cry about, girl, it doesn't matter. Just think how you're improving yourself. You're seeing nice things, serving at table, learning the difference between dishrags and table napkins, chalk and cheese. How else were you to know, poor thing, eh?' In the midst of all this I came and went, tossing pancakes, spreading them with jam, making cream sorbets, chocolate sorbets, coconut and water-lemon sorbets, red sorbets, green and blue and yellow sorbets, bitter sorbets and sweet sorbets, enough to turn me into a sorbet myself. And I served and cleared away, smiling at everyone, wove in and out, stepping now to the right and now to the left, my one thought to keep myself safe, to remain intact under the white man's words and gestures and incomprehensible grimaces. And all through those afternoons at Belle-Feuille, slipping in and out among the guests, I beat a special drum in my heart, I danced, sang every part, every cry, possession, submission, domination, despair, scorn, and the longing to throw myself off the top of the mountain, and all the while Fond-Zombi slept within me as though at the bottom of a great lake.

When there were no guests, and when it suited Madame Desaragne's mood, she would give me all Sunday afternoon off. But Madame Desaragne's moods were unpredictable: she was a weathervane and you never knew which breeze she had caught. Sometimes when she came back from mass she would sigh, and talk of a great gulf opening up at her feet, and of the ever-increasing wickedness of the world. 'Telumee', she'd say, her head bowed as if it was too heavy for her neck, 'Telumee, my girl, you must stay in today. I need you to say vespers with me. We'll say them together out of doors, in the yard. Two voices are more pleasing to God than one.' Other times, mass would reinvigorate her and she would step out of her carriage lightly, with a look that was abstracted and mysterious, smiling, her eyebrows faintly raised above a gaze astonishingly like a little girl's. Then I'd put cacao lotion on my hair and oil my braids, put on my print and take leave of Madame Desaragne. At the last moment she'd always seem rather put out, rather reluctant, secretly, to see me go. 'But really, Telumee, what are you going to do in Fond-Zombi? Get yourself a belly on credit? Learn to chuck breadfruit into salt water? I don't know how to put it, but try to understand me, girl: this is the only place around here where they make béchamel sauce.'

But in less than no time the hibiscus path and then the road were carrying me far away from Belle-Feuille, and a wind caught up Madame Desaragne's words and dropped them on Balata mountain, on the tops of the mahoganies, where they rang out for the birds, the tree ants, for God, for nobody.

Every Sunday the inhabitants of Fond-Zombi sallied forth to go to church in La Ramée, carrying their portion of want over the ramshackle Bridge of Beyond. They swarmed through the town with souls completely new, Sunday souls without a trace of prickles or sweat or canes. They jested, strolled, heard the news of marriages, deaths, drownings at sea, and notorious local love affairs. And they laughed, they laughed, till you'd have thought all they knew of life was laughter and pleasure. After mass they overran the surrounding districts seeking out relations, friends, fellow workers in the canes, anyone who on Sunday wanted to forget his weekday soul, for on Sunday they liked to think of themselves as respectable men.

When I came in sight of Fond-Zombi, by the mombin tree that

looked down over the last slope, it was an oppressive time of the day: everything looked dumb and asleep. At the least breath of wind, ripe fruit crashed to the ground. I was filled with a bitter smell, a serene happiness, and I felt I hadn't the strength to leave the shade. I looked the hamlet over from north to south, east to west. When examined like that, it didn't seem quite the Fond-Zombi I knew: some tin roofs had gotten rusty, hedges had been mended here and there, and Sunday seemed to lend the whole place a halo of mystery. Then in the midst of this torpor a shrill voice would be heard in the distance: 'Here she is – she's come!' The alarm had been given. Soon after, Elie would appear at the bottom of the hill, and not far behind him a little group of children and pregnant women who couldn't get down to the town, together with the solitaries who saw the world only from their doorsteps – Adriana, Filao, and a few others. Elie rushed ahead of the rest and arrived streaming with sweat, sending out before him a sort of long bitter look that got shorter and sweeter as he approached, as if to show me his infinite patience. He would sit down, take me in in silence, and finally say with surprise:

'You smell of cinnamon in spite of the mombins.'

'You smell of cinnamon too', I'd murmur.

Then he'd pull up his shirt sleeve, put his arm beside mine, and observe playfully:

'We're the same colour, no wonder we've got the same smell.'

But the others snatched me away from him, hugging me, carrying me, looking at me from every angle, sizing up the important person I'd become. 'How nice you look, how nice you look, dear – your braids have gotten longer again. Did you put cacao lotion on them? What a fine bamboo in the wind you're growing and what a fine flute you'll make. Whoever plays your music will be a lucky man, eh Elie? But first you'll play us a little tune of Belle-Feuille, won't you, love? For in our own way we've been waiting for you too.'

Elie drew away from the group and looked at me from a distance, just addressing a little nod to me from time to time, or a slight gesture of the hand, the way you might greet someone on the other side of the river. Escorted thus, I reached our cabin, where Queen Without a Name received me in her rocker, hunched up and wizened by a joy that made her face dim and bereft of life. But her eyes gave out a little flicker, and seemed to stand out from the rest of her face to touch me, question me, tell me how she'd been getting on lately. And, each time, everyone would fall silent before the eyes of Queen Without a Name, and someone would say timidly:

'Ah, Queen, you'll never die. What can happen to you now, and what kind of a feather is it for you, death? – a hummingbird's feather or a peacock's?'

And the Queen would smother still more the fire of her glance, and, rocking nonchalantly, just repeat the words, the way one states a well-known fact:

'I've never asked for anything, but I do see that with all these blessings I shall never die.'

And everyone would scuttle about, then settle down. Dresses crackled with all the starch in them, pipes gave out a light cloud of smoke. Sunday afternoon had begun.

'And now', Grandmother used to say, 'now we're among ourselves, tell us about the white men at Galba.'

The cabin could hold about five or six people, some sitting on the bed and the others on the floor leaning against the wall. But there were at least as many more out in the yard, pricking up their ears, and as soon as Grandmother pronounced these words, heads poked in through the open door, and anxious looks were bent on me, drinking up what I said in advance. Everyone wanted to know what life was like at Belle-Feuille, behind all those ramparts of green – how they ate, talked, drank, went about their daily lives. And above all, what was important to them in life, and were they at least glad to be alive? This was the fundamental question that concerned the harassed souls of Fond-Zombi. I hesitated slightly before answering, because I'd already talked to them on previous Sundays, and in fact all Belle-Feuille would have fitted into a thimble. My difficulty was evident to all those present, and someone brought glowing eyes close to me to say: 'There, there, get back the lightness of your breath, love.' All eyes were on me, and, faced with so much eagerness, I did begin to talk to them about Galba, visible and invisible; and unwittingly a different Belle-Feuille would issue from my lips, so that my listeners couldn't help seeing an ocean, with waves and breakers, whereas all I was trying to show was a bit of foam. For want of anything better I'd always end on the words with which Madame Desaragne had taken leave of me a little while before, the business of the béchamel. Those who knew the story already would laugh, but if there was someone there who'd come for the first time, they'd say with great interest:

'If it's so good tell us how to make it, for our own stomachs.'.

'Stephen, man', Grandmother would say gently, 'there's nothing good in béchamel, let me tell you. I tasted it once, and you can take it from me: there's nothing good about it. Telumee', she went on, turning to me, 'Telumee, dear flame tree, whenever your heart bids you, you can come and cook two slices of salted breadfruit over some wood in the yard here, and not worry whether the others have got their béchamel.'

And she'd season her joke with a free Negress's fine deep-throated laugh, and I'd be a human being again and not a maker of béchamel sauce. And my soul would rise up and float over all the faces, and I'd think that other rivers could twist about, changing their courses and currents, but what I wanted was a hidden life without foam, here at Fond-Zombi, under one roof and one man, surrounded by faces whose slightest eddy was as visible to me as ripples on the water. Everyone laughed with the Queen, leaving the whites to their béchamel; and, laughing, they were themselves again, ringdoves ever on the watch and juggling with sorrow.

Many of the faces changed from one Sunday to another, but there were three I encountered regularly on each of my descents to Fond-Zombi, and these I must mention. They were those of Amboise, Filao, and Adriana. Amboise was the reddish-brown Negro who'd saved Elie from the canefield. Up on their scaffolding they'd become friends, and every Sunday Amboise would be there in Grandmother's cabin standing on one foot, leaning against a wall, taciturn, rarely laughing, only opening his mouth to answer questions about the life of white people in France, where he'd dragged out an existence for nearly seven years. His views on the white people in France disconcerted us. He regarded them as burst bladders that had set themselves up as lanterns, and that was that. Filao was an old man who'd worked in the canefields, with a worn, grooved face like a nutmeg, slow-moving eyes, and an oblique uncertain gaze; he was always giving expression to some dream. He spoke in a tiny little voice, perhaps afraid someone would break the

67

thread of his reverie if he could be properly heard; and so everyone's eyes would be fixed on his lips, though whenever he opened them it was to say something like: 'Do you know what, my friends? I've some important news to tell you. Imagine, a little green lizard like me who runs from wall to wall without a roof of his own, well, yesterday . . .' Adriana was a stout Negress of about fifty with arms still nicely plump, white and yellow braids slightly greenish in places, and heavy lids forever lowered over blank eyes – so as not to see the world, or so as not to be seen by it? She was one of the host of waifs and strays who wandered from cabin to cabin in search of a thrill. When she opened her mouth her eyelids lifted reluctantly, and rolling the whites of her eyes she would utter strange words, words that seemed to come from elsewhere, none knew where. 'My lost sheep', she'd say, 'my little fleecy princes of the dark . . .' and then she'd recast her life, sweetly, innocently, knowing no one would like to contradict, to lift up her feathers and reveal her flesh.

'Ah', she'd say in a voice of happiness, of delight, with a kind of faint smile that suited her, 'when you see a woman's hair going white, let it be, for it is quite right to sacrifice oneself for one's children. Take me – I've six daughters, but if I wanted to I could open a shop this very day with all the things they send me from Pointe-à-Pitre. If I opened my cupboard and showed you the piles of new towels, the pleated dresses and everything, not to mention such trifles as sugar, rice, and cod that I don't even bother to mention, you'd really understand my position in the world. You see me in rags, with a hole in the roof, and you may think I'm in a bad way – but don't you believe it! Just drop in one day and I'll show you my cupboard, maybe.'

'Quite true', Grandmother would answer at once, backing her up firmly. 'You see people in torn dresses, lying down and getting up in ramshackle cabins, but who knows what they may have in their cupboards? Who knows?'

And old Filao, coming to the aid of Queen Without a Name, would say in his fluting voice:

'Someone speaks, and an angel hears in heaven.'

'Ah, words', another voice would say, 'what a blessing.'

'Yes, and what a pleasant afternoon, but here it is, nearly over', Adriana would say, heaving herself out of her chair. 'And if anyone isn't satisfied, let him lift his finger and tell us what else his heart can desire. . . . Brother Negroes, if one listened to you, you would never stop. Think of the lovers – when are they going to court each other if we stay here buzzing in their ears like a swarm of wasps? Words are words and love is love.'

And turning finally to me she would add mischievously:

'You're just right now, Telumee, like a ripe breadfruit. Too green it sets your teeth on edge, too mellow and it's lost its taste. Come back to us, my girl, don't wait for a wind to knock you off the tree and scatter you on the ground. Try to pull yourself off while you're just right.'

At that the cabin emptied, then the yard, and a little breeze reached us coming down from the mountain. Queen Without a Name pretended she had something to do, and she too vanished. We were left alone. There'd be a great silence and we'd breathe in the scent that rises in the evening from the very heart of the bloodworts. Outside, people were back from their visits, and in every cabin conversation was at its height. The village vibrated like a huge assembly. In the dusk the glowworms' lanterns twinkled faintly, then grew stronger and more brilliant as the darkness deepened. The lamps were lit, the last laughter died away. Sunday was over.

Elie was nearing the end of his apprenticeship and had arranged to be paid half in cash and half in sets of planks with which to build our future house. In the twilight of Sunday evenings he would talk about our cabin in such detail I would enter right inside it, walk along the veranda, sit down on one of the three chairs by the little round table, and lean my elbows on an embroidered cloth. He wanted me to be the one to go up on the roof and fix a red bouquet there. He'd let me know when everything was ready, by coming and serenading me at night at the Desaragnes'. We were sitting on the edge of the bed, and his eyes glittered in the half light, looking at me gently, warily, a little askance it seemed to me, as if he was afraid to show his resentment. I would caress him, and cling close to him, and the unhappiness would go out of his eyes, and he would murmur plaintively:

69

'But should you really be there, with your sixteen-year-old breasts, shaking the white men's doormats?'

'Don't try to be clever, Mr Sawyer – as soon as our house is finished I'll come and fill it as a candle fills a chapel.'

'I let you skip about, my little goatling. Your rope is long between my hands, but one day I'll shorten it – close up against your neck.'

'Long rope or short, when the goat wants to run away—'

'No', Elie would interrupt, laughing. 'I've got my eye on it, and if it makes a move I'll kill it.'

A clump of bamboo creaked in the evening breeze, and up in the woods the animals began to call to one another, freed from the heat of the day.

'I'm a new man', he'd say.

When she returned Grandmother prepared our meal in silence and we ate under the protection of her calm, her tranquil joy – outside, sitting on rocks, amidst the peace of the evening. And each time, as he went, Elie would touch one of the beams and say, 'That's how hard Telumee's head is.' When I woke next morning, fine mists swirled over Fond-Zombi, silence and dew were over all the village. Then I'd set out for Belle-Feuille, my eyes full of the vision of my future home. When, still early in the morning, I went through the Desaragnes' gate, the vision still followed me, and I'd sit down on the lawn with my legs stretched out in the cool grass for a last gloat over the brand new tin roof of my house shining in the cheerful morning sun, the red bouquet, the table, and the embroidered cloth.

Then Madame Desaragne's voice would be heard behind me:

'You gave me a fright, child. Haven't you anything else to do at this hour but sit on the grass? Fond-Zombi certainly has a very bad influence.'

And as I shook my head in bewilderment, still lost in my dream of glory, she'd add:

'Come, girl, snap out of it – the sun's high in the sky already.'

6

A leaf falls and the whole forest trembles. It all began for me with a laugh that would come upon me any time, anywhere, for no reason that I could discover. When my mind was troubled over it, I'd cheat it with the thought that I was laughing for Grandmother, Elie, Adriana, or someone else who might happen at that moment to need my laughter. But the people and servants at Belle-Feuille knew its meaning better than I, having heard it on other lips, and there was a sudden flurry, a sudden peal of compliments that made me fly so high I was breathless. One promised me the town, another the country. 'If you died now', they said, 'God wouldn't take you like that – he'd send you back on earth for your youth to shine forth. Oh no, heaven won't take a girl who doesn't shine for any man.' Meanwhile Christmas was approaching, there was great activity, parties and visits followed one on another at Belle-Feuille, and Sundays came and went without my being able to go to Fond-Zombi. The note of my laughter rose higher and higher. Even the guests noticed it and said to Madame Desaragne as I served the punch:

'You have the gift of surrounding yourself with beautiful things, cousin. How do you get hold of them?'

'Don't go by appearances', Madame Desaragne would say coldly. 'A Negro's a Negro, but since the music of the whip is no longer in their ears they take themselves for civilized.'

'Oh well, I'm more easygoing than you, Aurora dear. We'll talk about it again later, when they're really enlightened. Meanwhile, there's no one like her for serving punch – a pleasure both for the palate and for the eyes.'

One day as I was crouching in the tank washing the kitchen cloths, I felt a prickling sensation at the back of my neck. When I came to the rinsing, curiosity got the better of me and I turned

71

around, to see Monsieur Desaragne standing still in the middle of the yard looking at me out of grey eyes tinged with green and mysteriously quizzical. Although he was stoutly built he was naturally easy in his movements and seemed to draw support from the air, like a bird. At this moment, however, he was slightly unsteady on his legs. At last he sighed, turned away slowly, and reluctantly withdrew, while I thought in my heart: 'So now, my girl, you're finding out the white men's weaknesses.' But that thought was soon replaced by another, and by the time I went to bed that evening I'd completely forgotten the notion that had occurred to me in the tank. The air was heavy, there were no stars in the sky, no hope of rain. There was a knock at my door. The coachman sometimes came and asked me to prepare a custard-apple infusion when Madame couldn't sleep. So I got up and opened the door, and to my great surprise Monsieur Desaragne walked calmly in, shut the door behind him, and leaned against the wall. He was carrying a silk dress which he tossed to me, smiling, as if it were an understood thing between us. Then he came over to me and put his hands up my skirt, muttering: 'No pants, eh?' Trouble is something that takes you by surprise – a tick that jumps on you and sucks you to the last drop of your blood. At my age, and by no means ignorant, I'd thought myself safe from this sort of attack, but for all our experience we know no more about life than we do about death. I made no resistance as Monsieur Desaragne put his arms around me, but as he unbuttoned himself with one hand, I murmured softly: 'I've got a little knife here. And even if I hadn't, my nails would be enough.' He seemed not to have heard, and as he went on with what he was doing I continued in the same cold calm voice: 'Monsieur Desaragne, I swear to God you won't be able to go into any other maid's room because you won't have the wherewithal.' He laughed, I brandished my nails, and he leaped back in dismay, suddenly understanding what I was saying. He wore a faint, uneasy smile.

'What a little devil, eh?' he whispered, still with the same smile but his face going pale and set in the candlelight. 'So a dress isn't enough? Do you want a gold chain or a pair of earrings? Listen, I need a little singing Negress more lively than lightning, a little blue-black Negress. That's just what I like.'

Now he was not looking at me but gazing wistfully around,

72

object by object, at my wretched room – the bench that served me as a bed, the stool, the bit of mirror stuck on a nail, the apron, the bundle of linen hanging from a string. And it was as if I myself were spread all over the room, I myself from whom he, a melancholy smile on his lips, expected I knew not what. A tempest had swept down on Monsieur Desaragne; it had lifted up his white feathers, and I had seen his flesh. I stayed where I was, oblivious of my naked bosom and my skirt half up my thighs. An icy intoxication filled my head, and without thinking what I was saying I answered calmly:

'Ducks and chickens are alike, but the two species don't go on the water together.'

His eyes went very pale. He shrugged his shoulders, spread his fingers as if to let through a trickle of sand, and, resuming his royal sorrow, fell back step by step into the night, still gazing at me with a strange smile in the depths of his grey eyes.

My job as a maid entitled me to sleep in a little closet adjoining the stable, with an opening the size of a hand, which was fitted with a tiny shutter that I raised at night so as not to die of heat. This opening looked out over my employers' land, and in the distance, beyond the tall spears of the canes, lights flickered in the huddle of the Negroes' cabins. Christmas was nearly here, and as I lay on my straw mattress I could hear carols rising up from the cabins to the stars as if imploring love to descend – or trying to pluck it down from the sky. Now and then, borne by a breath of wind, I caught the rumble of drums, too, and I thought how the heart of the devil himself must hurt to see all that misery, and the Negro's ingenuity in forging happiness in spite of everything. There was a truce over there in the little cabins buried among the canes, there was a respite for the Negro, who became, I thought, all the more ingenious through doing all these magic tricks, dancing and drumming simultaneously, at once both wind and sail. The struggle with Monsieur Desaragne was a thing of the past, and I hadn't realized the victory I'd won, as a Negress and as a woman. It was just one of the little currents that would ripple my waters before I was drowned in the sea. But now a sadness came to me in the evening, as the Sundays passed away at Belle-Feuille and the vision of the

73

red bouquet I was to put on my house broke up and faded with each day. I thought my man had forgotten me, and a dream tormented me every night, a strange dream I couldn't decipher however hard I tried. It was winter, and I was a servant in some French town which I saw in terms of the descriptions I'd heard from Amboise. Snow was falling ceaselessly and it seemed to me quite natural. The white people had strange eyes – like bits of frosted glass that gave no reflection – but they were amazingly kind, and my mistress often asked me how the climate affected me. I told her I liked it very much, and she would laugh, disbelieving. This laugh tore me in two, and one day when she started it again I said to her calmly: 'I'm going to prove I'm not cold', and I took off my clothes and went out naked into the snow. She watched me in astonishment from behind the kitchen curtains. Then I felt my muscles stiffening until they turned to ice, and I fell down dead.

One night when the nightmare kept me awake and open-eyed on my pallet, I was made even more uneasy by hearing someone singing. I even thought I recognized Elie's voice. For some time past my room had been attacked by mosquitoes, attracted by a pigsty that had just been built behind it. 'I must be going crazy', I thought. 'But who'd have believed mosquitoes could have driven me so crazy I hear songs?' And then I remembered a promise Elie had made me, eternities ago it seemed now, and a serenade he was supposed to come and perform when the house was quite finished and lacked nothing but my red bouquet. The dogs belonging to the house barked, and the voice fell silent. But a little while later it rose once more into the night, farther away this time, on the other side of the road, as if it had gone out of reach of the dogs. And yet despite Elie's efforts to pierce the denseness of the night, or perhaps because of them, because of those sudden shrill flights, the words of the song communicated a great melancholy.

> Why live Odilo
> Just to swim
> And always face down
> Never
> Never
> Floating on your back
> One moment.

When I opened my eyes, at dawn, the sky was full of low-lying clouds like ships in distress pitching in the wind. A great silence hovered, and there were still patches of shadow over the objects in my room. I was seized with a desire for flight and space. The sun goes away at night, leaving you with your troubles, and doesn't rise any faster when you are full of joy. I slipped out into the growing light and went to the sink beside the tank. I ran cold water into my mouth, over my arms and shoulders, and over my tear-swollen eyes that felt as large as pigeon's eggs. Then I carried a little bowl full of water back to my room, crushed some patchouli leaves in it, and sat down by it to perform my morning toilet. My wages were hidden under a plank in the bench: three five-franc pieces – three whole months without one Sunday in which to take wing and rest my body. I took down my bundle and put my three coins in, then set out for the big house with it balanced on my head. Madame Desaragne was already up and about in the drawing room, notebook in hand. I went up to her and said:

'The mosquitoes were very bad last night. I need a rest.'

She started; then, looking at me closely, smiled timidly as people do at someone who's gone crazy.

'Yes', she said awkwardly and with a slight tremor in her voice, 'the mosquitoes were terrible last night. Go home, girl, as quick as you can, and don't linger on the way.'

A breeze caught me up and I didn't come to until I was on the road, far from the house with colonnades and bougainvilleas, in free possession of myself and my two breasts. By now the sun had emerged from the mountain and was on the edge of the sky, just behind the fleet of threatened clouds. I'd cried so much that night there was a veil of pink silk between my eyes and the sky, the road, the nearby canefields, the distant bluffs fading away into greens ever paler and more soft, and, right on the far horizon, Balata Bel Bois, still indistinguishable from the clouds. My legs had taken the road to Fond-Zombi, but my eyes never left the mountain: I was trying to make out the Bois Riant slopes, where my man sawed his planks. I laughed to myself, remembering that when a woman loves a man she sees a field and says it's a mule. There's air, water, sky, and the earth we walk on – and there's love. That's what keeps us alive. And if a man doesn't give you a belly full of food but gives you a heart full of love, that's enough to live on. That's what I'd always heard people saying around me, and that's what I believed. And now here I was on the way to Fond-Zombi, a woman in free possession of myself and my two breasts, and at each step I felt Elie's eyes against mine and his steps within mine, and though the people I greeted on the way thought I was alone, he was already within me. When I got to the Bridge of Beyond the sinking clouds had been swallowed up and the sun was darting blinding red flames into a completely green sky. On one side was the road leading to Fond-Zombi, cracked clay full of stumps and stones; on the other was a path running directly into the forest. Hesitation gripped me – I felt more nebulous than the foam on a mountain stream. And then I told myself that however much the river may sing and meander, in the end it has to go down to the sea and be drowned. And so, turning aside from the road to Fond-Zombi, I followed the path leading to Bois Riant, as if drawn irresistibly by the presence of my sweating Negro on those scaffoldings built by little men with ten fingers and two eyes. Even in the midst of my heart's confusion I had a vague feeling that the clearing I was heading for was mined; but it dazzled me and drew me towards it willy-nilly. And as I hurried along, running over hillocks and through muddy hollows, everything grew dazzling, appareled in the light descending from Bois Riant. I went, as in a dream, amid the smell of rotting vegetation. There was a river at the foot of the slope where Elie and his friend Amboise had their scaffolding. I climbed down the slippery slope, parted some branches, and bathed my eyes one last time – a few moments ago they'd started to weep again, I didn't know why. Here and there, around green rocks, the water was almost stagnant, then it flowed clear and transparent again farther on. Looking at my reflection, I thought how God had put me on earth without asking me if I wanted to be a woman or what color I'd like to be. It wasn't my fault he'd given me a blue-black skin and a face not overflowing with beauty. And yet I was quite content; and perhaps, if I was given the choice, now, at this moment, I'd choose that same bluish skin, that same face not overflowing with beauty.

Higher up, among the trunks of the mahoganies, I saw the sawyers' scaffolding. Elie was on the platform and Amboise was standing, legs apart, on the ground, while the jagged blade rose and fell in a cloud of sawdust. I sat down a little way off and gazed at the two toiling men – Amboise, a tall, gaunt, gnarled tree that had already let fall its fruits, and my Elie, with his slim body and the unformed wrists and ankles of the child I'd met a few years before by the river. A long moment passed away in this joyful contemplation. The planks fell, and turning calmly towards me Elie smiled, a gleam of apprehension in his eyes.

'It's not polite', he said at last in a voice that tried to be cheerful, 'it's not polite to look at people when their backs are turned, Mademoiselle Telumee Lougandor. Do you know I scented you at once in the breeze?'

At this, Amboise turned towards me his reddish-brown face, with its deep wrinkles and anxious piercing eyes, which lingered over me a while, then shifted away as if overcome by some strange embarrassment. For an instant I felt as if that look reached right down inside me. But by now Amboise was feigning indifference.

'Oh', he said to Elie in a drawling voice, 'so now some people claim to smell things in the breeze!'

And picking up his shirt as he went, the reddish-brown Negro took the path I'd come along, went noiselessly down the slope, and disappeared.

'Here I am drinking you up with my eyes', said Elie, 'and I haven't even said hallo'.

'It's for you to speak – you're the man.'

'You want me to speak, Telumee, but you know very well all that goes on in my heart.'

'Only the knife knows what goes on in the heart of the pumpkin.'

'Why do you talk to me of knives and pumpkins? Tell me rather about the little candle that was lit and went out yesterday evening in the room at Belle-Feuille.'

So, jesting, Elie approached, and when he was close and clasped me to him I remembered having seen that gleam of apprehension in his eyes before, under the flame tree at school, when he spoke about the virgin forest and the ways that might one day be lost.

'Ah', he breathed. 'I imagined you in fine lace sheets all starched and ironed, and here we are borrowing the bed of the fieldmouse and the mongoose.'

'Let's wait for the lace sheets then.'

77

A great laugh that came from the whole forest seized hold of us, and our two kites set off on their wanderings through the sky.

Opening my eyes, the first thing I heard was the sound of the stream in the ravine. My head was resting softly on a little bed of leaves, at the foot of a mahogany whose sloping roots surrounded me like the sides of a bed. Elie was sitting on one of them, gazing unsmiling at me with a frown of concentration. His face looked like the prow of a ship, capable of cutting through the wind and resisting life's onslaughts; I found it extremely beautiful. His arms were folded as if he were in school, and his bare feet scrabbled softly at the ground. Seeing I was awake he said ceremoniously:

'Get up and let me see you walk before me.'

And I, after a few paces:

'They say you can see these things. How is my walk – has it changed?'

'It's absolutely the walk of a woman.'

'So I should hope!' I laughed.

'So you are a woman', Elie went on gravely, 'and a faithful one, and I look at you and see you are like a fine breadfruit, just ripe, swaying in the wind. But the question is, are you going to come off the tree and fall ... and roll away?'

'It all depends on the wind. Some winds make you fall, others strengthen you and make you cling on tighter.'

'Fine words for a little breadfruit just ripe!'

He gave me his hand and we went down towards Fond-Zombi, seeing first the upper slopes, then the tops of the trees, then the rusty roofs of the little cabins, and lastly the dust of the road. The declining sun hovered just at the level of the sea, sometimes still, sometimes in motion again, as if it couldn't bring itself to leave the earth, to abandon the village. Darkness was not far off, and a warm wind blew in from the sea in short gusts. Elie still wore his air of gravity; his brow was still scored with two furrows; and I felt impotent, helpless, not knowing how to give him strength and assurance. But when I saw the little brand-new house there by the path not far from the cabin of Queen Without a Name, just under the Chinese plum tree as I'd wanted it to be, a sweetness descended

78

on me and I glowed like a charcoal oven, capable of warming the very depths of heaven. Grandmother was in her rocker, dreaming of life's illusions. She showed little surprise at seeing us coming towards her like that, in the dusk, hand in hand. She just stopped rocking and smiled a strange smile, as if she wanted to reassure the little girl standing there before her cabin, uncertain, hovering between heaven and earth.

'You've lost your job and you stand there laughing?' she said at last.

'I shan't be idle long', I answered mysteriously.

At this Elie frowned, turned to me and stopped me with a severe and distant look, as if to remind me of the seriousness of that moment and to ask me to put on my soul of honor and respect. Then, when he was satisfied with my bearing, he turned to Queen Without a Name and said:

'Queen, I come before you today as a man.'

Grandmother got up out of her rocker, and in a tone of deep gravity, the distant irony of which escaped Elie, answered:

'Know, my son, that I have put new drums in my ears, to hear you as one hears an old man of a hundred.'

'Well', went on Elie, 'as we're among grown-ups, I'll put no pebble in my throat to muffle the sound of my words. And I'll admit to you, Queen, that at this moment I'm in a bath that's very uncomfortable, now boiling and now ice-cold, whereas what every man wants is a little bath just nice and warm. You see, I know Telumee, I see her in the woods, I see her in the fields and at the bottom of rivers, but that's not how I want to see her. I climbed up on a roof especially to look down and see her tending to our little affairs. But I don't know if the day will ever come when I'll circle her finger with gold. I don't know, Queen Without a Name, I just don't know, but when I marry, my house won't any longer be a field without yams or gumbos or boucoussou peas – everything will be growing in it, from a bed to a veranda to keep out the wind. I'm not a gladiolus; I can't promise you whether I'll come up out of the earth red or yellow. Tomorrow our water may turn into vinegar or into wine, but if it's vinegar, don't curse me, but let your maledictions sleep in the hollow of the bombax tree. For tell me, isn't it a common sight, here in Fond-Zombi, the sight of a man being transformed into a devil?'

79

Was that the day for such words? Was it just an idea of Elie's, just an idea? Or was it a sign sent to him by spirits? A chill came over me. I wanted to ask him, to find out; but it was up to Grandmother to speak for me. And I saw the old woman's glance wander, travel to a placè unknown to me, then come back again to us, brushing against our bodies, against our hair, and finally settling on my brow and on Elie's, one after the other. Then, giving Elie a lovely peaceful smile, she answered:

'Don't frighten her, man, don't trouble the peace of doves for nothing. But since frankness calls for frankness in return, listen: we Lougandors are not pedigree cocks, we're fighting cocks. We know the ring, the crowd, fighting, death. We know victory and eyes gouged out. And all that has never stopped us from living, relying neither on happiness nor on sorrow for existence, like tamarind leaves that close at night and open in the day.'

'And if the day itself doesn't open, what becomes of the Lougandors then?' asked Elie.

'If they know there can be no more day, the Lougandors lie down, and then they die', said Grandmother serenely. Then, turning to me, she went on in the same steady voice: 'Sway like a filao, shine like a flame tree, creak and groan like a bamboo, but find your woman's walk and change to a valiant step, my beauty. And when you creak like the bamboo, when you sigh with weariness and disgust, when you groan and despair for yourself alone, never forget that somewhere, somewhere on the earth, there's a woman glad to be alive.'

Finally, assuming a little off-hand air, she drew Elie to her, and, kissing him gently, murmured just for him to hear:

'If you are shipwrecked, man, she will go down with you.'

And then came silence, with Grandmother shutting her eyes and Elie remaining still, huddled over his thoughts. All I could hear were the sounds and whispers of the neighbouring women who were crowding around the cabin now, eagerly straining to hear the slightest word. I squeezed Elie's hand hard and looked at him, and all my apprehensions changed into a delicate swirl of smoke that vanished into the air. Old Abel, alerted by the bustle, appeared with hands stretched out toward us, his little yellow eyes sparkling with mischief. In the heat of his emotion his face, usually so black, had taken on a strange wine color. And his cheeks seemed to have gone

80

suddenly hollow, the wrinkles making open slashes like those that you cut in fish. Without looking at us at all he went up to Queen Without a Name and said in a hoarse, rustling voice:

'What woes, what chains and woes . . .'

Then he went on, with a cheerful gurgle:

'Lord, the number of unfortunates that go about on the earth! Take Queen Without a Name, for example, and look at the bad luck that falls on her today, with my bar to the right of her and Telumee's cabin to the left. Oh the chains and woes!'

He let out a funny, childish laugh, full of innocence, and Queen Without a Name icily observed:

'Old Abel, everyone knows you're the only injured party in this affair—'

But, unable to keep it up any longer, Grandmother in her turn brought forth a little youthful laugh that leaped nimbly into the air carrying the rest of us after it, so that all the laughter, young and old, merged into one, issuing from a single human throat. Over on the other side of the road, the crowd laughed too, without knowing what it was all about. A pink light still lingered up in the sky, but the darkness was already gathering around the trees and at any moment now dusk would fall over Fond-Zombi. Grandmother picked up a fine round basket containing a coffee mill, some kitchen utensils, a bowl, a liter of kerosene, and some old clothes for us to use as a bed. Everything had been ready, waiting for us since yesterday. She handed Elie a lamp with a curved glass chimney, and the whole procession moved off, Queen Without a Name in the lead carrying the basket on her head, Elie holding the lighted lamp, me with my bundle, and Old Abel gaily bringing up the rear and scattering incomprehensible words into the breeze. The cabin was sixteen feet long by twelve feet wide, and mounted on rocks, like that of Queen Without a Name. A ladder was leaning against the roof. Old Abel went inside and came out with a red bouquet, which he gave to me, laughing. I scampered up the ladder and tied the bouquet to a rafter: there was a burst of applause from the crowd, which had remained a little way off so as not to disturb our privacy. Queen Without a Name crouched down beside three stones arranged to form a hearth, not far from the Chinese plum and a few yards away from the house. She lit the fire, drew three cobs of corn out of her bodice, and roasted them in the flame. When they were cooked she stripped off the grains and gave us some of them to eat, then poured half the remainder into Elie's pocket and the other half down the front of my dress, between my breasts, wishing us as many pieces of silver as there were grains. Then, everything needful having been done, she declared in a voice husky with emotion:

'And now that there is fire and cooked food, you may take possession of your house.'

When Queen Without a Name had gone we sat in the doorway of our house and watched the dusk descending over the village, the mountain, the sea in the distance – melting everything into one pink and blue mist, except for the little yellow gleams in the cabins on the ground, and the silver glitter of the stars above us. The people of Fond-Zombi were making energetic preparations for Christmas, and singing could be heard far off, and waves of accordion music rolling from cabin to cabin, hill to hill, as far as the edge of the forest. Sometimes there was the sound of carols, and the wind wafted the smell of gooseberries boiling merrily to be eaten on Christmas night. And I thought to myself that with smells like that in their nostrils women feel more like women, men's hearts begin to dance, and children don't want to grow up any more. After a while I arranged the clothes on the floor and we lay down on them, in silence, close up against one another, like two thieves, and we watched the village sink slowly into the night and disappear, as gradually as a ship being swallowed up in mist.

7

The next morning I woke with the feeling I was fulfilling my destiny as a Negress, that I was no longer a stranger on the earth. There was not a human voice to be heard, no barking of dogs. There were gleams of light on top of the mountain, but the village was an island in a sea of darkness. I looked at Fond-Zombi in relation to my cabin, and my cabin in relation to Fond-Zombi, and felt I was in my right place in life. Then I started to make my coffee and see to my other little chores with slow, precise gestures, as if I'd been doing these things at the same time and in the same place for a hundred years.

The sea breeze sprang up and a luminous mist spread over Fond-Zombi. House doors banged in the distance, and Old Abel appeared outside his shop, clapping his hands when he caught sight of me. Then Elie came, took the coffee I held out to him, and started sipping it, not taking his eyes off me for a moment. He had a shapeless felt hat pushed back on his head and was wearing his working drills. He said nothing, but looked at me with an expression of intense curiosity, his eyes dancing like wavelets in strong wind. Sitting down on a big rock, he put his empty cup down between his feet and said to it, with dreamy eyes full of solicitude, as if he were addressing something alive: 'You are beautiful by night, you are beautiful by day, and here you are in my cabin. What can God mean me to die of, after all that?' Then rumpling his tousled hair with an embarrassed air, he heaved a sigh and muttered, half glad and half sorry:

'All that ought to be ready is ready, so that for once instead of reproaching myself I can eat my reproaches in the forest as if they were sweets.'

He picked up his lunch box, all nice and hot, and I prepared to see him go and to watch him as long as I could on his way toward the river. But he didn't move, and there suddenly welled up from deep inside him, from the very marrow of his bones, a great powerful laugh like a waterspout in Lent, which immediately filled all the space around us. The laughter overtook the grass and made the leaves of the Chinese plum rustle, as for the second time that morning I felt I was in my right place in life. The fancies, terrors, and doubts of the day before were left far behind. Elie looked at me with satisfaction and pride, pulled his hat down over his eyes as if he didn't want to see anything but me that day, and walked off serenely towards the forest.

I began my first day as a woman nervously, uneasily, afraid of the comments, noise, and laughter of the neighbours. But I was surprised a little while later, when I went down to do my washing by the river, to see other women looking at me quite naturally, saying simply: 'It's a good thing, now and again, for one of us to have a new roof and caresses. It makes one believe in the sun.'

'Oh, so you were spying on me during the night?' I said, laughing.

And then the novelty faded away in the stream, in the gestures and laughter of the women doing their washing, and it was as if they'd always known in their minds that my destiny was to live on a branch in Fond-Zombi, under Elie's wing.

In the afternoon the air would suddenly go still, the roof was white hot, and I'd seek the shade of our Chinese plum. Then I'd feel as if something subtle and new was weaving itself around me, and around the cabin still wearing its red bouquet. One day I told Queen Without a Name about what I felt under the tree in our yard. Grandmother didn't answer right away: she looked at me searchingly, her scrutiny piercing into me like a gauge into oil. Her examination completed, she kissed my forehead, rubbed my back, and said:

'Good. I like to hear questions like the ones you ask. Look.'

Picking up a dry branch, she started to draw a shape in the loose earth at her feet. It looked like a spider's web, with the threads intersecting to make ridiculously tiny little houses. Then, all around, she drew signs resembling trees, and, pointing with an ample gesture to her work, said, 'That's Fond-Zombi.'

Seeing my surprise, she explained tranquilly:

'You see, the houses are nothing without the threads that join them together. And what you feel in the afternoon under your tree is nothing but a thread that the village weaves and throws out to you and to your cabin.' Pointing to one of the tall trees on the edge of her drawing, she made a vague gesture and whispered in a suddenly broken voice: 'That's where Jeremiah and I used to live.'

Then she slowly lowered the lids over eyes flooded with melancholy, and, with a regular, unceasing swaying of the head, seemed to travel into another time, another world, another light. I left her, taking care not to tread on any dead twig, any dry leaf that might wake her.

From then on, thinking of the thread floating near our Chinese plum, I began to go along the street in Fond-Zombi unself-conscious and assured, despite having set up house so recently. But a certain curiosity hovered about me, and some people fussed and wanted to know more. 'What exactly is the set-up, with Telumee?' Crude questions and direct admissions were not the custom. The people of Fond-Zombi restricted themselves to brief visits during which they gathered what evidence they could from a tone of voice, the resonance of a laugh, the ease of someone's movements. Some of the women even went to Queen Without a Name to try to find out if, under her skirts, Telumee had grown thinner or fatter. But the ruse failed and they were disappointed, for Queen Without a Name showed never a chink, was absolutely true to form. Fond-Zombi would perhaps be wondering still if Elie's friends had not decided to air the mystery, so as to know once and for all whether they should rejoice or lament, feel strengthened or weakened, when their thoughts came to rest on us. One evening they posted themselves outside Old Abel's shop, and when Elie got back from his forest, laughter over his eyes and lips smiling, a voice addressed him:

'What a rare commodity you've become, friend! Join us this evening and show how much you care for us.'

'We exist, my dear Elie, we exist just as much as anyone else. Come into Old Abel's with us and have a drink, as you used to.'

'Come now, a spot of rum, no one can refuse that', said a third, in a voice that would take no denial. 'It's as if a sick man refused soup.'

From Queen Without a Name's yard, where I'd taken up my position, I heard Elie laugh, the reckless laugh of a lucky gambler, and he murmured with some embarrassment:

'Friends, a Negro is always sick, but can't you see I'm in perfect health and in no need of soup?'

'Never mind the soup, that's not the point. The real trouble is that though you belong to the race of men, you're getting Telumee into one bad habit after another – anyone would think she holds the strings of your will. You can't even go home at the time you fancy any more. A man doesn't carry on like that, for heaven's sake – how do you expect to train her?'

Elie was wearing his usual old clothes, worn almost threadbare, but he seemed to be protected by some invisible power – armored, overflowing with confidence, immune from anything anyone might say to him. He raised his hat and gave them all a bold, innocent, invulnerable smile.

'Haven't you learned yet, Negroes', he said, 'that among any race there are always traitors ready to play into the enemy's hands?'

His easy and provocative way of talking, that inward glow, were irrefutable signs of a Negro who was happy. They all looked at him incredulously now, their faces brimming over with affection, and the air held a silence that seemed to herald something momentous. It was as if everyone were weighing life up, balancing the black man's folly and inborn sadness against the mysterious contentment that comes over you sometimes looking at nature, the sea, trees, or a happy man. Lost in these reflections, people shook their heads, cleared their throats at great length – kep, kep – and shrugged their shoulders as if to say, 'But what can I possibly know about all this?'

'Life is strange', one voice commented dreamily.

'Yes, no kidding, a black man is something in this world, after all.'

86

Since this scene had begun, Amboise, Elie's comrade, had stood apart from the rest of the group, following what went on with an indulgent eye. After a moment's hesitation he said suddenly:

'I am very happy to hear what you say, but there's one thing you still need to know, my friends, and that is that the man you see there with his head bathed in happiness and his eyes dusted with pride, he has all he needs to drink at home, strong liquor and scented rum. That's why he looks at us and doesn't see us, and why he doesn't say anything.'

All eyes converged on Elie, in anticipation of a word or a sign of approbation, and for a moment my man was wrapped in the shame and awkwardness that sometimes affect those favoured by fortune. Then he tossed them off and said:

'You know, fellows, it's not good to put just any seed in just any soil, and it isn't wise to say just anything to just any ears. There are many things, in fact, of which one shouldn't speak. But one thing I will say, my dear friends here present: a sweeter-scented rum than that in my cabin just doesn't exist.'

As soon as he'd finished speaking Elie paid no more attention to those who surrounded, loved, and blessed him – he was already roving among his thoughts, amid the reveries of one who is in bliss. Suddenly he set off along the road, staggering like a sleepwalker, and quickly disappeared into the dusk. Outside the shop, in the light of a storm lantern Old Abel had just hung up, the others looked as though they'd been visited and transfigured by the Holy Ghost in person. The women had been silent so far, and now they trembled, their eyes shone with wonder, and one said:

'I always knew all wasn't lost, for a woman.'

'That's why we bring children into the world', said another, timidly. 'Life is certainly strange.'

Looking up I saw it was a moonless night, with just a few stars. They seemed very close and warm and welcoming that evening, as tangible and comforting as the lights of some neighbouring village.

During the days that followed my little cabin was never empty. Peaceful and cool in the middle of its plot, with its bunch of faded roses still on the roof, it seemed to attract the women like a lonely chapel. They had to go in, look it over, warm it with their presence, and leave some gift, if only a handful of coco plums or peas. Mostly, they didn't even feel any wish to speak, but just touched my dress with a little sigh of pleasure, then looked at me smiling, with absolute trust, as if they were in the aisle of our church, looked down on by their favourite saint, who lit up the darkness of their souls and sent them forth to live in hope. They paid me a few vague compliments about what I stood for, there in Fond-Zombi, and left with airy dancers' steps, as if everything – life, death, even just walking along the street – was henceforth only a ballet that they must perform as beautifully as possible. And then the rumor spread through all Fond-Zombi, even to beneath the clear waters of its rivers, that good luck had descended on my body and into my bones, and that my face too was transfigured by it. Grandmother laughed, and when people asked her what one had to do to have such a blessed old age, she would answer in a trembling, husky little voice: 'I knew not what I'd sown nor what I was going to reap.' And the others would answer, with a touch of humour, 'Blessed is he, little mother, blessed is he who steers in uncertainty, who knows not what he has sown nor what he will reap.'

Old Abel had lost the glum expression of an old man who doesn't know what he's doing there behind his counter. He now had a kind of confidence and gaiety that all his customers well understood. They teased him about his wrinkles, which seemed to have changed into fine, purely ornamental traceries. Some asked him what one had to do to get such becoming lines.

'Ah, how do you do it, Abel? Who'd have thought we'd ever see you like this, beginning a new youth?'

The old man was pensive, following, furrow by furrow, with the finger of an artist, the rich pattern of the wrinkles, and marveling at what was happening to him. All of a sudden he seemed eager to know everything; he was aware of all that went on in Fond-Zombi, and had completely lost the detached and sometimes disagreeable look he used to have when some cane cutter was waving his arms about in front of his counter. Now he had the keen and watchful eyes of a ferret, and whatever anyone said he was passionately interested, shouting out, agreeing and disagreeing, joining in the chorus, and putting in exclamations of 'What fetters, what chains!'

to egg the speaker on and highlight whatever happened to be the subject. It became known that Old Abel's ears had been unstopped, and that the black man's troubles could enter in and make them hear. And so his shop became indispensable, the place where everyone went to organize and comment on life, to remake it nearer to the heart's desire. A small closet was added to the shop, and to distinguish it from the back room it was called the 'new bar'. Sometimes things got too much for Old Abel: his two thin green arms were not enough to sell cod and rum marmalade in the shop, and absinthe and vermouth in the two bars. Then he would let out a long shout from his stronghold: 'Oo-oo, Telumee! Oo-oo!' And I'd go running, and plunge into the din, into the sea of voices and shouting and singing that echoed with curious force, submerging everything, catching me up, bewitching me, opening up new and infinite perspectives and ways of looking at things unknown to me a few weeks before, when I hadn't yet discovered my right place in the world, and that it was right here in the godforsaken hole of Fond-Zombi. I came and went wide-eyed in the inner room, where the clumsily laid floor shook and trembled under my sturdy weight. And Old Abel couldn't help saying to me sometimes: 'One of these days, Telumee, the way you stomp about, my shop's just going to cave in between its four rocks, crash!' And the men would laugh at the thought. I myself laughed so much I had to sit down. And when I got up and could be serious again, when my eyes opened on the world again, it was rather as if my laughter lived on in the ears of those who had heard it. And the men who were still young looked at me gravely and said with solemn brows that I was a little Negress of laughter and singing, laughter and speed. At such moments I was firmly convinced that everything might change, that nothing had really happened since the beginning of the world. And I would go back to my cabin, to my life of a woman blessed, waiting, waiting. But it wasn't like that always. Sometimes, when I looked at myself in the glass, a fear would come over me, a disagreeable sensation, the thought that I was still the same black girl with stormy tresses, with sooty skin and roving eyes, who had hired herself out at Belle-Feuille and would not escape heaven's vengeance. Then I wouldn't know what to do with myself at the thought of disappointing so many – whether to go under the plum tree, into the woods, or by the river. But soon Old Abel would exorcise my folly. 'Telumee, Telumee, oo-oo'—and the world would reappear, and voices would assail and surround me, opening my eyes and ears. And I would give myself a good talking to. 'So, Telumee, you haven't started to walk yet, you haven't run and gotten out of breath, you haven't found your toes covered with blisters, and you're moaning and groaning already?' And so I would arrive all smiling, and pour out the absinthe and wash up the glasses and throttle my devilments. And the men when they saw me would call out: 'Ah, here you are, girl – it isn't worth calling life till you come in to serve!'

And Old Abel would come to my rescue from behind the counter, putting on one of his shows of rage:

'Let the woman alone, can't you? She's a woman and you're boors. Caper about, puff and blow as much as you like, my boys, but leave her be.'

It was one of the best times of my life, the period when Fond-Zombi grew tall, bloomed, and was radiant. A little wind of prosperity blew over the village, the canefields spread, new land was cleared, the banana trees bowed under the weight of their fruit, and shippers came from Basse-Terre and bought the crops where they stood. Unemployment had gone out of fashion, the women fertilized the vanilla with needles, and the saws hummed peacefully. There were never enough planks to satisfy those who wanted them, and Fond-Zombi grew and acquired shutters on its doors, kitchens of 'resolute' wood, and verandas where everyone sat and took the air, discussed the moon and stars, laughed, danced, and sped the time. In his forest, in company with his red-brown Negro, Elie sawed away indefatigably, and in the evening teams of tired oxen brought back piles of acomat, locust wood, red mahogany, and adegonde poles that vanished almost as fast as they appeared. Elie dealt them all out, singing like a thrush in a guava tree, a song that was always the same:

A day's work Monsieur Durancinee
A day's work
What a long day Monsieur Durancinee
What a fine day
A day's work Monsieur Durancinee.

Nothing was too good, nothing too expensive for our cabin, and on our iron bedstead there now lay the bedspread of my dreams, with flounces and the flowers of France that looked so strange to me, and that people said were heliotropes, the ones you scent your earlobes with. I looked after Elie as a mother looks after her child. His clothes were always mended and ironed and folded away in a drawer, and when I gave him his food I always served it on a dish and never put his slice of suckling pig straight onto his plate. All day, while my man was in his woods, I whipped around seeing to my garden and my hens and my linen and my pots and pans, and on Saturdays, with Queen Without a Name, I made preserved breadfruit flowers and crab patties that we delivered to Old Abel's shop. Every morning when I'd done the house I used to go a little way along the road and turn around suddenly for the pleasure of seeing it there on its four stones, a little cabin just the right size for us, distant, motionless, mysterious and familiar, like a tortoise sleeping in the sun. After the morning cleaning, my next favourite occupation was the washing. I hated doing it in a pan near the house and wasting the water from my jars, and however little there was to wash I used to take it down to the river. I liked to use plenty of water, and it seemed to me, when I unfolded a garment in the current, that I could see my man's weariness fall away and be carried off with the dirt, and, with the sweat from my dresses, most of my own fancies. I was especially fond of the wood, because of its palm trees intermingled with a tangle of wild bananas and Congo canes. The place had a kind of mystery, as if, in some long distant past, it had been inhabited by men who knew how to rejoice in rivers, trees, and sky. Sometimes I almost felt as if I too might some day look on one of these trees in the way it was waiting for. Once I was pounding my linen in the middle of the stream when Letitia came along, the one we used to tease about Elie when she was a little girl. She walked along the bank with her proud slow step, gliding over earth, stones, and leaves like a marauding snake. This was no longer the little thieving Letitia of old. In an instant the light in the wood began to waver, and my heart sank to see her so lovely over the water, looking at me from the rock where she sat as on a throne. With her thick yet transparent skin darkened by some strange coloured sap, she made me think of a waterlily on a pond. She gazed at me for a while without speaking, then, tired of watching me at

91

my washing, stood up, snapped off a Congo cane that was growing on the bank, stripped it swiftly with a knife, sucked it, and said:

'That's what you are for Elie, my girl—a nice succulent congo cane. But will you always have the juice to satisfy him? Not that I'm jealous of your flavor. But let me tell you this: to dance too soon is not to dance at all. So take my advice and don't rejoice just yet.'

Very likely she waited for an answer, waited there on her rock, and seeing there wasn't going to be one went off, for when at last I looked up Letitia had disappeared. There was the river, the trees, the sky, and, had it not been for the unhealthy sulphurous gleam of the sun I'd have thought I'd just had one of my fancies, my happy woman's fancies. But from that day on those words haunted me like prophecies – they began to blow in the sea breeze and in the land breeze, and when the river sang it was Letitia's words it repeated. Unable to bear it any longer, I went to Queen Without a Name and asked her by what signs one recognizes that happiness is going away. She murmured that it had never happened, at least to her knowledge, that one woman carried off all the happiness in the world in the hollow of her bodice, and that human beings had to die sorry to leave life behind. And she said, further:

'We Lougandors don't fear happiness any more than we fear unhappiness, which means that your duty today is to rejoice without apprehension or reserve. All Fond-Zombi is looking at you, and sees you are like a young coconut palm in the sky. All Fond-Zombi knows it is present at your first flowering. So do as you ought, my child: give us your fragrance.'

But Letitia's words crept into the sea breeze and the land breeze and the song of the water, and my soul could no longer find rest. My bones were filled with lead and my blood with bile, and I had become all suspicion about Elie. I scrutinized everything he did, the slightest change in his expression, in order to detect treachery, weariness, or cooling affection – but in vain. In the end his laugh came to seem to me the most suspect thing, the slyest. It made my food rank, the water I drank had a bitter taste, and sometimes his fresh boyish laugh seemed to me to contain such baseness and artifice that I despised myself for sleeping beside this man, and regarded myself as nothing and less than nothing. Not having any proof, I couldn't confide in anyone about my humiliation, and when I gave myself away by a cunning hint or allusion, Elie would at once revel in it and tease me shamelessly. One evening I thought the moment of truth had come. It was still light, Elie was on his way back from the forest followed by a team with a load of planks, and I was behind my plum tree, watching him, when Letitia went up to him right there in the street. They started to walk along calmly side by side, and my heart contracted at the thought that they no longer even sought the complicity of darkness. Letitia spoke out loud as if she wanted the whole world to hear her.

'So now you know', she said. 'When you're tired of Congo canes, remembering there are Campeachy canes too, and maybe I'm one of them.'

They were now quite close to the plum tree, and Elie, looking uneasily toward our cabin, in the shadows, answered in a whisper:

'To press one's wares is to cheapen them, madam merchant. That's why I'm lost in the Congo canes.' And, with a little enigmatic laugh, he added: 'Up there in my forest I don't hear such comical things.'

At that moment Letitia saw me, and as I emerged from the shadow she called to me carelessly:

'Telumee, my friend, where is it written that a man's made just for one woman?'

Her hair was done in four braids hanging down her back; she was wrapped in her skin as in a mantle of silk; I thought she looked magnificent.

'Letitia, Letitia, you are beautiful, it's true, but with the beauty of a waterlily that lives in stagnant water.'

'A lily in stagnant water? Maybe', she answered, smiling. 'But for all that you're a coconut flower right up in the sky, and when the breeze blows you'll fall.'

'Let's wait for the breeze, my waterlily – let's wait for the breeze to spring up.'

'As long as you like', she said, shrugging her shoulders. And with a laugh she glided off, sinuous and airy, scraping her long toes against the earth at every step. A gleam of light still lingered in the

93

sky, revolving slowly, as if the sun was loath to leave Fond-Zombi. I was back again in Elie's sight, a tall red canna, my soul light and free, and I said to my heart: 'Ah, Telumee, my girl, you were ready to moan, but your hour of sorrow has not yet sounded.' Already, without more ado, my man was unloading the planks and setting them out around our cabin, singing:

> Telumee what a pretty girl
> A girl a Congo cane ladies
> A Congo cane in the wind
> She bends forward and back
> Back and forward
> You should see her bent forward ladies
> You should just see her bent forward.

8

In the perfection of my rise, its speed and resonance, there was something disturbing, and I was puzzled at having obtained, all at the same time, the three crowns that can usually be hoped for only at the end of a long life. Love, the trust of others, and that kind of glory that accompanies every woman who is happy – these were gifts too great not to become dangerous in God's sight. So sometimes, in the shade of my Chinese plum, I would tremble with fright, trying to make out the exact moment when the Almighty would take umbrage at my crowns. But then a little breeze would come and play with my skirt, my sleeves, my braids, and I'd feel I could go on like that until the end of time, and it was as if I was already embalmed, powdered, and laid out happy on my death-bed.

Since the evening when Queen Without a Name had come with me to the cabin and roasted a few cobs of corn to sanction my presence under Elie's roof, I seemed to have entered another world; it was as if I never lived before, never known how to. When Elie looked at me, then, only then, I existed, and I knew well that if ever one day he turned away from me I should disappear again into the void. I watched him as a sailor watches the wind in fair weather, knowing not every ship reaches haven. The feeling I bore him overflowed on to every creature my eye lighted on, and I marvelled at the skill and agility with which man fulfils his destiny, however changeable, unpredictable, or excessive it may be. Life went on turning, suns and moons were engulfed and then reborn in the sky, and my continuing joy lifted me out of time. But meanwhile there were the dead children, the old who survived them, and friendship betrayed, razor slashes, the wicked waxing strong on their wickedness, and women with garments woven of desertion and want, and so on. And sometimes a long thorn slowly pierced my heart, and I'd wish I were like the tree called Resolute, on which it is said the whole globe and all its calamities could lean.

One evening when I was taking my usual stroll in front of my cabin, a neighbour stared at me so persistently that I asked her: 'Are you so fond of me, mother, that you wear out your eyes on me like this?' And the woman answered at once, as if she expected my question and had prepared for it: 'Everyone loves dragonflies, and you are a dragonfly without even knowing it. You know how to light up your own soul, and that is why you shine for everyone else.'

'If you think I'm a dragonfly, mother, perhaps I'll really become one.'

Then I went on with my stroll, thinking that if it was so obvious, the time must be near when every second would seem to me like a whole year. The shadow had almost reached the hamlet, the sun was disappearing over the horizon, a heavy perfume rose into the air and over the mountains and clung to a dull and melancholy half moon. A little while later I found Queen Without a Name sitting in her rocker. Here and there around her in the grass the toads seemed to be searching for a dew that would not fall. As I settled myself on a stone, the Queen said without looking at me:

'The breeze won't get up, it's as tired as I am. Will it get up during the night? Maybe, but everyone will be in bed and no one will get any good of it.'

'It's a season for zombies, not for men', I said, to amuse her.

'Why do you want to bother about men?' she said with a faint laugh. 'Many are zombies, and this weather suits them down to the ground. But what surprises me is that you're so good at seeing that spring keeps to its winter quarters. Have you come back to earth?'

It was my turn to laugh, and, this polite exchange concluded, I told her what my neighbour had said, and described my fears. At this moment I envied the Queen. I would have liked to be old and have lived my life already. And suddenly I asked:

'What is natural to man, then—happiness or unhappiness?'

'It depends', she answered.

'What should one do then, to bear—' I went on feebly.

'My child, you will feel just like one deceased, your flesh will be dead flesh and you will no longer feel the knife thrusts. And then

96

you will be born again, for if life were not good, in spite of everything, the earth would be uninhabited. It must be that something remains after even the greatest sorrows, for men do not want to die before their time. As for you, little coconut flower, don't you bother your head about all that. Your job is to shine now, so shine. And when the day comes that misfortune says to you, Here I am – then at least you'll have shone.'

We'd known many bad times, but after every other slack period, when no poisoned word had been uttered, Fond-Zombi and its inhabitants had warded off drought, unemployment, and depression – the canes grew green again, we took our place once more in the earth's orbit, the world went on turning. But this time everything seemed different: it was only the beginning of the season, but it was as if the men were tired already, exhausted with doing nothing. And only a few laughed and said to themselves: 'What else is there to do, and when a man is about to die who can stop him from laughing?'

Fond-Zombi's downfall began that year with a winter that astonished everyone. The village was attacked by waterspouts that transformed the streets into muddy torrents and swept all the goodness of the soil away to the sea. The fruit fell off the trees before it was ripe, and the children all had a painful little dry cough. We must wait for things to calm down, people said, forgetting that a bad winter can get the better of a good spring. And spring came, torrid and stupefying, stifling the pigs and devastating the poultry yards, while the banana leaves became hatchings of the wind, tattered finery scoring space and symbolizing rout. Fond-Zombi was like a desert. Evil seemed to hang in the air, the only tangible thing there was, and people stared at it, dazed, throughout whole afternoons. The women went about the streets in disconcerting haste, so that one only guessed how thin they were, and what sadness was in their eyes. They glided along like shadows, and when they passed each other made a little evasive gesture which meant, 'We must block evil with our silence, and anyway, since when was sorrow a subject for tales?'

From the start, before the pigs died, before the hens' tongues

97

were swollen by the pip, even before that conversation with the neighbour, I knew the hour of the abyss was approaching for me. Elie seemed to find the sun tarnished, dulled, and you could see from his glance that here was a man who had stopped seeing wonders. Not a single new cabin was built in Fond-Zombi – only shanties, hovels of cardboard, and patched-up shacks. All the timber that should have been sold piled up around the house like flotsam on the shore. Elie kept on going to his forest, all alone, out of sheer obstinacy, but he hardly ever laughed now as he set out his planks of locust wood and red mahogany. After a good swig of rum he would wander about the yard examining each plank minutely, then stretch his idle arms out in the darkness, gingerly trying his muscles, swaying now to the right and now to the left as if the weight of his body was too great to support. One evening when he seemed even more depressed than usual I started to hum a little beguine to remind him of old times. But he looked so scandalized I stopped short. He seemed to be saying; 'Don't you realize, my poor Telumee, that the time for songs is over?' Next morning, as I was handing him his old lunch box that he used to take to the forest, he snatched it from me and threw it down, shouting:

'Can you see one little house post going up anywhere, that you dare to give me this?'

I was transfixed with surprise. I couldn't take my eyes off the food lying scattered about, with little ants running over it already. When I looked at him again, Elie was scratching his head gloomily and glaring wildly at the sky, the piles of planks nearby, and the trees in the distance, as if he didn't know whom or what to vent his anger on.

'Oh', he moaned quietly, 'what I've always feared is happening. We no longer live on solid earth, Telumee, we're out at sea amid the currents, and what I wonder is whether I'm going to drown outright.'

'What I wonder is, what fish would ever eat you, with that tough hide', I said, trying to be light and reassuring.

'Tough, you say. Don't be too sure.'

And he turned away and went slowly off towards the village, in search of the others, equally disenchanted, who now gathered to drink and bicker and even, sometimes, fight; to lose their savings at dice, and fritter the hours away on the same adegonde verandas where not long ago they had talked of the stars and the meaning of life.

From that day onwards Elie spent most of his time amid the bruised and shattered souls of Negroes without jobs, and when he staggered home he wouldn't have anything to eat, but just spat out jets of brown saliva and muttered: 'A long time ago . . . I used to saw wood . . . but now I've found friends who are fond of me, so what does it matter?' Sometimes he would come back from these gatherings quite changed, and look at everything with a mysterious, knowing gaze, as though he possessed the secret of all existence. I used to envy him those bird of prey's eyes looking down on life from on high; I too wanted to know the secret that was told on the verandas now that Fond-Zombi had left its place in the earth's orbit. One afternoon, wishing to acquire the same look as my Elie, I decided to go to one of the meetings. That day, all those with nothing to do were gathered at the other end of the village, on the veranda of Madame Brindosier, already old and crowned with white braids, but still keen on stirring up evil. She crouched on her heels some distance away from the rest, under a flame tree, her eyes fixed admiringly on the group of bold demons cursing and yelling and boxing on her handsome veranda. Every so often she would stand up and lean over the balustrade.

'It gets worse every year', she sighed. 'Men go further and further downhill, and it isn't that which kills them.' And her fine gold-speckled brown eyes were filled with artlessness.

Slipping in among the crowd outside the balustrade, I hid my face behind one of the smooth planks Elie had brought back from the woods a few years before. The first thing I noticed, at the other end of the veranda, was the tall reddish-brown Amboise, looking down pensively on the spectators. Then I became aware of the continual hubbub that reigned inside, punctuated by hoarse bids on the dice and a ceaseless flow of gratuitous insults. At that moment two men were going for each other with an air of fierce resignation. Elie was egging them on and singing drinking songs, hollow-cheeked and red-eyed, the veins in his temples swollen with rage and helplessness. Suddenly he let out a crazy laugh and the fight broke off, as if no longer capable of masking the confusion of men's minds and hearts.

'It's hot as hell', he panted, 'and I'm dying of cold'.

Then, snatching up a bottle of rum, he drank till he was out of breath, stopped to say a few words, and punctuated them with a long jet of brown saliva, as if to show that for him speech itself was nothing but bitterness and disgust.

'Which of you can answer and tell me exactly what we are hunted by – for we are hunted, aren't we?'

Amboise emerged from the crowd and murmured in a distant voice, such as one uses to the wind and trees and rocks:

'Friend, nothing hunts the Negro but his own heart.'

A huge disappointment spread over every countenance, and Elie shouted, full of wrath:

'Why talk to me about the Negro's heart, when what it's all about is my two arms and my trade as a sawyer? You think you've got a monopoly of all the world's wisdom, Amboise, and you're really only an acomat fallen among rotten timber!'

Amboise looked long at the face of his friend, his brother of the forest.

'Alas', he said at last, 'the Negro's heart is a dry land no water will improve, a graveyard insatiable for corpses'.

And coming over to me among the crowd, he drew me away with a firm hand, while behind us, in the hubbub on the adegonde veranda, the fighting began again. We went through the village in silence and he left me as soon as we were in sight of my cabin.

'You certainly found what you were looking for', he said, and disappeared.

That night Elie came home even later than usual, and, dragging me out of bed, started to beat me unmercifully without saying a word. From that instant dates my end, and thenceforward shame and derision were my guardians and my angels. Elie would come in in the middle of the night and put on superior airs: 'I am a shooting star, Negress, I do what I please, and that's why you're going to get up and warm up my supper before I have time to bat my eyelids.' I didn't cry out under his blows – all I did was cross my arms to protect my eyes and temples. But this only increased his fury, and he would thrash me with all his strength, saying, 'For you six feet of earth and for me penal servitude, my girl.' I was covered with blue and purple bruises; soon not a square inch of my flesh was presentable. Then I began to flee the light of day, for a women's misery is not a tourmaline she wants to flash in the sun. Every evening when night fell I would hide my purple skin in the dark and drag myself to Queen Without a Name's. She would make me lie down, light a candle dedicated to suffering, and massage me gently with carapate oil warmed in the palm of her hand.

'It's abominable', she'd sigh as she rubbed my arms and legs. 'He ought to send you away instead of knocking you about like this. But things like this never go unpunished, and I'm sure he'll get what he deserves.'

Her oracular tone made me shudder.

'Don't curse him, Grandma. He's drowning, and if you curse him it's all over with him.'

But she would shrug her shoulders and sadly shake her head:

'I don't need to curse him, woman. He's taking care of it himself.'

One day, when people had stopped believing in Him, God caused it to rain: the earth was flooded, the roots watered, and with them human hope. Soon the banana leaves stretched out like the sails of windmills, and the canefields foamed and sang beneath the wind's caress. Gradually all the verandas emptied of their demons. People stared at each other wide-eyed, in silence, and with a certain touch of mutual admiration, and went about the streets as light as ships without ballast. The planks around our cabin had faded: they served as nests for termites, the rain had rotted them. Elie never set out for the forest again. He was crushed, weighed down by his own body, his soul, his breath. People looked at him awkwardly, and he remained alone and friendless, with a gulf in his bosom that swallowed up everything. He bought a horse with the last of our money, and stayed away from Fond-Zombi as much as possible, spending his time in the neighbouring districts, stirring up trouble in them, issuing his famous challenges. He would ride full tilt to Le Carbet, Valbadiane, or La Roncière, instal himself in a bar, down a full glass of rum, and suddenly bawl out to all and sundry: 'Is there a man among you? In less than three rounds I'll send him back to his mother's womb.' In this way he came to be called the Hunted One, and Old Abel himself said: 'I acknowledge my part

101

in Elie's head, his body, his arms and legs, and even the reed flute between his legs. But I acknowledge no part in his heart. The gulf of the hunted ones is in his bosom, and the way he's heading now he'll go right through the thirty-two communes of Guadeloupe, and soon think the whole world too small for him!'

When he returned from these excursions Elie would call me a black cloud and swear he'd dispel me. He would indulge in strange kinds of violence, choice cruelties that he called his specialities, his little pleasures. Some days he would weep, wild-eyed, and approach me with lips parted as if to speak of truce, and of bygone things that might come back again. But no sound would ever emerge from him; all he did was watch the sky resignedly, and after a while take to the road again. One evening as she was rubbing me with oil I asked Queen Without a Name:

'Grandma, doesn't he realize I love him?'

'In the state he's in, my child, your love is of no use to him – the whole world might love him and to him it would be of no use. Alas, if only men could love not with half their heart but with the whole heart God has given us, then no one would deserve to die. But as you see, no one is immortal, and that is how the world goes around.'

I grew extremely weary. I had had enough of living. I was drunk and swollen with sorrow. Elie beat me now without a word, without a look. One evening I sank into the void. I heard and didn't hear, saw and didn't see, and the wind passing over me encountered another wind. When he was tired of beating me Elie would sit in a chair with his head in his hands and try to work out ideas, kinds of barricades or ditches that separated him irrevocably from me and from himself and from the whole world. He would sit like that for hours, not moving, his only thought to try to counter each of the bruises dealt by life with an even more perverted and sinister notion, though the contest never came out in his favour. He went away, came back, went away again and never looked at me any more. I sat in the shade of my Chinese plum, languid and non-existent, and sometimes, under the tree, I fell asleep and dreamed there was a bubble inside my body that filled me up and floated me to heaven. Passers-by looked on me as a kind of apparition. They took the precautions one takes with a spirit enclosed in flesh; as they approached my cabin their conversation would fade to a cautious murmur. Both children and grown-ups seemed to dread frightening me, lest I should fly away. A few stray dogs did bark at me, but even their yapping only confirmed the general idea that I had been changed into a zombie.

For now I heard and didn't hear, saw and didn't see, and the wind passing over me encountered another wind.

9

The woman who has laughed is the same one as she who will cry, and that is why one knows already, from the way a woman is happy, how she will behave in the face of adversity. I'd liked that saying of Queen Without a Name, once, but now, under my Chinese plum tree, it frightened me, and above all it saddened me, for I saw clearly that I didn't know how to suffer. When I was at my height I could show the way to be happy, but now here I was succumbing under my first burden. And yet I knew very well only she who has not filled the jar of her life during the rainy season is to be pitied, and was not it filled, my jar, with all those years with Elie? But when I told myself this no consolation came, and I stared at myself intently, and the sun set and the night fell, and the same sun rose next day, and I saw there was no longer any thread linking my cabin to the others. Then I would lie on the ground and try to dissolve my flesh: I would fill myself with bubbles and suddenly go light – a leg would be no longer there, then an arm, my head and whole body faded into the air, and I was floating so high over Fond-Zombi it looked no bigger to me than a speck of pollen in space. But it was seldom I attained such happiness; usually the most I could do was contemplate my ravaged life with serenity, watch it unfold before my eyes like a significant but harmless dream, a painful mystery that astonished and eluded me. I still clung, really, to the hope that Elie would come back to me, that his muddied soul would clear. There are muddy waters that flow majestically, and if they clear, nothing is more limpid and profound. It was that moment I was waiting for, it was for that man I watched.

Now Elie would say indulgently to anyone who cared to listen,

'Telumee is a strong wind, and if she courts the clouds what can I do?' He applied this maxim rigorously, only coming to the house to cut down the grass in the yard, which sometimes got to be as tall as a man. If I was lying in the grass, floating, he would push my legs out of the way with the point of his machete and work over the place where they had been in silence, without a glance at me. He worked fast, set fire to the green grass, and went as he had come, his handsome face lit by a vague, awkward smile. I might have turned into a foaming fish or a dog without any legs, and still not have aroused the least flicker of interest in his eyes. It was as if I was already rotting underground, and I said within myself, 'How one can deceive people – they think I'm alive, and I'm dead.' I no longer knew where he lived, what bowl he ate out of, or what hands washed and ironed his clothes. He had given up rum for absinthe, which hung between him and the rest of the world a veil the same color as itself, murky, shifting, uncertain, and it was through this he moved. One evening he jumped from his horse, rushed into our cabin, and collapsed on the table with his head in his hands and his eyes shut. I lit the little pink glass lamp that Queen Without a Name had given us, and saw by its light that Elie was green in the face and streaming with sweat. A wave of tenderness swept over me. It was as if I were seeing him in the middle of the Blue Pool, a boy, looking for our crayfish. I went over to mop his brow and said, 'You're a strange colour, man. Aren't you well?'

He looked up at me with eyes I'd never seen before, the eyes of another man – or were they those of a devil? They were cloudy, sad, cold, their only light a flicker of scorn:

'Your breasts are full', he said in a slow, forced voice, 'your breasts are full and your womb is deep, but you don't know yet what it is to be a woman – you don't know it yet'. And with this sibylline pronouncement, he got up abruptly, rammed his hat down over his eyes, and vanished into the night.

As soon as she heard the horse galloping away, Grandmother used to rush over to my cabin to see if anything had happened, and then she'd anoint my arms and legs, massage if necessary the places bruised by Elie's fists or feet, rub my forehead, for heart and hope, and pour a little lotion of herbs on my hair to give me back scent and colour in the eyes of my man. It was because of her I ate and drank; she even did all my errands, for I couldn't bear to have people looking at me in the street and whispering, 'A fallen acomat, with a vengeance.' It has always been so. Whenever misfortune touches the acomat and it falls, drops in the dust, those who used to envy its splendour cry: 'It was a rotten tree from the beginning.' And that was why I never left my cabin now, but clung to it as what we call the 'guilty crab' clings to its shell. When Queen Without a Name had bathed me and given me something to eat and drink, we used to spend hours just looking at each other in silence, and as soon as she started to say Elie's name I'd put my finger on her lips, for her heart was overflowing with bitterness. I wouldn't, wouldn't hear it said that I'd mounted a crazy horse, a man ill-grafted in his mother's womb, who was falling to pieces limb by limb. So, when I saw her lips tremble, I put my finger on them, and we sat there like that watching the hours, bearing our load in silence. I still hoped. I told myself the earth had never been known to have enough water, and the day would come when Elie would thirst for me again. I only had to wait, to be ready to take up my life again at the very moment where it had stopped. But that evening, after Elie's mysterious words, my heart suddenly swelled with despair, and I asked Queen Without a Name:

'But, Grandmother, what is it that pursues him – what is he hunted by?'

Grandmother gazed intently, first at one point in space and then at another, then at my whole person, and, looking at me with the lovely tired eyes that seemed to have scanned the surface of things visible and invisible, and to have known, in their time, they too, terror, horror, and despair, she murmured very gently:

'There is boiling water and the foam on top of it, and man is both at once, water and foam. But it's only the foam that pursues Elie, and that will not disappear tomorrow. And that's why I say, if you don't run away while there is still time, you'll be submerged by it. Telumee, my little crystal glass, I beg you – as I am untangling your hair now, untangle your life from his, for it is not laid down that a woman must bear hell on earth. Where is that laid down, where? Listen – the day will come when you'll put on your dress of life again, and everyone will see that your taste hasn't changed. Already there's a man who comes to my house to talk to me about you, a good man who adores you once and for all. You know him, I know him, and I can tell you he loves you as a sensible man loves a fertile

106

piece of land, which will nourish and support him to beyond the grave. Sometimes, you see, the back dies for the shoulder and the shoulder knows nothing about it. And today I want you to know this man's name, so I'm going to tell you.'

Surprised, I went over to Queen Without a Name and murmured, laying a finger over her lips:

'Please, Grandma, don't go on. Do you think I like suffering, and that I'd stay with Elie if I could do otherwise? Where have you ever seen another monster like me, eh, mother?'

Queen Without a Name smiled. Her eyes lightened, as if for the first time she saw right into my depths, down to the smallest pebble lying on the bottom, and, raising her fine arched brows she said:

'My child, you have a stormy man who sleeps in the arms of darkness. But who knows? Perhaps you are right when you say muddy waters sometimes flow majestically, and if they clear, nothing is more limpid and profound. Yesterday I went up to see Ma Cia in the woods, and she told me an evil spirit had been sent against your cabin, to fill it with desolation. To begin with, the spirit entered into Elie's body, and that is why his blood fights against itself and tears him apart bit by bit. Ma Cia told me to tell you she isn't asleep up there in her forest, and as Elie has gone to pieces bit by bit, so she will put him together again. The first thing is to take the spell off your cabin, so that the spirit no longer has any power over you. Tomorrow I'm going to burn some herbs she gave me, to chase the spirit back at once to his master. You know, Telumee, evil is very strong, and that which breeds in the heart of man is quite enough for man's shoulders to bear without evil spirits putting their oar in.'

First thing the next day, Grandmother took some coconut shells and set them out around my cabin. Then she burned in them incense, balsam, vetiver roots, and magic leaves, producing a fine cloud of green smoke, slow to disperse, which soon surrounded my house with a protective halo. While she attended to this, I turned toward the red disc of earth where Ma Cia lived, and I seemed to see Elie being put together piece by piece as she had predicted. Ah, I thought, smiling in my heart, he'll have to admit a Negress isn't a cloud, and he is not a wind strong enough to disperse anything. And for the first time for a long while I took a comb and did my matted hair: I washed it and made it shine with oil, I started to look after myself and my house again, and that very day the place began to look as it used to. But at the end of the afternoon, Elie, informed by someone or other of what was going on, arrived foaming with rage. He kicked the smoking shells over and yelled that he wouldn't have any witches around his house. Traps would be set all over the ground from now on, and woe betide anyone who set foot on it. After this warning he turned to me and shouted mockingly:

'You think you're still a little girl at the Blue Pool, but if you don't know it already I tell you you're a grown-up woman with full breasts under your dress. And soon I'm going to teach you what the word woman means, and you'll roll on the ground and scream, as a woman does roll and scream when she's handled right. You're trying to get away from me, runaway Negress with no forest to go to; you leap into the air and float, but you won't escape a man like me, and white hairs are not going to scare me.'

A group had gathered by the side of the road, and Elie strutted about as he spoke, shouting loud enough to be heard in Old Abel's shop. He also glanced around from time to time, hoping for some sign from the spectators, some mark of admiration or contempt. But seeing that was what he wanted, the people turned their backs on him, and he and I remained alone in the middle of that strange space still traversed by small green wisps of smoke. Then Elie pointed to me with a curious gesture and began to laugh, saying, 'A dried fish slung on a plate, that's what you look like.' And as I remained silent with terror, he came at me with his fist raised, intent on scattering me like a pawpaw fallen from the tree.

'Where are your tears and cries now, spirit of the highways, flying Negress – where are they now?'

From then on he never let a day pass without seeing me, without coming to teach me what it means to be a woman. I saw him coming far off, his handsome face filled with a calm that faded as he approached the cabin. And suddenly his mouth twisted, his nostrils twitched, a kind of icy fury came over him, and he'd throw himself on me raging. 'You want to run away from me, my fine crow, you think I'll let you fly in the air, but you're not going to court the clouds, because I'm here, and here to stay. And I can tell you this – my mother's womb brought me forth, but it will never open for me again.' Every time, after he'd gone, when he'd finished scattering me body and soul all over the floor, I used to go and lie

108

in the grass, close my eyes, and try to bury Fond-Zombi and myself in the depths of my memory. But the paths of the sky were closed to me, I could no longer take refuge in the air, and though I lowered my eyelids I remained below, stirring up cold, dead embers with a bitter feeling that I was still wide of the mark, the certainty that I had many more discoveries to make before I knew exactly what it meant to be a woman.

Thus did the days go by for me, growing heavy with new shames and unavowable fears, while my memories themselves gradually abandoned me and disappeared into the mist. All the beautiful words and all the things I'd thought I understood had happened to someone else, some living flesh, not this dead flesh indifferent to the knife – some woman with the heart to do her hair and dress and watch other living creatures.

But man's mishaps have never made the sun shine any less bright, and at the year's end, the days vied with one another in splendour. It was Advent, and songs trailed away, were lost and taken up again from cabin to cabin and hill to hill right up to the edge of the forest. The Negroes' soul, fallow and full of thorns throughout the year, grew clear, and people passing one another in the street would look at one another jestingly. Some would even quip:

'Does not the wild pig's tail grow bushy when it's hunted?'

Straight came the traditional reply:

'It does indeed grow bushy, man, and what are all of us in Fond-Zombi but a pack of wild pigs on the rampage for spoils?'

Then they would smile delightedly, artlessly, pleased with their definition. And they would go on their way pensively, with the slow, grave, unconcerned tread they deemed appropriate for the last days of December.

A few days before the holiday people began to go up and down in front of my cabin without saying anything, just to prove to me that there couldn't be a gap in the weft, and that however much I wanted to fly and become a wind I had two hands and two feet exactly the same as them. And then, when they went by my yard, it was as if they deliberately laughed louder than before, some of them even singing cheerful songs and hymns of deliverance with such zest I wondered if they were singing only for themselves. So they went to and fro in front of my cabin, and from time to time a woman would break away from a group, lift imploring arms heavenwards, and cry in a high-pitched voice, 'Be born, come down to change our fates.' And hearing her I'd have the strange feeling that she was throwing me a thread in the air, throwing a light, light thread toward my cabin, and then I'd be visited by a smile. Meanwhile the weeds in my yard grew until they covered me completely, and I felt like a neglected garden, left to its brambles and thorns.

One day, Christmas Eve, there was a great to-do on the other side of the road, and I could hear hymns, faint laughter, and the sound of grass trodden on. Suddenly these human voices, this laughter, these mysterious and apparently aimless energies reached my house, my plot, the Chinese plum under which I was sitting. Straightening up a little, I could see Adriana and Ismene and other neighbors settling themselves down on the verge of the road opposite my yard. They squatted on their heels in a circle, bolt upright, just as if they were in a house, and looked in my direction without saying anything, as if to let me get used to their presence. Some time passed like this, then they began to chat among themselves, quietly and naturally, addressing the very air and wind, and the first words I heard were: 'Ismene, we want only coloured rum after midnight mass, so see that your syrup's right, you lazy little louse.'

Adriana had plumped down right in the grass with her podgy arms stretched around her knees. The women around her were gathered like chicks about their mother. Suddenly the black mass of her head turned towards me and she said in a slow, deliberate voice:

'Have you heard the news, my friends? Queen Without a Name is sick and soon we shall hear her knell.'

There was a pause, then a voice answered reproachfully:

'Queen Without a Name told us not to say anything.'

'But, my dear', said another voice, 'don't you see this person can't hear or understand? I even wonder whether we'll ever see her again as she used to be, in the flesh'.

'Yes, you're right, something stops her from touching land and she could still go sailing through the air for a long time without ever setting foot on any continent.'

'You set out on a fine raft and after a while the paint goes, and

110

the mast and the sail, and the boat starts to let in water. And it's always like that. Why?'

'And yet she had a face that was promisingly marked, spaces between her front teeth, and features that seemed made to attract good luck. I thought for once at least everything would go well, and there'd be for once, here at Fond-Zombi, a woman's life as light and white as cotton. Oh well, it'll come in the end, the day when God puts his rope right around Fond-Zombi and drops it from the highest sky into the deepest ocean. And the salt will purify and dissolve it all, all the unending awfulness.'

At that point Adriana heaved herself up and I saw her enormous bulk silhouetted against the grass, the setting sun making that towering flesh look like a block of granite. Opening her eyes as if reluctantly, she said in a dreamy, wistful voice:

'Do we know what we carry in our veins, we Negroes of Guadeloupe – the curse of being a master, the curse of being a slave. It's true, you're right, Ismene, something stops this little Negress from touching land, and she may go on a long while, a long while, voyaging like that. And yet I, Adriana, I beat my breast and tell you she *will* come to shore.'

'She will', Ismene declared at once, ingenuously, 'she will come to shore, she will, she will'.

Then, addressing me directly from the other side of the road, the good Adriana said in a vibrant voice that was almost a cry:

'Telumee, dear little countrywoman, you stay in your grass, there's no need to answer us today. But one thing I wanted to tell you this Christmas day: you will come to shore.'

Adriana, having spoken, turned away toward Old Abel's shop, and the other women rose up after her, smoothing their crackling skirts, and, chattering around her, scattered about the village. I stayed among the tall grass, under the little cage of foliage around my Chinese plum. Night was near, and somewhere in the distance singing arose, shrill voices still imploring, Be born and change our fates. And I thought of the mountain of pain I was giving Queen Without a Name, and of all the starched skirts she had to put on so that no one should see her thinness or her sorrow.

I had the feeling Adriana had said something about Grandmother – but what? I couldn't remember. Only a vague dread arose in me at the thought. Every so often the singing stopped and an accordion

111

took over, and the rambling, melancholy sounds filled me with pity. Then I wondered what I was in this world for, what I was doing under this Chinese plum. I'd gone hunting, I'd lost both the dog and the hare, half of my soul was broken and the other half debased. By now the moon had come out, and its serene, sparkling light dulled and killed the beauty of the stars. The whole countryside was as clear as day, but the cool and mystery of evening rose on all sides, and over there among the shining grass at the side of the road the trees' shadows danced in the wind. In the moonlight a broad shape with two heads appeared, coming from Old Abel's shop. It advanced toward me like a spirit, gliding along slowly without touching the ground. Now it was brushing the grass in my yard, and as it thus approached I shut my eyes, overcome with fear. Suddenly there was the whisper of human voices, and the enigmatic countenance of Letitia appeared among the weeds, on top of a long thin neck like that of a wild goose. Letitia was bending over me, her arm hooked around Elie's waist, and she murmured, in a languid, caressing voice:

'What a heart she has, this little woman, and how well she knows how to bear suffering.'

'What are you doing in my house, Letitia?'

'Your house?' she said carelessly.

'Elie, Elie, what is she doing in my house?'

'You wouldn't see', said Elie in a vexed tone, his eyes lost in a dream. 'Didn't I tell you over and over to find a hole to hide in, my poor little crab without claws? Why have you stayed here as if you were tied by the ankle? Every day I goaded you more, and still you didn't leave. Why?'

'Why?' repeated Letitia sourly.

'She's a little Negress that flies', Elie then said in a strange voice half cruel and half gentle, 'she wouldn't see. But perhaps this evening she will learn what it means to be a woman'.

And, suddenly overcome with irritation:

'Are you still there, you headless crab? You haven't any hole on the earth to go and hide in? But you've got to vanish from this house – backwards, limping, or flying, you've got to go. Now, right away.'

Letitia listened to him with half-closed eyes, as one listens to heavenly music. Then she came nearer to me and said pityingly:

112

'You can see you have to go now.' Then she added softly, smiling: 'But if you want to stay, we'll give you a blanket and you can lie down at the foot of the bed. Only you'll have to try to stop your ears with cotton wool, because I make a lot of noise at night.' And she writhed her beautiful guitar-like body in front of me.

Elie clasped her tight, and they both began to laugh. They'd already forgotten me.

I hurried to my cabin, lit a candle, and hastily began to gather my things together in Queen Without a Name's tablecloth, for I could see I had to get every smell of myself out of the place as soon as possible. Away in the village I could hear the buzz of voices, and then came accordion music that made me clasp my hands to my breast, for it pierced me to the heart. But I had to manage to see it all as though it were happening to someone else. This thought consoled me, and I put my bundle on my head and went calmly out of the house. But at the last moment I couldn't help saying to Letitia:

'Won't anything in the world really please you except my place and my house?'

She seemed genuinely astonished.

'Little coconut flower', she said woefully, 'where have the bells been ringing for you? Your house? What house is that? You're no more at home here than anywhere else. Didn't you know the only place on earth that belongs to a Negress is in the graveyard?'

She smiled sadly, and I remembered the little roving girl, everybody's child, who knew every house in Fond-Zombi. But suddenly terror seized me and I started to run. I ran through the tall grass to the road, and went along it, still running as if pursued by a spirit, in the light of a moon that now changed, taking on reddish hues and swelling and thrashing in the sky like an octopous under attack. Then, when I came to the Bridge of Beyond, I felt tired, and sat down on a mound by the support of the bridge and wept.

The sun never tires of rising, but it sometimes happens that man is weary of being under the sun. I have no memory of the days that followed. I learned later that I was found next morning sitting on

113

a stone in Queen Without a Name's back yard, completely bemused. I stayed there several weeks without moving, no longer even able to tell day from night. Queen Without a Name fed me and brought me in at night, like a chicken that has to be protected from mongooses. When anyone spoke to me I was silent; they said that of all things in the world speech had become the most alien to me. Three weeks went by like this. So as not to weaken in front of me, Queen Without a Name went, for the first time, to speak her grief in the street: 'My child, my child, her mind has gone, her mind has gone.'

One day, coming up to me without a word, she suddenly pulled a needle out of her bodice and pricked my arm.

'You see', she said, 'you're not a spirit – you bleed'.

Then, raising her arms to heaven and moving her old bones with difficulty, she went back indoors. As she bent near and pricked me, her face had seemed quite flattened and crushed, without mouth or nose or ears, a sort of shapeless lump from which nothing emerged but her lovely eyes, which seemed to exist independently of all the rest. A little while later Grandmother heard me singing at the top of my voice, standing up on my rock, singing so loud it was as if I was trying to drown another voice that was singing at the same time, the voice of someone whose singing I refused to hear. Still singing, I ran to the river and jumped in, immersing myself again and again. Then, dripping wet, I went back to the cabin, put on dry clothes, and said to Grandmother: 'Queen, Queen, who says there is nothing for me in the world, who says such foolishness? At this very moment I have left my grief at the bottom of the river. It is going downstream, and will enshroud another heart than mine. Talk to me about life, Grandmother. Talk to me about that.'

10

What really cured me were all the visits, all the attentions and little gifts people honoured me with when my mind came back from wherever it had been. Madness is contagious, and so my cure was everyone's, and my victory the proof that a Negro has seven spleens and doesn't give up just like that at the first sign of trouble. People came to Queen Without a Name's, filling the house with their chatter, bringing me fruit, aromatic herbs, and incense for having escaped the claws of evil. And then they looked at me with screwed-up eyes, as at one who has come back from far, very far away. 'Ah', they said gravely, 'here is the stout one, the Negress with seven spleens, four breasts, and two navels. Right, right, stay as you are, woman – don't go buying a pair of scissors to stick in his heart, for that fellow's not worth a pair of scissors'. I would laugh, and acquiesce in silence, and all these words, this laughter, these marks of attention, helped to lift me back in the saddle, to hold my horse's bridle with a firm grip.

Sometimes old thoughts arose in me, shooting up like whirls of dust raised from the road by a herd of wild horses galloping by. Then Grandmother would try to whistle up a wind for me, saying we should soon be going away, for the air in Fond-Zombi didn't agree with my lungs now. Since my return it was as if she'd suddenly sprouted wings, as if, at last, she was going to be able to fly. She was still rather tired from all the recent trouble, and had to be helped into her rocker. But her eyes flashed, thrilled at the thought of all the fine things awaiting us. 'Ah', she'd say, her cheeks bright with excitement, 'ah, there are so many places in Guadeloupe, and as soon as I'm better we'll put our cabin on Amboise's cart and put it down on La Folie hill, on Monsieur Boissanville's estate. I used to know him, he won't refuse us a bit of land. And when your peas and yams start to yield, you'll be a woman and a half'.

And so through all her last days Grandmother was whistling up a wind for me, to fill my sails so that I could resume my voyage. And listening to her, I would come to believe in her mirage, and add a veranda to our future home for the pleasure of seeing the Queen rocking there in the cool and just snuffing up the wind. And the days went by, and I forgot I was a fallen acomat, and began to feel the beauty of my own two woman's legs again, and started to walk. At first Queen Without a Name laughed about it. 'You walk crooked, Telumee, but you do walk.' Then she stopped smiling and pointed out that I'd taken on the walk of a woman . . . the walk of a woman who's suffered, she said finally.

'And how does one recognize it', I asked, 'the walk of a woman who's suffered?'

And Grandmother answered:

'By the special, incomparable air that belongs to someone who's said to herself one day: "I've helped men to suffer enough, now I must help them to live."'

Queen Without a Name had always said that the day she took to her bed it would be to die. I joined in her projects for the future, pretending to think her invulnerable, but all the time she was getting weaker, and the candle she had caused to shine for us was about to go out.

As her face grew thinner her eyes had suddenly grown larger, as if to take in every nuance that reached her of people and things – a hen, the shadow of a bamboo swaying in the wind, fine rain made transparent by bright sunlight. When she looked at you it was as if you were being given a little piece of her knowledge, a morsel without bitterness or hatred, ringed about with a halo of gaiety that stayed with you long after you'd left her. One day I found her in bed, very ashamed at not being able to get up. She had complained of bedsores recently. I settled her on her couch, and after she'd made me twist and turn in front of her so that she could look at me, as on that first day when she'd brought me from L'Abandonnée, she asked for some dittany custard flavoured with vanilla. As I

116

bustled about with pots and pans, blew up the fire and crushed some dried dittany, the dark came down with the usual splendour of evenings in Fond-Zombi, alighting like a caress between the houses and the trees. Grandmother's hair, spread out on the white pillow and damp with sweat, surrounding her wrinkled brow with pale, watery gleams that made her look as if she were wearing a crystal diadem. But deep in her eyes there was a mischievousness, a boundless comfort, a gaiety that made her very much alive – perhaps more alive than ever, as in the bloom of her youth. After she'd eaten her custard I took her head in my lap, and she talked to me of the balance of nature and the planets, the permanence of the sky and the stars, and of suffering, which after all is only another way of existing. The window was wide open, and from our bed we could see the sky and the highest peak of the mountain still in sunlight: the light seemed to make everything larger, revealing a tree or a bamboo stem to us in its eternity. Turning toward me, Grandmother whispered: 'Telumee, my little ember, although you see me so glad, don't think I'm just rejoicing at death. No. I must make you a confession: for three months Jeremiah has been with me. He hasn't left me day or night. You see, knowing my time was almost come, he couldn't wait any longer and came to be near Toussine.'

'Where is he now? Is he in this room?'

'He's sitting by my pillow, and from time to time he strokes my hair, and wipes my brow, and when I'm too hot he fans me with his breath.'

I could feel the presence of something strange, of approaching death, but stare as I might into the darkness I could see nothing unusual. As we were talking, completely happy, thinking of nothing but our joy in being together, night suddenly fell, enveloping all the disorder of the world. Then Grandmother began to breathe very calmly, and after a few sighs of pleasure:

'You see', she said, 'I have found rest again with Jeremiah. He has prepared a comfortable place for me, and I'm going away to fill it. As for you, my child, you mustn't stay in Fond-Zombi. Your eyes mustn't go on seeing that man and that house. If you go away perhaps your heart will recover, and the root of your luck will grow and bloom again.'

'I'm to abandon my ship, Grandma, and let it sink alone?'

'Ah, Telumee Lougandor, you mustn't think it's your fate to feed the fire of hell. Don't let that be recorded in your book of life, for it's something man and heaven and the trees all hold in horror.'

I promised I'd leave behind the dust of Fond-Zombi, and we stayed a long while without speaking, she with Jeremiah and I seeking my woman's heart in the shadows. Outside, the stars looked as if they were dancing around the moon, and it was as if all beauty and even life itself had taken refuge in the heavenly bodies. The sky seemed alive, swept by waves, emanations, and you had the feeling it was a realm that excluded men but whose mere existence was enough to comfort them. Suddenly Grandmother grew lively: propping herself up on her elbows, she started to talk about her youth, and of her mother, Minerva, as sharp as nails, she said: 'Yes, a real tease, and I'll tell you why I say so. Long ago, when Jeremiah started courting me, he used to come to the house every afternoon. He'd go straight into the kitchen, and there the two accomplices would tell each other all sorts of things about me. Mama was never as radiant as she was at that time, and my Jeremiah would go into her kitchen and they'd spend whole afternoons together. Jeremiah told her about how he'd like to live with me, what he thought of me, and what I meant to him. And poor Minerva drank up his words like honey, because, as she told him, she could see he was a sensible man, capable of appreciating God's wonders at their proper value. But there was one thing I hated: as soon as my fiancé had left she'd come out of the kitchen, spread out her full skirt with yellow dots, and sing:

> I want a fisherman for a husband
> To catch me a fine sea bream
>
> I don't know if you know
> But I want a fisherman
>
> Oh oar before, he pleases me
> Oh oar behind, I die.

Queen Without a Name had a little thin thread of a voice, diaphanously light, which almost hurt to listen to; but her face glowed as it had done long ago when Minerva teased her. Then suddenly her voice broke, and I began to weep without knowing why, sparse tears that ran in silence down my cheeks.

One day I found Queen Without a Name lying down clutching her heart with both hands, like someone trying to hold back a runaway horse. After a moment her breathing grew quieter and she fell into a heavy doze. Streaks of shadow chased here and there over the hamlet, and there were threatening clouds. High up in the sky one white star twinkled like a pearly shell on a beach of black sand, and suddenly, seeing the star, my grief grew lighter. Grandmother opened astonished eyes and, quite revived by her little nap, tried to sit up. She looked as if she were just about to make one of her little jokes, but suddenly she fell back and beckoned me nearer, nearer, nearer still, until my ear was right by her lips, to hear her say: 'Today and tomorrow will have the same sun and the same moon, but I shall be no more –' and at that instant she smiled. My heart smote me to see her smile, and I asked her, in a voice that in spite of me held a note of reproach:

'So, Grandmother, you're leaving me and you smile.'

She took hold of my face and put her lips right against my ear.

'It's not death I'm so pleased about', she said, 'but what will come after. The time when we'll never leave each other again, my little crystal glass. Can you imagine our life, with me following you everywhere, invisible, and people never suspecting they have to deal with two women, not just one? Can you imagine that?'

Word by word, Queen Without a Name's face was shrinking. I didn't know how to tell her to be quiet, and she went on whispering in my ear, pointing to the soft rain falling from the sky. 'It's not tears, just a light mist, for every human soul is bound to regret leaving life.' And an extreme gentleness came into her voice as she murmured on: 'Listen – people watch you, they always count on there being someone to show them how to live. If you are happy, everyone can be happy, and if you know how to suffer, the others will know too. Every day you must get up and say to your heart: "I've suffered enough, and now I have to live, for the light of the sun must not be frittered away and lost without any eye to enjoy it." And if you don't do that, you won't have the right to say "It's not my fault" when someone seeks out a cliff and throws himself in the sea.'

I could hear laughter outside, human voices. It was raining gently, and I couldn't believe Queen Without a Name was dying. She closed her eyes, was silent for a while, then whispered to me to put some water on the fire to warm, for she wished to attend to her own laying out. When she'd finished I helped her put on her pink nightdress, her best, kept ironed and folded ready for a long while, for she'd always wanted to make a rose-colored entrance into the other world. As I was putting her into the nightdress she signalled to me that time was getting on, and this amazed me: I'd never imagined dying could be like this, so quiet. When she was dressed and powdered and her hair done, she seemed really pleased with herself and the world. Her eyes went slowly around the room, and she said: 'Telumee, sorrow exists and, everyone has to take a bit of it on his shoulders. And now that I've seen you suffer I can close my two eyes in peace, for I leave you with your own panache, your own air. And now, as soon as there's no more mist on the mirror, go and fetch Ma Cia – she'll see to everything. Above all, don't go lamenting, for if you do that for me, what is a mother to do who survives her child? And don't go being frightened of a corpse . . . don't go being frightened . . .'

She still moved her lips, trying to speak, but her tongue was heavy and she said no more. Her head was resting in my lap; I stroked it. After a moment she began to drowse, breathing feebly, more and more feebly. Her hands, her breast, gradually ceased to move, and I realized that she was dead.

As I was sweeping the floors, twilight crept over the sky and a light rain, almost a mist, covered the earth. I'd always heard it said that a virtuous soul never leaves the world without regret; and that was why this dew was falling – dew, not rain; not tears, but only dew. A little while before I'd gone down with a torch in my hand to announce Queen Without a Name's death. While matters were taking their course, I busied myself putting the house in order, cleaning and scenting it so that everything would be as it should be when people started to come. From time to time I looked at

120

Grandmother, but without fear, just wondering if her soul had left her body yet, and whether she was with me now. Calm thoughts came, strangely peaceful: it was as if some force were entering into me; life seemed amazingly simple. For the first time I began to think about the life I had lived with Elie without trying to distinguish, without trying to keep the good and throw away the rest. There weren't two separate parts – they had taken place in one and the same person, and it was well, and I rejoiced at being a woman. I felt light and decided. I fixed some torches, lit the lamps, and welcomed in proper style the people who began to flock to pay homage to Queen Without a Name. They brought cups, glasses, pots, roasted coffee, and vegetables for the soup at daybreak; and everyone went over for a moment to pray and look at Grandmother's face. She looked as if she were sleeping; there was a faint smile on her lips. After making the sign of the cross and sprinkling holy water in the four corners of the room, everyone wondered:

'What can she have seen, the Queen, to make her look like that?'

After a brief exchange of observations, some of the women set about hanging embroidered sheets from Vieux-Fort on the walls. Those whose function it was to pray arranged themselves busily on either side of the bed and began to fill the room with litanies and the De Profundis. Now and then one would get up from her chair to go and fix a flower on the wall, and then the praying would begin again. Outside in the yard some men were putting up an awning and setting out tables, stools, and little individual benches, and a group of neighbours were chopping up the vegetables for the soup and gossiping desultorily:

'There must be something in the air today ... Jeremiah must be in raptures this evening, and Lord! after such a long separation.'

Under the awning one man sat nonchalantly on his drum, while others talked, guffawed, drank whenever they felt like it, and got up some gambling. There was dice, dominoes, and a rock that one group passed from one to another while chanting a rough, monotonous song:

> Accursed one, accursed one
> Even if your mother's accursed too
> Say a prayer for her.

121

And the rock went from hand to hand, faster and faster, each player banging it on the ground before passing it on to his neighbour. The rhythm accelerated, the noise of the rock grew louder, and the tune could barely be distinguished when a man got up and said:

The Queen is dead, gentlemen. Did she ever live?

We do not know

And if tomorrow it is my turn, shall I have lived either?

I do not know

Come, let's have a drink.

A sea breeze had arisen and bright clouds were invading the upper reaches of the night. I had sat down on a bench in the midst of all this commotion and was tapping a rock diligently against the wood on my own account, trying not to let anyone see how lost and heartbroken I felt without Grandmother's little lantern. Adriana appeared, and Ma Cia immediately after, without a torch, as befitted a habitué of the dark, and with a parcel wrapped in newspaper tucked carefully under her arm. She cast a look all around, screwed up her eyes in some kind of satisfaction, and said:

'It's as if the Queen were alive and watching over everything with her fine white Negress's eyes.'

Going through the rows of benches she greeted the entire company and went into her friend's room. She stroked her hair and gazed at her for a long while in astonishment. 'There you are, and yet where are you now? She was an enigma, that woman', she said smilingly.

It was now black as pitch, without moon or stars, and our house seemed alone in the world, surrounded by darkness. The flames of the torches flickered to and fro in the evening breeze, and people's faces became shifting and uncertain. The preparations were over and a kind of torpor weighed down on everyone's spirits. We were seated in a circle in deepest silence, balancing the weight of the dead and that of the living: the atmosphere was one of deep uncertainty. I was between Ma Cia and a woman whose eyes were covered with a blue film. It was Ismene. She was very slight, with a round dimpled face; her intensely black skin had faded with age, so that sometimes it seemed not to be coloured at all. She was a contemplative kind of woman, who examined people coolly and yet always shut her eyes when she spoke to you, as if she couldn't talk

122

and size up a human face both at the same time. She wasn't keen on speaking at all, so we were very surprised when she said in a hesitant, questioning voice: 'To see so much misery, be spat at so often, become helpless and die – is life on earth really right for man?'

Ma Cia lit her old pipe, lowered the lids over her fine eyes of faded velvet, and said tranquilly:

'I beat my breast before Queen Without a Name, and say: there are some whose life makes no one rejoice, and there are those whose death, even, comforts people. That's a fine stone in your garden, isn't it, Queen?' she ended, smiling at Grandmother.

'How good her death is', little Ismene went on, eyes shut, in her everlasting voice that was half tears half laughter, 'and how I wish I'd known her in the days of her youth. I would have told you about her . . . if I'd known her'.

A thrill ran through all present, and all eyes turned towards Ma Cia, who had her hand up to her eyes as if she were gazing dazzled into the past.

'It's true', she said. 'To know the Queen properly you need to have seen her at L'Abandonnée, in Jeremiah's time. Her body was a whole catalogue: two legs like two flutes, a neck more flexible than the stem of a milkweed. And what can I say about her skin? And then she was always blinking her eyes as if she was right in the sun, and that was why everyone in L'Abandonnée said: "Toussine? she will become a rainbow and leave her mark on the heavens."'

'That's right, that's right, Queen', said a man, turning toward Grandmother's bed.

Madame Brindosier was sitting near the door, in the background, her hands resting demurely on her ample stomach, while her great artless eyes roved from one to the other, from face to face, on the lookout for a weakness. Judging the time had come, she preened herself in her chair and said in a soft, insinuating voice:

'Unfortunately, though, rainbows come one after another and none lasts any longer than a falling star. If one knew one would never get out of the calabash again, would one ever go in? If you ask me, God's blame is on every living creature, and in the end, for Him, goodness and wickedness are all the same – He kills you.'

'What's all this about blame?' said Ma Cia, vexed. 'If God blames and kills, let Him. But He can't prevent a Negro showing Him the

123

weight he accords to the soul of another Negro. The truth is, Ismene, man belongs as much to heaven as to earth. No, man is not of the earth. And that is why he looks, why he searches for another country, and there are some who fly at night while others sleep.'

Ismene was aglow, and in her excitement she started to speak, staring at the whole assembly, in her curious hesitant voice, sure of nothing but its own insignificance:

'Ma Cia, have you ever seen another country when you were flying about at night?'

'Alas, little chimera, I can't tell you about anything like that, but though we are almost nothing on the earth, I *can* tell you one thing: however beautiful other sounds may be, only Negroes are musicians.'

Then we felt the soul of Queen Without a Name, and we sang until morning, and said what Queen was, and recalled all the events in her life, and everyone knew exactly the weight she had been accorded here in Fond-Zombi. And the next day, at her funeral, just after the last shovellful of earth, we all thought she was going to sprinkle us with her regrets, for there were clouds flying low over the graveyard. But it was only pretense, the last little dodge she played on us, and that day it was in a rose-coloured sky that the sparkling sun sank into the sea on the edge of the horizon.

11

Man is not a cloud in the wind that death scatters and destroys at a blow. And if we Negroes at the back of beyond honour our dead for nine days, it's so that the soul of the deceased should not be hurried in any way, so that it can detach itself gradually from its piece of earth, its chair, its favourite tree, and the faces of its friends, before going to contemplate the hidden side of the sun. And so we talked and sang and drowsed for nine days and nine nights, until Queen Without a Name's soul should cast off the weight of the earth and take flight. On the tenth day the people took away their handsome Vieux-Fort sheets, their cups and plates and benches. Grandmother's last party was over, all the voices were still, and I was alone in the vague light of dawn as it grew yellow on the heights and backfired on the tops of the trees. I felt naked, I found a voice, and it was that of Ma Cia. 'Telumee, my girl, know that I shan't die like Queen Without a Name, my eyes bewitched by the light of the sun. For in reality I am blind and see nothing of the splendours of the earth. And yet I tell you, he who loves you has eyes for you even when his sight is extinguished. Let us go up into my forest, woman – it will warm you and soothe the regrets of us who are left behind.'

Thus did I leave Fond-Zombi and follow Ma Cia into her forest, to live in the cabin where she lived with the spirit of her dead husband, Wa. She did a bit of gardening, massaged the sick who came to see her, took the spell off the Hunted Ones, turned away the evil eye. Close to her, I felt myself become a spirit. Every morning I woke up drenched in sweat, resolved to leave the forest and live in my own body and woman's breasts. After four weeks I went down back to Fond-Zombi. Going by the Chinese plum, I saw Elie's cabin deserted, the yard overgrown with weeds, abandoned. Old Abel made no mention to me of his son's departure, and suggested he should come with me to Pointe-à-Pitre to ask Monsieur Boissanville for a piece of land, as Queen Without a Name had suggested. He had to go into town himself to buy things, and, seeing my lack of enthusiasm, he agreed to go and see Monsieur Boissanville on my behalf. I went back to Queen Without a Name's cabin, flung open the doors and windows, and began to sweep the floor with a passion and energy that made me smile. Next day Amboise presented himself on my doorstep with a beautiful white caplao yam in his hand. I had been expecting him, and seeing him standing there so proud in the doorway, yet with a strange little gleam like that of a hunted dove in his eyes, I remembered what Queen Without a Name had said to me on her deathbed: 'He's loved you for a long time, Telumee, and just remember Amboise is a rock that can't be moved, and who'll wait for you all his life.' For me he had been like Elie's shadow at the time when they both sawed planks in the forest. And as he stood by the door, a great tall reddish-brown man with anxious eyes, deep wrinkles, and nostrils like two organ pipes, I smiled inside myself and thought that instead of inventing love these great lumps of men would have done better to invent life. Meanwhile Amboise took a step forward, put the yam gently in my arms, and said:

'Hallo, Telumee. How is life with you?'

'It isn't. I just watch it pass away.'

'A wounded woodcock doesn't stay at the side of the road', he said.

'Where does it go then?' I asked.

'Yes, indeed, where does it go?' he laughed.

Then he added gravely, in a way that suddenly touched me:

'I just wanted to say . . . even in hell the devil has his friends.'

He gave an awkward little laugh, turned on his heel, and vanished. I didn't see him again until a week later, the day my cabin was moved to La Folie.

The cart set out at dawn – four oxen drawing two long beams with wheels on which was perched Queen Without a Name's cabin, emptied of everything that could not stand the journey. A crack of the whip and the team moved off, Queen Without a Name's cabin started out and went through the village, followed by all her other worldly goods – her table, her rocker, her two round baskets full of plates and saucepans, all balanced on the heads of the neighbours who were accompanying me. After the Bridge of Beyond the procession turned into a muddy gully leading directly up toward

126

the mountain. By the end of the day, shouting, swearing, wedging the wheels at every halt, the men brought the cabin onto a little plateau of sharp-edged grasses with woods in front, woods behind, and a few animals' droppings scattered about nearby. Once the cabin was set up on four stones, everyone drank and joked and said how lucky I was, and after all this to-do, intended to hide their sadness, the Negroes of Fond-Zombi went off down the hillside, leaving me to solitude and night. Suddenly one shape turned back. I recognized Amboise, and was filled with emotion at his tall figure and the already furrowed face from which the eyes looked out without bitterness. A deep constraint swept over him, and he made a gesture as if to wipe away the wrinkles from his face and the greying hair that separated him from me. Then he smiled and said tranquilly, in a perfectly steady voice:

'Telumee, you have put on your robe of courage, and it would be ungracious of me not to smile at you. But what is going to become of you here, in this corner out of reach of the hand of God?'

'Amboise, I don't know what is going to become of me, the flame tree, the poisonous manchineel, but there is no middle way, and this hill will speak and tell me.'

'This hill will speak', said Amboise.

I watched him go, then went back unafraid to the unknown shadows of the hill, for that evening uncertainty was my ally.

The next day, after my first night as a free woman, I threw open my door and saw that the sun was the same colour as at Fond-Zombi, and I left it to roll through the sky and scorch the root of my luck or make it sparkle, as it should decide. The place in which I'd set down my cabin was particularly lonely, and when I looked east across the green undulations of the canefields, I saw a kind of impenetrable barrier of huge mahogany and balata trunks holding back the world and preventing it from reaching me. Two or three wooden cabins and less than a dozen mud huts were scattered about the neighbouring slopes, among clumps of wild acacias and groves of mountain coconuts with ceaselessly churning leaves.

La Folie hill was inhabited by wandering Negroes, the motley

127

rejects of the island's thirty-two communes, who lived there exempt from all rules and without memories, surprises, or fears. The nearest shop was nearly two miles away. Without one familiar face or smile, the place seemed to me unreal, haunted. The inhabitants called themselves the Brotherhood of the Displaced. The wind of misfortune had deposited them there on that barren soil, but they tried to live like everyone else, to thread their way as best they could between lightning and storm, in everlasting uncertainty. But higher up the mountain, right in the depths of the forest, there lived some souls who were really lost and who were called the Strayed. These people did not plant seeds, did not cut cane, and neither bought nor sold. Their only resources were a few crayfish, a bit of game, and wild fruit, which they exchanged at the shop for rum, tobacco, and matches. They disliked money, and if anyone slipped a coin into their hand they would look offended and drop it on the ground. Their faces were impassive, with eyes that were impregnable, powerful, immortal. And a strange force unfurled in me at the sight of them, a sweetness made my bones grow weak, and without knowing why I felt I was the same as them, rejected, irreducible.

The most mysterious one among them was a certain Tac-Tac, so called because of his voum-tac, the great bamboo flute slung forever over his shoulder. He was an old Negro the colour of scorched earth, with a flattish face from which two deep-set eyes opened on you in wary surprise, constantly astonished at seeing animals and men again. He lived farther away than the others, at the very top of the mountain, in a little shanty up in a tree, which he reached by means of a rope ladder. His little shanty, his bamboo flute, and his garden in a clearing, that was all – every two months he would come down to buy rum, and in between he wasn't to be visited. He didn't like it, didn't open his lips to anyone, hadn't time, he said. But every morning, when the sun had barely appeared in the tops of the trees, we heard the tooting of a flute: it was Tac-Tac taking off with his huge bamboo, eyes shut, veins standing out on his neck, it was Tac-Tac starting to speak, according to him, all the languages on earth. And he blew with his whole body, in fits and starts – long, short, short, long, short, long, long, long long, long – which travelled straight through the vault of the forest and into our bosoms, in shudders, in sobs, in love. And it lifted you straight up

128

off the earth, as you opened your eyes. He was up already, standing up in front of his long bamboo flute, and you couldn't help hearing him, for it kept coming back – voum-tac, voum-tac – and it got you just as you were opening your eyes, and so there it was, nothing to be done, Tac-Tac took off with his bamboo, pouring out all that had filled, him, all that he'd felt.

All through the week I turned my little plot over and over, pulling up weeds and burning them, burning the big trees down where they stood, planting immediately the land thus reclaimed from the forest, putting in roots and boucoussou peas and gumbos. And on Sunday I would set out towards the red disk of Ma Cia, who had been calling me since dawn from over on the other side of the valley.

Instead of taking the road down the hill, which would mean going up again through Fond-Zombi, I cut straight across to Ma Cia's part of the forest by a shortcut that ran among the uncultivated slopes and along by the canefields of the Galba refinery – by the factory with its vats of juice, its four culverts, its white chimney towering over a landscape of canefields belonging to the factory, of cabins belonging to the factory, and of Negroes inside the cabins, also belonging to the factory. I went as fast as I could because of the smell of cane trash and sweat, and once I'd forded the river I was in the blue shade of Ma Cia's part of the forest. She was never in the clearing when I got there, but there was always a big earthen pan waiting for me outside her cabin, in the sun, full of water dark with all kinds of magic leaves – paoca, calaba balsam, bride's rose, and power of Satan. I would jump straight into the bath and leave behind in it all the fatigues of the week, making sure to cup my hands together and ladle the contents nine times over the top of my head. When I'd gotten out I'd put on a pair of pants and sit in the sun, glancing around from time to time to make sure the undergrowth didn't suddenly sprout eyes. Then I dressed, and did my hair by a mirror fixed to the trunk of a mango tree. And suddenly I'd hear a little dry cough behind me, and without turning my head I'd say, 'There you are, Ma Cia – it's you, isn't it?' and she'd clear her throat, a deep hem-hem, and I was right, there she was.

Then in the utmost silence we'd shell coffee beans, dig up the day's vegetables, and give the hens some boiled bananas. Noon soon came, for I liked working beside her, in the light of her eyes. We would sit down under the mango tree for a meal that was always the same: rice and red beans that had been simmering since dawn, and a sempiternal pig's tail. As she ate in a dream and seemed to be elsewhere, I'd say:

'To see you, Ma Cia, anyone would think you were at your last gasp.'

And she, tranquilly:

'I'm not at my last gasp, I'm thinking.'

Then she'd take a glass of rum, toss it off, smack her lips with satisfaction, and give a little trill of laughter deep down in her throat:

'Speaking like that to an old woman like me – haven't you any respect for grey hairs?'

She'd shake her head, bend on me the dazzling yet painful beam of her aged glance, and we'd get up and go for a walk in the forest, where Ma Cia initiated me into the secrets of plants. She also taught me the human body, its centres, its weaknesses, how to rub it, how to get rid of faintness and tics and sprains. I learned how to set people and animals free, how to break spells and turn sorcery back on the sorcerers. But whenever she was at the point of telling me the secret of metamorphosis, something held me back, something prevented me from exchanging my woman's shape and two breasts for that of a beast or flying succubus, and so there the matter rested. At the end of the afternoon our conversations came to take on a certain tone, always the same, at once mysterious and disappointing. We were bathed in light, which came in waves through the wind-stirred leaves, and we'd look at each other amazed at certain words, certain thoughts we'd had together; and suddenly Ma Cia would lean forward and ask roughly, point-blank, 'Have they succeeded in breaking us, crushing us, cutting off our arms and legs forever? We have been goods for auction, and now we are left with fractured hearts. You know', she'd add, with a deprecating little laugh, 'what's always worried me is slavery – the time when barrels of rotten meat were worth more than us. However much I puzzle over it, I cannot understand'.

And she'd shake her head hotly, and her eyes flashed, and little spurts of saliva would come into the corners of her mouth, as with children when they start to gabble before bursting into tears. A sadness veiled the light of her eyes then, and she uttered all kinds of mysterious phrases in the angry, plaintive, childlike voice she sometimes had since the death of Queen Without a Name. One evening just as I was about to leave she signalled to me to wait. 'Telumee', she said, 'don't panic, don't faint with shock, if instead of finding me a Christian you find me in the shape of a dog'.

'Why would you do that, Ma Cia? Have you seen everything, then, as a woman?'

'Over and over. But that wouldn't make me change out of human form. It's just that I'm tired, you see – tired of my two feet and my two hands. So I'd rather go about like a dog and have done with it.'

I kissed her goodbye with a heavy heart. Since she'd started to wear those strange childish expressions, solitude hadn't agreed with Ma Cia.

The next day, as I was at home digging a furrow in the garden, lo and behold a big black dog appeared, with a tail surprisingly small in proportion. I wasn't thinking about dogs or men in the shape of dogs, and I calmly went on scratching away at my plot. When the furrow was finished I put down my hoe, and found the dog straight in front of me, still looking at me with the same curiosity. I paused to examine him in my turn, and was struck by his eyes – brown, with a peculiar sheen, they gazed straight at me without a flicker, just like Ma Cia's eyes. A cold sweat began to trickle down my neck, and I asked softly: 'O dog, are you just passing by, or was it me you wanted?' Since the dog didn't move, I shouted, 'Off with you! Go on!', broke a branch from a nearby medlar tree, and gave him a whack. He let out a yelp and disappeared among the grasses.

I went back into the little cabin and lay down on Queen Without a Name's bed, sweating, trembling, weeping. When Sunday came some force drove me to the enchanted forest, and I found the house empty, the doors and windows open to the wind, and the black dog lying at the foot of the mango tree that bore my little mirror. Ma Cia was waiting for me, her forepaws crossed one over the other,

131

and as I came near I recognized her curious mauve, fluted nails. She looked at me in her usual manner, not lowering for an instant her light transparent eyes, with their deep gleams of irony. I sat on the grass and stroked my old friend, weeping. 'What do you want of me, Ma Cia? Tell me! What do you want? And why have you turned yourself into a dog – they can't speak! Why have you put an end to our little talks? See, see how you frighten me, lying there as if you weren't a human, born of a human womb.'

As I spoke my grief grew easier and went away, until at last I only felt a little sad. It was as if I wasn't on earth any longer, in the cool of our mango tree, but in some solemn place where time had ceased and death was unknown. Ma Cia began to run around me licking my feet and hands with relish. Already I was beginning to get used to her new shape, and I said, smiling: 'Since you're like that now, Ma Cia, stay that way, and I'll come back next Sunday and shan't forget to bring you some sausage.'

I suddenly felt like going for one of our usual walks, and Ma Cia came with me, frisking about and yelping happily. A bit later, on the stroke of eleven, I went back to her cabin and put on the rice and beans to simmer, and we ate it as we had always done, in the cool shade of the mango tree. It was the same on the Sundays that followed. I arrived early with a little bit of manioc sausage, her favourite dish, and gave it to her on a clean plate, saying always: 'You see, Ma Cia, I haven't forgotten you – but where are my red beans and my rice?' And she would frisk about and lick my hands at great length, and go with me everywhere I went, and in her beautiful brown eyes there was a kind of deep, dumb appeal that put my heart to rout. I talked to her, recounted the events of the week, told her all I hadn't liked to tell her before, when I felt I was just a little girl come into the world by mistake. Then one Sunday when I went up to see her as usual, with a bit of sausage, I didn't find her in her customary place under the mango tree. I went into the house; I searched the undergrowth all around it; I went into the forest and called her until late in the night. But she had gone, and I never saw her again. Gradually the little creatures took over her cabin, and it collapsed one day, eaten up by wood lice, termites, and suchlike.

12

Ever since I'd come to La Folie I'd been supported by the presence of Queen Without a Name, who wielded half my hoe, held half my machete, and bore half my troubles, so that thanks to her I really was a Negress that was a drum with two hearts. At least that was what I thought, until Ma Cia changed into a dog and disappeared. Then I realized that the protection of the dead can't replace the voice of the living. The swamp was under my feet, it was the moment to be light, agile, winged, if I didn't want life to be a failure just because of one woman.

All the things I'd planted had come up, they'd be ripe for the next harvest, and I could already see myself going down with a round basket on my head to the market at La Ramée. Meanwhile I missed the root vegetables from Ma Cia's garden, the oil and salt and kerosene and boxes of matches she used to get in exchange for her services as a witch, and which she used to share with me every Sunday. If I didn't want to die of hunger before the harvest I'd have to go and work in the canefields belonging to the factory. But I feared the cane worse than the devil, so I lived on wild fruit, which made me go yellow and gave me strange fancies, hallucinations. One fine morning when I opened the door of my cabin, I saw a calabash of rice at my feet. In the days that followed it was malangas, a little jar of oil, and even two or three pieces of preserved tamarind. One night, posted behind my cabin, I saw a shape cross the road furtively, like a thief. A few seconds later it reappeared against a shaft of moonlight, and I recognized the little narrow-brimmed straw hat belonging to Olympia.

She lived just below me, on the other side of the road, and when she didn't stay indoors I caught vague glimpses of her through her variegated hedge of kawala bushes. That day, when she came back from the canefields, a sweetness was in all my limbs and, dropping my hoe, I went down the slope towards her cabin. She was sitting on a little bench under her arbour, her face severe and rather stiff, as if to warn me from the outset that she wasn't of the same age or order as I, and I wasn't to think myself by any means on the same shelf. She sat there motionless, looking me over, appearing to study my every step as I walked toward her. But this tactic, disconcerting as it was, had been employed by more than one of the women in Fond-Zombi, and refusing to be intimidated I introduced myself, telling her in due form who I was, and the name of the woman who'd brought me up, ending up by saying I'd come to ask her to tell me about the canefields, for I was to start work there the next day.

Olympia looked at me intently.

'I know everything, everything', she said in a strange voice. Then, thinking better of it almost at once, 'No, I don't know everything.'

She seemed to have forgotten me, gazing first at the hill, then at the mountain, and finally at the sea, which at the end of the afternoon was visible as a thin silver strip. Suddenly she got up, went into her cabin, and after a moment came out again carrying another little stool. Inviting me to sit down, she gravely told me she was called Olympia, and offered to let me come and fetch embers first thing in the morning to light my fire. She gave them to everyone, for her it was a kind of duty, yes, a duty, she insisted. And as I thanked her and said that from now on I would be like the others and come and fetch embers from her too, the ice gradually began to melt between us. Bending on me eyes wide with curiosity, she began by saying that this was the first time I'd been away from my usual surroundings – wasn't it? – whereas she'd left many places behind before ending up on this hill, in the middle of the Brotherhood of the Displaced. Oh, but it wasn't the quietness that had attracted her, nor the wildness of the people, for both were found side by side here as everywhere else. What had pleased her about La Folie was the quality of the spectacle it presented: 'All colour, all flame, all ready to confront the eyes of Christ', she concluded admiringly, laughing softly at the thought of the fine sight the Negroes of the hill offered Him. And leaning towards me she spoke to me of this one and that, of Tasia, who never minced her words, of Vitaline and Leonora, who lived in the same house and loved the same man, of all who came into her head, showing them off to me with the eagerness, delicacy, and detail of an embroideress unfolding her finest work. Lastly, beaming, she pointed to the curtain of balatas and mahogany trees covering the head of the mountain. 'But all that's nothing', she whispered. 'It's up there that the most lost of our displaced ones lives, the man with the voum-tac. He can justly say he knows all the languages in the world, languages as they ought to be spoken. At any rate, when he takes his bamboo flute it's not a lying dog's words he tosses into the air, it's actual truths that rise up to heaven, I can tell you that.' And still gazing at the curtain of trees beyond the canefields, she murmured as if to herself: 'And you, little girl – what do you think of words?'

Olympia's eyes went from the sky to my face, from her little multicolored hedge to my face, and finally she said as if by way of conclusion that I was right not to accord importance to speech. She seemed pleased with me, and even said I was very young to be an equal member of the brotherhood. I looked at her in surprise, waiting for a sign, for some explanation of these mysterious words, but none came. Night was approaching and I could scarcely see her face. She had become just an ordinary shape sitting rather stiffly on a bench; perhaps it was the half light that gave me the courage to ask her again about the canefields.

Then Olympia stood up, filled a glass of rum to the brim, and said apologetically: 'Oh, the canefields.' Then she drank her rum, lit a pipe, and said no more.

The next day while it was still dark, I went down to Olympia's and she gave me some embers to start my fire, as she was to do for many years, until I left La Folie. Then, when we'd each cooked something to put in our lunch boxes, we set out in silence along the road that led down to the valley and the canefields belonging to the sugar factory. We walked along in the fading light of the stars, both followed and preceded by workers going in the same direction – a

135

procession of dim and haggard ghosts, with here and there the flash of a machete, or a mouth laughing in the darkness, or the sparkle of a ring in the ear of the woman just in front of us, who moved along like a somnambulist, carrying her sleeping baby in a basket on her head. Others had whimpering children trotting along with them, sometimes two or three clutching the same skirt and being dragged through the dawn like fish, eyes shut, lips puffy with sleep. Olympia walked along calmly, her machete carried flat over her shoulder like a gun, a bottle of rum on her head and her legs completely covered with rags tied on with creepers. I walked beside but a little behind her, as if to show her superiority. And seeing the children of the canefields, I wondered where my own were all this time? In my belly, hanging on to my guts, that's where they were, and that's where they'd stay until further orders, I thought to myself.

Down in the valley the canefields undulated in the breeze, and the cutters arranged themselves in a line to attack the wave with one movement of a hundred machetes. They were followed by the binders, who separated the spikes, the straw to be used for fodder, and the sections full of sap, tying up the latter quickly and piling them up behind their appointed cutter. Already, by the edge of the field, a little sugar train was heading fully laden towards the tall chimneys of the factory, glowing red in the distance. A foreman told me what my job was, and I found myself plunged at a blow into the heart of malediction. The machetes skimmed low, the stems fell, and the prickles flew everywhere, like splinters of glass, into my back, my nose, my legs. On Olympia's advice I had put tight bandages on my hands, but the infernal prickles stuck into the cloth, my constricted fingers wouldn't obey me, and soon I tore off the bandages and entered outright into the fire of the canes. Olympia laid about her with her machete like a man, and I collected up behind her, running bent over, tying up bent over, sorting out and heaping up as fast as I could so as not to be left behind the other women performing their task around me without a murmur, anxious to complete the twenty piles that made up one day's work – twenty piles of twenty-five bundles, representing ten thousand sweeps of the machete, and representing also several bits of zinc with the factory initials on, dried cod, oil, salt, 'France' flour and rum from the factory, molasses from the factory, unrefined sugar from the factory at the factory-imposed price, abracadabra, two sous where there was only one before. Gradually I entered into the malediction, made myself accursed, and a few days later I was no longer tying up the canes but going in among them with my old machete, among the flying prickles and the swarms of bees, and the hornets that rose with the sun, attracted by the heavy, intoxicating fumes of fresh cane sap. I already worked at the same pace as Olympia, doing the same turn as the men, and I soon realized that Mama Victory's wrists, the ones she'd put at the ends of my arms, were of steel. We started work at four in the morning, but it was not till nine that the sun was high enough to fall on us in earnest, piercing through straw hats, dresses, and human skins. There amid the fire of the sky and the prickles, I sweated out all the moisture my mother had ever put in my body. And I understood at last what a Negro is: wind and sail at the same time, at once drummer and dancer, a first-class sham, trying to collect by the basketful the sweetness that falls scattered from above, and inventing sweetness when it doesn't fall on him, and at least he has that if nothing else. And, seeing that, I began to take little nips of rum, then big glasses of it to help the sweat flow out of my pores. And I folded up a leaf of tobacco and filled my pipe, and started to smoke as if I'd been born with it in my mouth. And I thought, it's here, in the midst of the cane prickles, that a Negro ought to be. But in the evening, when I got back to La Folie in my sacking apron, my face and hands all torn, I'd feel a faint, smiling sadness come over me, and then I thought that groveling about like that in the canefields I'd turn into a beast and even the mother of men wouldn't know me. I'd push open my door, eat a bit of something hot, light a stub of candle for the Queen and say the Lord's Prayer, then I was on my pallet with my eyes closed to it all. Sometimes I didn't even undress, just fell like a stone. And the sun rose, and I set out again with the sweat of the day before, the prickles of the day before, and I got to the fields belonging to the factory, and I wielded my machete, and I lashed into my affliction like everyone else, and someone would start to sing, and the affliction of us all would flow into the song. And that was life in the canefields. And from time to time I'd stop and try to put things in order in my mind, and I'd say to myself, already smiling and soothed, 'There's a God for everything – a God

137

for the ox and a God for the carter.' And then I'd tell my body again, peacefully, 'This is where a Negro ought to be.'

Now, on Sunday mornings, I went down to the town with the rest of La Folie, and laughed and paraded about till evening. I was in affliction, I bore my yoke, I pulled and I whinnied – was affliction to make me miserable too? So it was laughter in the square outside La Ramée church, and cheering little visits to the nearby bars, while the people from Fond-Zombi that I ran into by chance looked at me in amazement – sweating, tousled, shocking, amidst my Brotherhood of the Displaced, Olympia, Vitaline, Leonora, and the rest, whom I stuck to like glue. When the bells sounded the end of mass Olympia would lead us to the church to scare the virtuous. She would wave her arms about jeering at all respectability and shouting: 'Slavery is finished – love me and you can't buy me, hate me and you can't sell me.' And scandalized remarks would rain down, and everyone would put in their word about Olympia, who could undo a mass as a tidal wave the ocean. Sometimes a neighbour or acquaintance from Fond-Zombi began to approach me, then at the last moment turned away with an expression of pain. Two or three times, too, I caught Amboise looking at me, with an indefinable expression of amusement, fear, and perhaps remembrance of what I used to be. He was barefoot, like me, and wore a soiled shirt and pants; there was nothing to distinguish him from the old reddish-brown Negro I'd known in my youth. But now, to me, he looked like a prince: his walk, the set of his head, his two organ-pipe nostrils – and his sombre, distant gaze was exactly that of a prince. And when his eyes happened to rest on me, by chance, I turned away embarrassed, ashamed to think that such a fine man had loved me. One Sunday as I was sitting in a bar in the town, in the midst of the Brotherhood of the Displaced, I heard Amboise's voice saying softly behind me:

'Telumee, Telumee, how is life with you?'

I felt a pang, and answered carelessly over my shoulder, without turning around, so that he shouldn't see my new face:

'Still nothing, Amboise, I just watch it, see it passing away, that's all.'

'Listen', he whispered, 'I've come for a serious talk. Are you still on your own . . . as you were before?'

'On my own, Amboise, in solitude itself.'

After a moment's silence the well-known voice went on softly behind me:

'Remember what I said – even in hell the devil has his friends. Of course that's just a manner of speaking, because if one of us two is a devil it's me.'

'Many thanks, Amboise, many thanks for the word you've just spoken. But the trouble is, today I'm a woman without hope, and I don't know when it will come back.'

I'd spoken very quietly, lest the drinkers around us should notice. I waited for some while, and hearing no answer turned around at last, to see an empty chair, a tobacco pouch left on the table, and by it an untouched glass of rum. I wondered what I had said to drive Amboise away, and the depth of my degradation oppressed me all that afternoon, as I knocked back one rum after another and acted in the usual outrageous fashion, laughing and strutting about worse than ever. Back at La Folie I said I wasn't feeling well and left the drunken company, went back to my cabin, and slowly lowered the stick that barred my door. Then, lying on my pallet, I slipped out of the world to join Grandmother, sad at the thought of the line of noble Negresses that had died out with her. My ship had run into the sand, and where was the wind to come from to set it afloat again?

The next day, as I quietly occupied my place in the world in the midst of the prickles, I heard Amboise's voice rise into the air, and bitterness smote me and my body weighed me down. Then the bitterness went, and all that was left was the surprise of hearing that voice rise among the canes, for Amboise had always said his sweat would never feed the white man's soil. I wanted to see him but didn't like to turn toward his voice. Up above the mountain the sun was white-hot, and the cutting had begun long before. The time had come to fight against sweat, weariness, and the soul's rout, and suddenly Amboise started to sing a lively caladja that floated over the herd:

> In those days there lived a woman
> A woman who had a house

Behind her house was a Blue Pool
A Blue Whirlpool
Many, many are the suitors
But they must bathe in the Pool
Bathe for the woman
Who will win her?

And from all sides the chorus, cutters and binders, sang the refrain:

The young men who bathed there
Are in the estuary, drowned.

I hadn't opened my mouth, for the bitterness had just returned, and I was afraid I might unwittingly spread it, let it overflow onto the shoulders bent among the canes. But suddenly, I don't know how, my voice escaped me and soared high above the others, piercing, lively, and gay, as in the old days, and Amboise turned toward me in astonishment, and my face was bathed in tears. And he at once turned away again, and the singing went on until noon. Then came the midday break, and those who lived in the cabins belonging to the factory went home, and there remained those who had brought lunch boxes. I chose the shade of a bombax tree at the edge of the field, and Amboise followed me in silence. Once under the tree I tucked my dress up between my thighs and sat on a flat rock with my legs one on either side. I rested my elbow on my knee and balanced the box in the palm of one hand; then, with the other, I began to delve into my malanga purée with the tips of my fingers, as a woman should. I pretended not to know Amboise was there, and every now and then gave a little shake of the head as if to drive away something, some persistent thought I couldn't place. And in this way I tried to run away from myself, and my eyes roved the sky and scrutinized the road. And Amboise saw my anguish, and was afraid it would be like that until I died. After a long silence he spoke:

'Telumee Lougandor, the Negroes sweat so much it makes the white men's wives tired just to see it.'

It suddenly struck me he hoped to make me laugh, though he spoke in a voice that was grave and sad. This amused and distressed me at the same time, just as in the fields, before, his voice had amused and distressed me, this tall red Negro who obviously didn't know his place. And surprised, amused, distressed, I wondered if it was myself he wanted to make laugh, Telumee, Telumee of La Folie, or the young woman without hope. And I wouldn't let myself laugh, for I couldn't find a satisfactory answer. And the break ended, and we went back, thoughtful, into the fire of the canes.

On the days that followed we sat in the shade of the same bombax tree, I on the flat rock and the man a little way away, propped against the smooth trunk. We ate always in the same silence. And during those bright days none treated me with disrespect, as sometimes happens in the canefields, for Amboise's machete was my umbrella. And then, one morning, he unobtrusively put a bundle of his canes in my heap, and I couldn't keep back my tears. And my singing soared so high that day that the overseers on horseback, some way away, made sure they had their guns in the holsters of their saddles. But I was far away from all that, far away from the sun, far away from the prickles and the foremen, and all I wondered was whether Amboise had put the bundle in Telumee's pile, or in that of a woman in distress, or, worse still in my eyes, if it was a kind of tribute to the memory of Queen Without a Name. And that was why, later, sitting under the bombax, I broke the silence with these words:

'Amboise, I know you – you have a nature stronger than that of many men, but you are as cowardly as all men are, too.'

Amboise seemed not to have heard. He said nothing, turned a thought over in his mind, and stared at his hands as if to take them as witness to what he was about to say.

'Telumee', he said abruptly, uneasily, 'you are more verdant and more shining than a siguina leaf in the rain, and I want to be with you. What do you say? Answer'.

I looked at him for a while, thinking if men have invented love they'll end up one day inventing life. And so here I was about to take my place, to help this man hale life from the depths and set it up on earth. But I replied extremely coldly, in a slow, reserved voice:

'Amboise, I am just a bit of wood already battered by the wind. I've seen the dried-up coconuts stay on the tree while all the green ones fell. Life is a quarter of mutton hanging from a branch – everyone thinks they'll get a piece of meat or liver, but most of them get only bones.'

And I added, with great difficulty, afraid of looking foolish and losing what remained of my dignity:

'And it's in the knowledge of all that, Amboise, that I accept your proposal.'

13

We'd agreed Amboise should come to me in three days, on which date the sky was born again and with it the moon, always favourable to new unions. Amboise wanted me to go to him, but I preferred to wait for him in my own place under my own roof. I first prepared the cabin, tidying up outside and clearing the path, and washing and scrubbing the inside as if it were a person I was getting ready, but a person who'd seen service – a woman, not a girl. At the same time I trained my heart to turn to stone, for I didn't think it was hard enough to take a man into my home. I looked forward to living, but in a sweet sadness that perhaps belonged to the end, when the taste for living is gone. Sometimes I saw myself in a cockpit in the middle of a fight, bloody, now one bird and now the other, the spurs, the pecks, now one and now the other, and these visions always came out of the blue, at the most unexpected moments, when I suddenly started to laugh and found pleasure in the sound of my laughter, or when I bent over a verbena that grew by my cabin and suddenly found pleasure in having a sense of smell.

The last hours of the third day went by very slowly. I'd bathed myself, steeped myself in one of Ma Cia's concoctions until the last prickle had gone from out of my skin and from under my nails. Then I'd washed my hair and done my braids with cacao lotion, put on my Sunday dress, and set some congo soup on the fire – the plop of the bubbles filled my ears as I sat on a stone in the doorway, watching the slim crescent moon that had appeared above the mountain. Silence hung over all the hill. In front of their cabins the people, warned by the spirit of the place, looked silently towards the valley, awaiting, they too, my hour. Suddenly the faint sound of a drum was heard, and the gleam of torches appeared on the slopes, forming a kind of luminous trail that wound along the road until, now, it reached the hill of La Folie. The neighbours, men and women, went to meet the visitors, while I sat still on my stone, listening to the beat of my heart, soft, smooth, singing. The crowd was in front of the cabin, with Amboise in front, lightly beating a chest drum. Behind him came a country fiddle, a rumbling sillac, and some chachas wielded by Adriana, Ismene, Filao, and several others from Fond-Zombi. They all came up and gave me a brief greeting, just a nod, as if they'd only said goodbye to me yesterday, and my life had flowed along in the same clear water, without surprises and without trouble, since the first day they'd seen me, as a child, in the house of Queen Without a Name. Amboise came up to me last, and I couldn't look at him. I sat there on my stone, suddenly exhausted and devoid of strength. He bent forward, took my swollen hands, and stroking them gently, murmured, jesting:

'No doubt about it, woman is a cool stream that kills.'

Then he added slowly, with just that touch of mockery in the voice that lets you say things without seeming to:

'Ah, a woman like this is as high as a mountain, and if you feel you can't rise to it, bite your tongue and hold your peace.'

Everyone started to laugh, glasses and bottles passed from hand to hand, and the crack entertainers gazed around, weighing up the audience so as to choose the right jokes. Everything was ready, the celebrations could begin. Amboise sat astride a drum, threw back his head, and slowly raised his right arm, as if all he'd ever seen or heard, everything he knew from today and yesterday was at the tips of his outstretched fingers. At that moment the rest of us disappeared from his sight, and for him it was an instant of perfect solitude. Then his hand struck strongly, and his throat let forth the traditional call to the spirits, to the living, the dead and the absent, bidding them come down among us and enter the circle hollowed out by the voice of the drum:

> I tell you we are coming
> We are coming, the Rhoses
> I tell you we are coming.

Olympia entered the circle first, lifting up her dress generously on either side as if to indicate that she opened her womb and her bosom before the company. All round and full, she made one think of a breadfruit covered in curls, and when she started to dance she was

144

a breadfruit that's knocked off the tree with a pole and rolls right down the hill, along paths and tracks, falling and rising with such energy she made us forget the ground beneath her feet was really flat. Her skin glowed, a light came to her full smooth cheeks, and her eyes looked up to heaven gazing at what they had always been waiting for. Amboise followed her closely, and when she seemed about to come to earth again, triggered off his drum so that it drew her out of herself once more, freed her of her arms and legs and body, of her head and her voice, and of all the men who'd trampled and torn and slashed her charity. She whirled and bent and straightened up again, snatching away our anguish with a gesture, lifting our lives to the skies and giving them back all clear and cleansed of impurity. And then the impulse began to die away, she stopped, panting, in the middle of the circle, and another dancer at once came and led her back to her seat with a friendly gesture, then took her place and began to talk about herself and her dreams, the life she would have liked, and the life she'd had.

Amboise uttered one summons after another throughout the night, and people came and went in and out of the circle, while I sat on my stone, not wanting to resist the drum and not wanting to yield to it. Early in the morning, Olympia pushed me silently into the middle of the circle. Everyone stopped talking. I stood motionless in front of the drum. Amboise's fingers tapped the goatskin lightly, as if looking for a sign, for the rhythm of my pulse. Seizing my skirt in either hand, I started to whirl like a top out of control, back hunched, elbows raised above my shoulders, trying in vain to parry invisible blows. Suddenly I felt the waters of the drum flow over my heart and give it life again, at first in little damp notes, then in great falls that sprinkled and baptized me as I whirled in the middle of the circle. And the river flowed over me and I bounded and surged, and I was Adriana, down and up, and I was Ismene of the great pensive eyes, I was Olympia and the rest, Ma Cia in the shape of a dog, Filao, Tac-Tac taking off with his bamboo, and Letitia with her little narrow face, and the man I had once loved and crowned, I was the drum and Amboise's helping hands, I his little hunted watchful dove's eyes. And now my hands were opening on all sides, taking lives and refashioning them as I pleased, giving the world and being nothing, a mere wisp of smoke hanging in the night air, the drumbeats issuing from beneath

145

Amboise's hands, and yet existing with all my strength, from the roots of my hair right down to my little toes.

It was my first and last dance that night, and with it the strange celebration ended. As we stood in the door and watched the people going, one of them gave a little shout and pointed to a patch of pink sky that had just appeared over the highest peak of the mountain, above the volcano. The rosy light soon spread over half the sky, and seeing it, the one who had shouted murmured as if in a dream: 'And now may ugly souls be absent.'

A few laughs, a few stifled sighs, and on a last general goodnight we shut the doors of our cabin behind us.

In that fine season of my life, the root of my luck came up, and the days were like nights, the nights like days. All we planted flourished, came forth well out of that scarcely cleared patch of hillside, full of rocks and stumps that sprouted afresh every year, sending up bright green shoots above the sun-baked mass. After each harvest Monsieur Boissanville's representative would seize half our produce, and we lived on the rest, which provided us with oil, kerosene, and a new dress or pants when necessary. I can see nothing in those years but contentment, good words, and kindness. When Amboise spoke of lemons I spoke of lemons in reply, and if I said use the knife he would use the axe as well. We enjoyed pricking out the seedlings, raising the furrows, setting the seeds in the womb of the earth. Our plot sloped gently down to the bottom of the valley, to a little stream grandly known as the torrent. At the bottom of the slope the earth was black and rich, just right for bringing forth long yams, crisp and juicy. The nearby torrent gave us its water and the shade of its trees. Amboise dug and broke up the clods of earth, and I crumbled them into a fine rain between my fingers. Every year this out-of-the-way place appealed to and attracted us more. As our sweat seeped into the soil, it became more and more ours, one with the odor of our bodies, of our smoke and of our food, of the eternal smoke, sharp and stinging, from the bonfires of green acomats. A square of paccala yams sprang up along the bank, and all around, hundreds of bindweeds intertwined their soft yet thorny creepers, like a writhing soul producing its

146

own fetters. The yams were surrounded by a double row of gumbos, and on another patch, just nearby, malangas, sweet corn, a few standard bananas and plantains grew in a dense tangle. The garden improved every year, and we spent most of our time there. A little arbour of coconut fronds sheltered us when it was hot, and the words we spoke seemed to perch on the leaves of the trees nearby, making them stir cautiously in the wind. There under the shelter we used to speak of all things past and present, of all our eyes had seen, of all the people we'd known, loved, and hated, in this way multiplying our own little lives and making each other exist several times. As the years went by we knew everything about each other, our deeds and thoughts, the voids within us. We often spoke of the Negro's decline, of what had happened in ancient times and still went on now, without our knowing why or how. Amboise was then in his fifties, with red-streaked white hair, and beneath the apparent calm of his expression one sensed the effort of holding back an inner flood, a stormy torrent that he restrained with all his strength. Passionate and anxious, I asked if it mattered much to him that we were Negroes in the dirt. And turning to me he said in a voice that tried to be peaceful, reassuring, empty of all anguish: 'Telumee, dear countrywoman, he who has never left the level path to fall in the gutter will never know how much he is to be venerated.'

The noon break was nearly over. Then we'd leave the shelter and go back to work under a sun that moved as we did, following us, stooping when we did, then going on, getting lower, getting lower and lower until it levelled glowing brands against us. Sweat would trickle off our bellies, but we wouldn't give in, and then in the end the sun would grow weary and weak.

But at the beginning of the afternoon nothing stirred, the birds were silent, drowsing in the motionless, scentless trees. Here and there on the ground, red scabs of earth would crack open and out would come the indefatigable ants. Then we'd sit near the shelter, in its shade, and there would follow one of my favourite hours. I bent over the hearth of stones and took the hot vegetables out of the pot and cut long twists of cucumber over them from a cucumber that went limp in the steam. Then I picked some half-ripe pimentos and arranged them on the edge of each plate, and, sitting on the ground, our knees relaxed and our toes exposed to the cool air, we would begin our meal. Amboise would take a slice of vegetable on the prongs of his fork, dip it all around in the hot sauce, then look at it for a moment and put it in his mouth, chewing it much longer than necessary, as if he couldn't bring himself to cease from tasting it, as if each mouthful had its own flavour that he must follow through to the end. So it became a great and mysterious celebration, a silent argument for the continuation of life, life in all its forms, and especially those no one can buy, such as a satisfied belly visited by all the fruits of the earth.

At the end of the afternoon, when the animals had been brought in, Amboise would strip off his thick, rough, ragged clothes, the colour of our soil, fold them up, and put them on the dome-shaped top of a young orange tree. Then, naked in the light of the setting sun, he waited for me. And that was another hour I loved, for his muscles, at rest, hoped for me, and I came and poured over him the citronella-scented water I always remembered to put to warm in the sun in the morning. The water flowed over his body with a murmur, its scent saturating the air as if it were sap, while Amboise splashed about making long spurts of water that soaked and drenched and carried me away. Every day I put on my canefield dress, my second skin, two flour bags softened by frequent washing and steeped in my sweat. It was a shapeless, lifeless object, held in around the waist by one of the Queen's scarves, the one with pale yellow checks the colour of a setting sun. I folded it across and tied it so that it would support my back as I bent and straightened up, straightened up and bent, all day, sowing and hoeing. I wasn't any good at doing my hair in the current fashion, swept up or back, and every morning my head would be covered with braids that I tried to sort out as prettily as possible and arrange in a crown on top. Got up like this as I sat in the shade of the cabin, I was nervous when Amboise looked at me, afraid that in his look there might be a touch of regret or disappointment. But he could read me like a book, and he'd throw back his head to get the land breeze that always rose at evening, and then, bending on me his clever, passionate, innocent glance, he would say how pretty I looked in that dress that fitted my shape, without fashion or paint. 'For, he would add, smiling, "it's corpses and those who have something to hide that are rouged and dolled up."'

148

He was born in Pointe-à-Pitre, in a little cabin that sheltered three generations of Negroes, including an old woman who'd been alive in the days of slavery and showed one breast marked with her master's brand. In his youth he had worked in the Carenage factory, unloading trucks of sugarcane from Grand-Terre, and one day during a strike, without quite knowing why he did it, he flew at the throat of a mounted gendarme who was galloping through the crowd. He didn't care to talk about the time he spent in prison. Apparently, at the beginning, the beatings only made him kick, but then he became more tractable, having come to see his position as a Negro in another light. The man who shared his cell explained the world to him, saying gravely: 'My friend, a white man is white and pink, God is white and pink, and where there's a white man, that's where the light is.' Amboise had already heard from the lips of his grandmother that a Negro is a well of sins, a creature of the devil. But in prison, his head splitting from beatings, Sunday sermons, and the words of the man who shared his cell, he came to be horrified at the 'blackness' of his soul, and wondered what he could do to wash it clean, so that one day God might look at it without aversion. And that was how, he told me with amusement, he got the idea of going to France, where he lived for seven years.

He didn't like talking about France either, lest certain words, certain descriptions, should suck up people's souls and poison them. In those days Negroes were rare in Paris, and used to congregate in the two or three hotels that made no objections. The people in his hotel were chiefly musicians, waiters, and dancers; there was even one who earned his living actually 'being' a Negro in a cage, yelling and throwing himself about like a lunatic, which according to Amboise was just what the whites liked to see. As for himself, having no special skill he fitted little bits of iron in various kinds of hole from morning till night. At first he admired the strength of character of the white men, who all had an air of solitude and self-sufficiency, like gods. The most difficult thing about the first few months was that he felt under no obligation whatever to go on living: he might disappear at any moment without anyone noticing, because nothing depended on him, he corresponded to

149

nothing either for good or ill. But at the end of two or three years he felt as if he were living in a nightmare, one of those nightmares he used to have as a child after certain bedtime stories. As soon as he left the hotel he felt as if he were going through places peopled with evil spirits, strangers to his flesh and blood who watched him go by with complete indifference, as if for them he didn't exist. He spent all his time now warding off invisible blows, which apparently these people strike at you without even thinking. However much he straightened his hair, parted it on one side, bought a suit and a hat, he still went through an invisible avalanche of blows in the street, at work, in restaurants. People didn't notice his efforts, didn't see he had to change everything, for in a Negro what part is good? That's what Amboise asked himself during his seven years' stay in France. He could never say what took place inside him, and how by the end of the seven years he had come to regard white men as mouths that cram themselves with misfortune, burst bladders that set themselves up as lanterns to light the world. When he got back to Guadeloupe all he wanted to do was go barefoot in the sun, and speak the words of long ago in the streets of Pointe-à-Pitre. 'How are you doing, brother? Don't let go, hold tight, for it's a tough fight, man, really tough.' That was his dream, that and to plunge into the deep water of the women here, to stroke our wild short hair that never grows any longer. He'd washed all white ideas out of his head, but he bore no grudge. Those people were on one shore and he on the other, they didn't see life from the same side, that's all, brother.

After a few weeks he had taken up with his former life again, his old habits, his little job at the Carenage. And he maintained total silence about France and the whites, even avoided looking at those he passed in the streets of Pointe-à-Pitre, with that air they have of floating somewhere above their bodies and only being there against their will. One day as he saw one of them approaching along the sidewalk he suddenly felt a mysterious desire to slit his throat. There was nothing special about the man, he was just one white flesh among others, with white thoughts running right across the grainy white skin of his brow. Meanwhile Amboise had gripped his knife down in the depths of his pocket and was preparing to stick him like a pig right there in the middle of the Rue Frébault. But at the last moment the thought of what he was about to do stopped him. During the days that followed, the spirit that had entered into him returned to the charge: now it was an unbearable torture, a constant struggle between the longing to cleave a white skin and the horror of doing such a thing. His will was no longer his own, so he went and placed it in the hands of a wizard, who said to him in terror: 'Amboise, my son, I can do nothing for you, for you are inhabited by the spirit of Satan himself and you are under his orders.' And the next day he said goodbye to his friends and plunged into the farthest hills of Guadeloupe, reaching the foothills of the mountains, far from the streets of Pointe-à-Pitre, far even from the canefields, far from any white face. That was how he came to be a sawyer in our forest at Fond-Zombi.

Here, when he spoke of France, people looked at him as if he were a lost sheep that had strayed and seen so many things it had been driven mad. So Amboise fell silent, and as a dumb protest would go many days without opening his mouth. He would often stand bolt upright or lean against a tree, a chair, or the wall of our cabin, all the weight of his body on one leg, the other tracing circles and arabesques on the ground while he calculated and plumbed the depths. His neck would seem to go out of joint, his head was no longer in a straight line with his body but stuck out sideways toward the sun, so that he was forced to lower his eyes to see what was going on below among men. And in his eyes there was a sort of constant alert, as if at any moment he might hear the word that would comfort him forever, as if that word might come from any mouth at any time. But it did not come, he never heard it, for no one here could utter it, and my own mouth was sad and silent. Then he would bend over me and say gently, in a voice that came from the very abyss of solitude and cold, 'Telumee, we have been beaten for a hundred years, but I tell you, girl, we have courage for a thousand.'

We spent such times like two octopi attacked at the bottom of the sea, shooting out ink so as not to see. But he always came back to shore in the end, to the godforsaken land of Guadeloupe that so much needed to be loved. But at first after he got back he would feign indifference, saying man is only a fish that eats other men, and that he had given up blaming sharks. The sky was the roof of the world, the house was vast and various, but the doors were all closed, and there was no way from one room to another. And picking up his old pipe he filled it with an air of longing, and turning to the sky, sent up to it a few puffs of smoke.

With the years these absences from the world grew rarer, then disappeared, giving place to a calm and peaceful astonishment at the Negro's vagaries, his beauty as of something unfinished, something perpetually springing into life. We could only be seen like this by one who had crossed the sea, and known the temptation of being far away from home, of looking at our country through foreign eyes, of denying it. He said enemy hands had got hold of our soul and shaped it to be at war with itself. And now people pricked up their ears and listened to him, because of the way he said all this, and some looked at him wide-eyed, vaguely dazzled, trying to see their wavering lives more clearly. And if someone said the Negro deserved his fate because he couldn't summon up the energy to save himself, Amboise always asked him the same question: 'Tell me, brother, what energy will save the tethered kid from the knife?' And everyone smiled, and we felt we were like the kid tethered in the field, and we knew the truth of our fate was not in ourselves but in the existence of the blade.

When he came to me Amboise was just in his fifties, and since then he had aged steadily, though his body was still full of youth and vigour. That was why people laughed and said, 'You know who I mean? The man with the father's head on a son's body.' All those years had gone by, new streams had come to the rivers, and I hadn't felt the passage of time because of this man who bestowed on me a breath of eternity. Our waters had mingled and merged, and little warm currents ran through them all day long. And at that good time in my life it seemed to me that even the wicked themselves lived in peace, practising a kind of activity indispensable to their fulfilment, and I looked on them with an indulgent eye, the eye I had for the sting of bees, the translucent tail of the scorpion, the plume of those marvellous saffron flowers that poison you at a mere touch of the finger. For our plowing we'd bought an ox that had come to know Amboise's voice, and slowed down to listen when he was saying something interesting. I loved the ox, and every day I congratulated myself on being of this world.

152

Towards the end, in the last few weeks of Amboise's life, strange rumours circulated throughout the countryside and even reached our little cabin on the hill at La Folie. It was said the cutters at Grande-Terre had gone on strike, led by some bold Negroes who knew how to talk to the factory in a way that could really be called talking, and who'd got a raise of two sous for a man and one for a binder. Amboise made no comment on this, but his eyes lit up with a strange gleam that soon appeared in the eyes of all the men around, in La Folie, in Valbadiane, in La Roncière, in Fond-Zombi, and even in the cabins of the Negroes living in the valley, in the very shadow of the factory. The price of food had risen steeply in the last few years, but the tokens with the factory's initials on had not produced any offspring. The shops had closed their credit books long ago, and the people who worked in the canefields grew exhausted, and their children became like birds on the branch, left to the mercy of heaven. Tongues wagged, necks stiffened, and some asked where were the laws of the land if the very shops wouldn't give credit any more. The foremen, who scented trouble, shouted threats from their horses, and galloped uneasily back and forth along the rows of cutters. But the words went on their way and generated other words under the tall heads of the canes. A strike was called, and woe to anyone who went to the fields, for he might find death instead of bread. One evening three men, from Fond-Zombi, Valbadiane, and La Roncière, came to our house and asked Amboise to represent the three communes next morning at a meeting with the factory authorities. The people at Grande-Terre, they explained, had found some clever men to present their grievances to the owners, and that was why they'd got their two sous. But in the out-of-the-way communes around here, Amboise was the only man who had travelled, the only one who could find, in the French of France, words that would both win over the hearer and express the Negro's determination. What did he say?

I saw my man go off into a long reverie, and as he chewed at the stem of his pipe and puffed a wisp of smoke into the air, one of the three envoys said curtly:

'Amboise, what energy will save the kid from the knife?'

Amboise took his pipe out of his mouth, smiled at the reminder of his own words, and said quietly and tranquilly:

'You are right, brother.'

From dawn onwards the hills echoed with lambis shells being blown all over the district, rallying the undecided, the fearful, and the disillusioned. From all sides ragged processions of men in tatters straggled towards the factory, moving forward in a stunned silence, heavy with centuries of fear and bitterness. Once near the factory, a single column was formed with Amboise at its head, followed by the three men who had chosen and sought him out. As soon as the column entered the yard a white man appeared at the top of the steps leading to the office. Amboise stepped forward and said in a high clear voice that shook a little:

'Some cutters came the other day and talked to you and received nothing but threats. What do you think – is a working man a bird? And are his children the young of a bird? I beat my breast and ask you: who toils here, who plants the canefields and cuts them and burns them? But everyone knows an empty sack cannot stand up. It falls, it cannot help but fall. So we have come to ask you if you've decided to make the sack stand up. What is your answer?'

'My answer is still the same.'

And the man from the factory turned on his heel and disappeared. And everyone started to shout and shove, trying to rush into the factory all together to sack it and tear it apart. At that moment someone inside switched on the boilers, which had vents opening into the yard. Jets of scalding steam fell on those jostling one another outside the building. Three were burned to death, including Amboise, others injured, one blinded. The mounted gendarmes who had arrived in La Ramée during the night and been at the ready since dawn, charged the crowd, now bent on destroying both the staff and the buildings of the factory. No one ever found out who had released the jets of boiling steam. Amboise was wrapped up in a sack and carried on four men's shoulders to our cabin at La Folie. After a wake at which no one spoke and there was no singing or dancing, he was carried hastily to the graveyard at La Ramée, for the burns had accelerated the process of decomposition.

At dawn I would go and sit in the shade of our palm shelter and watch Amboise eat, chewing slowly in his pleasure, and then the citronella-scented water would splash over his skin and the smell would fill the air, the inside of the cabin, and even the sheets on our bed. In the evening I would bar the door and the night would go by as of old, in the same glory, the same bodily enchantment that gives and takes and is annihilated. After a few months I was waxen, corpselike. People begged me not to live with a dead man – he would exhaust me and wither me up, and before long the earth would take me in its embrace. I must pull myself together before it was too late, go down to the grave with sharp acacia branches and whip it as hard as I could. But I couldn't struggle against Amboise. I waited for him every evening, and the life flowed out of my body in a continuous stream. One night he appeared to me in a dream and asked me to help him join the dead – he was not properly one of them yet, because of me, just as because of him I was not properly living. He wept and implored, saying I must keep up my position as a Negress to the end. The next day I cut three wands of acacia and went down to the graveyard at La Ramée, and I whipped Amboise's grave, beat it and whipped it.

14

The old men still remember that strike; they called it the Strike of Death. It went on for several days and then petered out, like a wave that comes and goes, leaving a scrap of foam behind it on the sand. As the Negroes had come to their senses and gone back of their own accord, the factory announced that the two sous were granted. For a little while longer the lambis shells kept the earth fresh, damp and shining around the three new graves. Then the sun, the sweet beak of the birds, and the careless feet of children reduced those graves to the common destiny of all. It had all happened too quickly – the deaths of some, the return of the others to the canefields, to life; and heaven sent down disfavour on Fond-Zombi, La Roncière, Valbadiane, and La Folie. There was one waterspout after another, followed by a red sun that burned off the skin in lumps. And in the morning there were never any of those marks as long as a man's body and as light as a child's tread that bear witness here below to the passage of God. Every night you could hear the clanking of chains dragged by the dead, slaves murdered here in Fond-Zombi, La Roncière, and La Folie, where Amboise had bravely perished. And when disease entered the mouths of the domestic animals, people shook their heads and were silent. They understood.

My eyes were two tarnished mirrors that no longer reflected anything. But when people brought me cows foaming at the mouth, their withers covered with black scabs, I did what Ma Cia had taught me, and, first one and then another, the animals began to want to live again. The rumour spread that I knew how to do and undo, that I knew secrets, and with a vast waste of saliva I was raised in spite of myself to the rank of seer and first-class witch. People climbed up to my cabin to put in my hands the grief, confusion, and absurdity of their lives, bruised bodies and bruised souls, the madness that screeches and the madness that is silent, the woes undergone in dreams, all the mist that enshrouds the human heart. I watched them coming with boredom and lassitude, still imprisoned in my own grief, and then their eyes would intrigue me, their voices wake me out of my sleep, their sufferings draw me to them like a kite extricated from the topmost branches. I could rub and massage, I could send back certain darts whence they came, but as for being a soothsayer I was no more a soothsayer than I was the Virgin Mary. Yet people pressed and begged me, forced me to take their troubles on my shoulders, all the woes of body and soul, the shame and scandal of wasted lives. Then I'd light a special candle and make signs, some that I'd learned from Ma Cia and others I'd heard about, and others again that came to me out of nowhere, because of the foam and the cries.

One day there came to my cabin, from the commune of Vieux-Habitants at the other end of the island, a middle-aged woman carrying in her arms a little girl of four or five whose body was covered with running sores. The weather that day was uncertain, with a leaden cloudless sky hanging low over the dark mass of the trees, and I was disturbed by the presence of this woman so afflicted and so far from home. With her eleven children, she had, she said, done enough to increase the world's woe, and this one, the last, might have taken root somewhere else than in her womb. But this seed wouldn't die, although it was the very scrapings of her bowels, and she'd called her Sonore so as to be sure of hearing her and not neglecting her breath of life. She had grown fond of this obstinate little thing, and now. . . . So she had brought her to me, and was handing her over into my charge.

I began to ponder, thinking on my own entrails, which had not born fruit, of the leaden sky, and the woman's distress. And, receiving her child from her hands, I felt something inaudible and long forgotten stirring inside me: it was life. The woman sighed with relief and went away. I started to treat the child with senna, santonica, and the sap of herbs. I gave her baths of cassia lata, put garlic on her joints, rubbed her gently from head to foot. She expelled the worms that had been devouring her, her feeble mewings became real cries, and gradually the abscesses became

157

scabs, then just pink scars that I washed in water warmed in the sun. The child could scarcely stand, but already she tried to follow me everywhere, her face wreathed in an indescribable shy smile. A year went by like that. The mother came to see her and went home alone, reassured. Sonore stayed with me, my young shoot: she put forth all her leaves, she stretched herself out in the light, and when evening came she would sit quite quiet in my lap by the lamp, listening to me tell old tales: Zemba, the bird and its song, the Man Who Tried to Live on Air, and a hundred others – and then all the stories of slavery, of hopeless battles, and the lost victories of the woman called Solitude that Grandmother had told me long ago sitting in the same rocker where I was sitting now. I had begun to grow young again, and several people tried their luck, leaving offerings of crayfish or peas outside my door. But I only laughed and tied ribbons on the little girl's braids: she went down the hill to school now, and would say gravely to anyone who asked her about me: 'She is steel grass, my mother, for she bends before no man.'

Sonore had soft, chubby flesh, and when I touched it I felt as if I had the taste of mango in my mouth. This surprised me, for I'd never heard of such a thing, of any woman having in her mouth the taste of any child. Those who saw her for the first time saw nothing but a soft little sun-charmed animal. She seemed to be made to live, just to live, as the birds sing and the fish swim; her very nostrils inspired such thoughts – quivering nostrils opened wide on the world, perfectly shaped for breathing the air and making her live. But there was something fragile about her still, in the nape of her neck, for example, in the transparent tips of her fingers, in the still hesitant walk that made you think of an infant still, though it was only a hesitation of the soul, a little inner trembling before life. Her frailness, her dependence, her infinite richness astounded me. She was very proud of my talents as a witch, and when I explained my ignorance, my inability to decipher the spirits' messages, she would remain deaf and dumb, thinking it was some kind of ruse. I tried in vain to shed my reputation, restricting myself more and more to rubbing, preparing potions, and helping the little ones into the light with my own hands. I wouldn't take any payment, and people were disappointed and stayed away, thinking that, as sometimes happens, I'd lost the greater part of my power. Then I could get

158

back to my garden, and there I soon noticed that the plants appreciated my influence, apart from the corn and the Angola peas, which didn't like my hand, and certain male trees that need to be looked after by a man. I had produce to sell all the year round, and I was already thinking of adding an extra room to Queen Without a Name's cabin, the first step towards the shop that would one day save Sonore from the canefields. She had left school and taken over from me, washing, cooking, ironing, going everywhere, weeding, knowing everything, ignorant of the world's evil. I had white hair now and dewlaps under my chin. I had fads too, old woman's maunderings, revolving one idea all day long: the hope that is contained in a child. Meanwhile Sonore had acquired certain curves, and I teased her about her 'splendours', as I called her little breasts and buttocks. I told her she was just as everyone who'd seen me said I used to be when I was thirteen: shaped like a guitar. This idea amused her greatly, and she didn't omit to ask me what sort of sound I made when I was played for the first time. And as she bent on me the straight clear beam of her childish gaze, with perhaps a tinge of mischief in the depths of the bright black candid eyes, I grew confused and muttered evasively, in a dream: 'Ah, cunning little octopus! The music was over long ago.'

Curiously enough, since I'd abjured witchcraft some of the local women accused me of paralyzing people's wills and stealing the fruit of their cows' bellies: in short, I had invented and created all man's suffering, I was one to be feared. But Sonore was still with me, and in the evening, at sunset, she would always have a good word to reassure me: 'Well, Ma Tel-Tel, all they say about you is nonsense. People don't know you, they don't know the way you breathe.'

Then she'd come close and put her arms around me protectively: 'Ma Tel-Tel, is it we who weep for loneliness in the evening when we've shut the door behind us?'

She murmured this in a strange, comforting voice, the voice of an adult to a child, and as we started to laugh in the darkness, for pure pleasure like a couple of rascals, I thought within myself that she set off the whole village, as the red canna sets off the whole forest.

*   *   *

159

At about this time a wanderer from Côte-sous-le-vent built a bamboo cabin on the other side of the torrent bounding the plot granted to me by Monsieur Boissanville. He was an old man with a dull sooty skin, and bleary eyes with reddish streaks that lit up innocently at the least sight of a human being. Taken in isolation his features were unremarkable, but they didn't fit one another: you couldn't see what that short flat nose was doing with these delicate feminine eyebrows, this thin indrawn mouth, this perfectly round smooth face, these few tendrils of white hair dotted about the round skull. With his little thin arms that he was always flinging about, he looked rather like a bat; one always expected some strange shrill squeak to issue from his nostrils. He said his name was Medard, but the people of La Folie, with a sort of spontaneous mockery, immediately called him Angel Medard, and this name stuck. He planted a few vegetables, set nooses for raccoons, and presumably lived on grass and fresh air. When, in the evening, a thin column of smoke rose on the other side of the stream, Sonore would say unhappily, 'I wonder whether he's not cooking a pot of stones just to make us think he's having supper too.'

A few days after his arrival rumors began circulating about him. The only name that really suited him was the one given him by the people of his own village: the man with the dancing brain. It was only a play on words, but it gave away the secret of one born to evil. God had made Angel Medard to corrupt the world, and that was why the world had set its mark on him, its own inescapable claw mark. It happened in La Boucan, his native village. One day after some sordid squabble his brother had stabbed him, laying open all one side of his skull: you could still see the place throbbing under the hair. People said that if his head had been whole and the stem of his thighs able to stand and shoot some shining trail into woman's womb, the spread of evil would have known no end. But God himself had set limits to the power He had given him. As soon as this rumour became known, it drove everyone away from him: as they went along the road the children threw stones at his bamboo cabin. Seeing him slink along in his darkness, his head tilted towards the side that was cut open, like a wounded bird, Sonore would say very quietly: 'Ma Tel-Tel, he can't just disappear off the face of the earth, and I beat my breast and tell you these people won't be satisfied until he does.' I didn't quite know what to think, and I said to myself that the wickedness of the Negro is like a gun loaded with blanks, while the wickedness of life is a gun loaded with bullets that pierce and kill you. Shortly afterwards, when I went into the new shop in La Folie, Angel Medard was standing at the counter trying to buy a bottle of rum. A dusty, silvery light was falling from the sky, and somewhere, near the river perhaps, a woman was singing, in a very sweet voice, the story of a deserted lover. Two or three Negroes were chatting on the veranda, glasses of anisette in their hands. The waitress winked at them, then, laughing, put a bottle full of kerosene on the counter. 'Have one', she said to Angel Medard, offering him a glass. He looked confused and turned grey, and seeing this the others laughed all the more. I had asked for a litre of rum, and when Rose-Aimee brought it I pushed it along the counter towards Angel Medard. Meanwhile a thin, disagreeable thread of a voice came out of my mouth and said: 'You haven't ever looked at me properly, do you know that? Haven't you ever noticed I've got a dancing brain too?'

Medard gazed at me out of his dull eyes, in which there arose a little flame of incredulity. Next day he came and stood in our yard, introduced himself, sat down, said nothing, and went away. Gradually he unfroze and used to cut wood for us and bring Sonore wild medlars. He spoke, and no animal howls came out of his throat. He would roam about near us now like a domestic pet that is always under your feet but not in the way. Every morning he would come to our place to drink his coffee, dig a few vegetables, make a furrow, fasten the roof where it had come loose in the wind. Little by little I came to do his washing and ironing, and to leave a place for him at our table. Later, when the rains came and I knew he must be wet as a dog in his bamboo cabin, and I saw him with water running off him every morning and his eyes fierce with lack of sleep, I fixed up a curtain dividing our house in two, and put a mattress down in a corner by the door for Angel Medard. When he came to live in my place the local people thought the world had come to an end, and that this was a sign of the times. An almost imperceptible shudder ran through them when they came near me, and beads of sweat stood out on their upper lip when they talked to me about him, saying he was a well of the world's crimes. Why did I have to go fishing in those troubled waters, when there were so many that were clear and limpid? The people of La Folie knew better than I did, they knew all there was to know about the existence of evil, they could look at one plant and say, 'Water it', and at another and say, 'Burn it.' Evil was in the world long before man, and would still be there long after the human race was annihilated. Thus this particular case had a significance far beyond La Folie itself; it had slipped out of their control, but they would watch the consequences carefully, so as not to go against the will of God. Who I was they no longer knew, but if asses didn't die, what would the vultures live on?

Angel Medard started to surround Sonore with a web of delicate little attentions, green coconuts, pet chicks for her to raise, crayfish, malacca apples, sandals woven by a man's hand that she woke to find waiting by her bed. He gave her dream names, he could transform everything: when it was raining he'd say the sky was blue and go on saying it till the child clapped her hands and said what a beautiful day it was. Sonore's feet, fingers, and eyes were those of a fairy. No dresses or ribbons were too dear, he'd say, scouring the mountains for whole days to bring back a hare or a pair of doves or hearts of cabbage palm that he would exchange at the shop for some trinket. He invented a bird language, and sometimes she would hold out sesame seeds in the palm of her hand and he would peck at them with funny little cries and twists of the head that made her peal with laughter. Then Sonore would stroke his cheek, and he would turn to me and say plaintively that he'd suffered the unpredictable assaults of life, that monster without saddle or bridle, but nothing had ever stuck to his flesh or entered his blood, everything was always new to him and each vile trick retained all its power of surprise, because he had kept the heart of a child. By slow degrees he came to have whims and fancies, imaginary illnesses, gluttonies, all sorts of childish demands I didn't like to refuse because of Sonore's affectionate indulgence towards him. If I was angry he would tell me to relieve my nerves on him to get relief. I was a person of luck, he said, and to contemplate me was all his delight, he, a dead man without happiness. But meanwhile the food would be badly cooked, the mattress scratched him all night, and even his shirts weren't ironed as they used to be. If I swept the floor I deliberately swept the dust in his eyes; if I served something piquant it was in the hope of taking the skin off the roof of his mouth; and when I did Sonore's hair he said I pulled

162

her braids as hard as I could because I was jealous of how beautiful they were. I didn't know what to do – I didn't want to keep him in the house, and I didn't want to turn him out, because of Sonore. People had always avoided him, so that, like a violinist without a violin, he hadn't had a chance to show what he was really like. And now because of me he had an instrument. An early riser, he would use what was left of his brain to hatch tricks that would make me wish I'd never been born. That was his only object really, for life was of no importance to him on his own account. He no longer cut any wood, never pulled up the smallest tuft of grass, kept his precious sweat intact in the marrow of his bones. And if, when Sonore wasn't there, I brandished a knife over his head, he'd repress a smile and take heaven to witness, saying tearfully that a man cannot prevent anything, either his coming into the world or his death. And so as the days went by my brain gradually crumbled, and I could never catch Angel Medard with his hand in the bag of his villainy. I learned later that he'd talked to Sonore in secret about her foster mother Telumee, who got up and lay down with spirits. I was a charmer of children, I only wanted to make use of her in her innocence, delivered over body and soul, hair and sweat into my witch's hands. Who knew whether her mother had left her here, entrusted her to me, of her own free will?

He had harnessed fate's chariot to the child's shoulders, and all he had to do now was crack the whip. One evening when I came in from the garden I found the house empty. While I was slaving down in the valley he had got my child's clothes together and taken her to the main road, where they caught a bus to the commune of Vieux-Habitants. I never saw Sonore again. People say she's living peacefully in her native village, still as bright and smiling as ever, despite armfuls of children. There is a time for carrying a child, a time for bringing it forth, a time for watching it grow and become like a bamboo in the wind. And what is one to call the time that comes after that? The time for consolation. But that evening, sitting alone in my cabin, I didn't yet indulge in such thoughts. I didn't weep, I didn't touch my bottle of rum, I only thought that the door of grief is never shut.

The next day I went down to Rose-Aimee's shop and bought the largest pair of scissors there was, tailor's scissors with big handles so that you could get a good grip. Olympia happened to be in the shop, disheveled, her eyes red-rimmed with rum, her eternal narrow-brimmed hat askew on her head. Seeing what I was buying she came over uneasily and stammered, ashamed like the rest at not having said anything while there was still time:

'Telumee, dear friend, don't soil your hands for an empty bubble. Medard is nothing, less than nothing. It's I, Olympia, who tell you so.'

I gave no answer. I had become a red ant, and I spoke only in the depths of my bowels.

Angel Medard reappeared at the end of the week, early one afternoon, and began to prowl around my cabin in ever-decreasing circles, as if the better to gorge his eyes on my distress and abandonment. But my house was more spotless than ever, the sand in the yard shone like a new sou, and I was in my Sunday best with my hair properly done and decked out from head to foot, going about my business as if to say however fiercely life used its spurs it would never pluck out my feathers. In desperation, Angel Medard went off to the shop and drank without stopping until evening, in a bar deserted by all the usual customers. When night came, a fine moonlit night, white and blue and dusted with stars, I went indoors, shut the door but did not bar it, and went to bed with the scissors open against my stomach, under the bedclothes. Soon I heard cursing and swearing coming from the direction of the road, then the door flew open to reveal an unsteady figure standing in the moonlight against a background of pale sky, bamboos bending in the wind, and mountains huddled together in the distance like a strange flock of drowsy animals. Angel Medard stumbled, lolled his mad head to right and left, raised his arms, let out an oath, then stepped forward and seized all he could lay hands on, glasses, plates, baskets of provisions, chairs, and stools, and hurled them all through the open door. I lay motionless in my bed, with the table still standing between us, between the patch of darkness where I lay and that gale of madness. From time to time he would look at me, and my stillness increased his fury: he waved his arms, yelled that he was my master and would gamble me away at dice whenever he felt like it, and that I was going to go hurtling down, me and my house and my bed, right down to the bottom of the hill, and forever. Then he suddenly rushed at me, a long kitchen knife appearing from nowhere in his hand. But he caught his foot on a chair lying overturned on the floor, went spinning through the air, and a moment later hit the corner of the table, which was driven right into his temple, just in the dancing part of his brain. He let out a terrifying grunt and remained on his knees by the table, his head held down by the wood that had been driven into it. Then there was silence.

Fearing a trick, I held the scissors open still against my chest, under the bedclothes. But after a while Angel Medard began to groan gently, like a baby, and with the scissors still in my hand I got up, lit a candle, and went over to the figure crouched by the table, in the moonlight that reached right into the middle of the room. Angel Medard was rolling his eyes in the darkness, and his hand clutched the wood of the table as if he were trying not to cry out. I went nearer and asked if he wanted me to free him, get the corner of the table out of his head. But he signalled to me not to move, that everything was all right. There was no trace of fear in his face, and his eyes were fixed on me with the astonishment of someone looking not outside but inside himself, someone who discovers, not without but within, something he never suspected till now. Every so often, abjectness would momentarily take possession again of his face, with its slack pinched mouth and eyes that were filling with murky black. It was as if little short twisted branches bristling with thorns were growing through his head, but he at once pruned them back and his eyes were once more like a clear, calm, peaceful river flowing quietly towards the sea. Now I knew what he wanted, what he had always wanted deep inside, below the sac of gall over his heart. Kneeling down, I wiped away the sweat that was streaming down his cheeks and said in a clear, distinct voice that I tried to make as peaceful as his new face: 'We see the crows and we say, They speak a foreign language. But no, the crows do not speak a foreign language, they speak their own language, and we do not understand it.'

Angel Medard smiled and I held his hand till dawn, kneeling beside him, while people gathered in silence outside, gazing at the scene unfolding before their eyes and trying to puzzle out a story, a story with a meaning, with a beginning and an end, as you have to do here below if you want to know where you are amidst the chaos of men's destinies. When morning came they helped me to wash Angel Medard, helped me dress him and lay him out properly

165

on my bed. Someone was already measuring the corpse, and the people of the valley came and went, sprinkling the house with holy water and gazing at Angel Medard's enormous brain under the bandages I'd tied around his head, just above his closed eyes. I sat upright on a little stool, thinking how Angel Medard had assumed the appearance of a man in the world, but he was not a man, for he had never been given a soul. He was a poisonous manchaneel tree growing on the bank, hoping people would touch him and die. I had touched him, and here he was, felled by his own poison. Everyone in this world was given two lungs thirsty for life, but they did not often get to be full of air. The first person who happened along squeezed your lungs in his hands and stopped you breathing, and if you turned yourself into a fish and went under water to breathe, people still said the bubbles your gills sent up into the sun were too bright. That was how it had been with the two of us, Angel Medard and me.

Outside, everyone was getting ready for the wake, in a hubbub of shouts and cries that stopped short at the door of the cabin. Every so often they would peer in at me sitting up straight on my little stool, and give me long curious looks, knowing, expectant, working out and weighing up I knew not what idea, what new delusion. And thus it was all through the night, all through that strange wake. But when the dawn rose on Angel Medard's coffin, the dancing over, the violins put away, the people came to me and said, their faces full of serenity: 'Telumee, dear, Angel Medard lived like a dog and you made him die like a man. Ever since you came to La Folie we have tried in vain to find a suitable name for you. Now you are very old to be given a name, but until the sun has set, anything may happen. So as for us, henceforth we shall call you Telumee Miracle.'

15

It's a long time now since I left off my battle robe, and a long time since I've been able to hear the battle's din. I am too old, much too old for all that, and the only pleasure left me on earth is to smoke, to smoke my old pipe here in my doorway, curled up on my little stool, in the sea breeze that caresses my old carcass like soothing balm. Sun risen, sun set, I am always there on my little stool, far away, eyes gazing into space, seeking my time through the smoke of my pipe, seeing again all the downpours that have drenched me and the winds that have buffeted me. But rains and winds are nothing if first one star rises for you in the sky, then another, then another as happened to me, who very nearly carried off all the happiness in the world. And even if the stars set, they have shone, and their light still twinkles there where it has come to rest: in your second heart.

The town of La Ramée is set on a hill sloping down to the sea. The only hurricane-proof building is the little painted stone church near which I live. There are a few small houses clustered around it, with its modest cemetery where cassias and flame trees cast a great red human shadow over the graves. At the foot of the hill is a vast beach of black sand, which would be very fine with its almond trees and scattered fishermen's cabins deep in foliage, were it not for the huge clouds of mosquitoes always surrounding the men and beasts that live there. The inhabitants say indulgently there never should have been such a place on God's earth, that they made a great mistake in living there, they, their parents or their grandparents, for it is probably a bit of earth that escaped the hand of the Almighty. They have talked like that for a long time, but people are born and die, generations succeed one another and the town is still there, and so everyone has come to admit it will hold out as long as sun and moon are in the sky. La Ramée is really not only La Ramée itself, but also the whole hinterland of which it is the heart – Fond-Zombi, Dara, Valbadiane, La Roncière, La Folie – so that by settling here, with my back to the sea, I am still facing, even if only in the distance, my own great forest.

Up there, near her, near the smell of her, I couldn't forget Sonore. Mothers sent me their daughters to wash and braid and foster, saying I'd find another Sonore there in La Folie, but some mooring that tied me to La Folie was broken. I tried to live in Bel Navire, Bois Rouge, and La Roncière, but nowhere could I find a refuge. One day in desperation I went to Pointe-à-Pitre, but I didn't last long there either. For anyone used to having tall trees, to having the song of a bird to apply to a sorrow, the town is a desert. Without a breadfruit tree, a currant bush, a lemon tree, I felt at the mercy of hunger and beggary, and the country called me. Then St. Anthony in person intervened and set me down here in the town of La Ramée, on a piece of land granted by the commune, behind the church, a few yards away from the graveyard. Here I have an old woman's garden, a little stove, and a pan in which I roast peanuts to sell in the church square. I like to get up with the sun, pick a watermelon, gather up a coconut with its milk cooled by the night, arrange my paper twists of peanuts in a basket, and put it on my head and go crying and selling my wares in the street. While the sun goes about its business, I go about mine. The people here are fond of me – I have only to call a little boy as he goes by and he's off to fetch water for me at once. Sometimes the women of La Folie come and ask me to go back there: 'Mama Miracle, you are the tree our hamlet leans against – do you know what will become of the hill without you?' Then I remind them of what I really am, not a tree but an old bit of dry wood, and I tell them what they are really trying to do is stop me from disappearing under the leaves. They laugh, then go home in silence, for they know I'm only trying to keep up my position as a Negress, to keep up the way I carry my soul. And so I have reached my role as an old woman, tending my garden, roasting my peanuts, receiving visitors standing up on my two legs, and decked in starched skirts so that they can't see how thin I am. And then in the evening as the sun goes down, I warm up my supper, I pull up a weed or two, and I think of the Negro's life and of its mystery. We have no more marks to guide us than

168

the bird in the air or the fish in the water, and in the midst of this uncertainty we live, and some laugh and others sing. I thought I would sleep with one man only and he abused me; I thought Amboise immortal; I believed in a little girl who left me; and yet, without quite knowing why, I don't regard any of all that as a waste of time. It may well be that all suffering, even the prickles in the canefields, are part of the glory of man, and it may well be that looking at it in a certain way, from a certain angle, I may one day be able to grant a certain beauty even to Angel Medard. As I dream like this, night falls without my noticing, and sitting on my little old woman's stool I look up suddenly, disturbed by the phos-phorescence of certain stars. Clouds come and go, a light appears, then disappears, and I feel helpless, out of place, with no reason for being among these trees, this wind, these clouds. Somewhere in the darkness can be heard the discordant notes, always the same, of a flute; they get farther away, cease. Then I think not about death but about the living who are gone, and I hear the sound of their voices, and it is as if I saw the various shades of their lives, the colours they were, yellow, blue, pink or black, faded colours, intermingled and distant, and I try to find the thread of my life too. I hear the words and the peals of laughter of Ma Cia there in her forest, and I think of the injustice in the world, and of all of us still suffering and dying silently of slavery after it is finished and forgotten. I try, I try every night, and I never succeed in understanding how it could all have started, how it can have continued, how it can still survive, in our tortured souls, uncertain, torn, which will be our last prison. Sometimes my heart is rent and I ask myself if we are men at all, because if we were, perhaps we would not have been treated like that. Then I get up, and by my moonlight lamp I look through the shadows of the past at the market, the market where my people stand, and I lift the lamp higher to look for the face of my ancestor. And all the faces are the same, and all are mine, and I go searching, and I keep walking around them till they are all sold, bleeding, racked, alone. I shine my lamp into every dark corner, I go all over this strange market, and I see that heaven's gift to us is that we should have our head thrust into, held down in, the murky water of scorn, cruelty, pettiness, and treachery. But I also see that we are not drowned in it. We have struggled to be born and we have struggled to be born again, and we have called the finest tree in our forests 'resolute' – the strongest, the most sought after, the one that is cut down the most often.

That is how my thoughts go, my old woman's reveries, as the night flows quietly over my fancies, then ebbs with the first cockcrow. Then I stir on my little stool, shake off the drops of dew, go to the little barrel under the gutter, and in my cupped hands I take a drop of water and rinse it around in my mouth to wash away the dreams of the night.

Life is certainly strange. You have hauled your boat up on the beach, fixed it firmly in the sand, and yet if there is a ray of sunlight you feel the warmth, and if anyone pricks this old bit of dry wood the blood still comes.

For a long time, almost half a century, every time anyone happened to speak of Elie, the son of Old Abel, I stopped my ears and walked away, not wanting to know if he was dead or alive, or that he had ever existed. Then in the last few years oblivion started to come, and I heard some say he was dead, others that he was in France, and others again that he lived by begging in Pointe-à-Pitre. Then, quite recently, I was told he was coming back here to die, to lay his bones in La Ramée churchyard, in the hope that some Negro would remember him on All Saints' Day, come and put a candle on his grave and say a few words to him.

After I heard this I stayed home for a few days, listless, revolving all kinds of ancient thoughts, seeing again how the clear water turned into blood. And then the other week, as I was sitting on my stool getting my wares ready for next day, old Elie began to go up and down, without saying anything, by the hedge of rose laurels that separates my place from the road. I was sitting roasting my peanuts, and I saw him going back and forth past the hedge as if he'd forgotten something. I was blind, dumb, and well protected by my laurels, and I watched Elie going up and down the road like a mad ant looking for a nest, occasionally looking towards my hedge with an innocent, childlike gaze. I was sitting down, cold to the marrow of my bones, I thought all God's sun would never make

170

me warm again, and I let Elie go up and down the road, then go away in silence, his back bent over his gnarled stick.

And then last Sunday, as I was doing up my paper cones, I saw through the leaves the same vague ungainly figure, holding the same gnarled stick; and this time a felt hat had made an appearance on the mountain of Elie's hair, as tousled as ever, as dancing, as full of verve and vagary in spite of the snow that covered it. Pulling down the frayed cuffs of his coat, he put his head over my pink hedge and started to call out:

'I said hallo – hallo, everyone!'

His face was all wrinkled, but, how shall I put it, they were not real wrinkles, I saw no hollow or furrow in that skin – it was like a newspaper which you've read and crumpled up, but which has straightened itself out again though it can never be as smooth as it was. Perhaps he had heard the sound of the wings of death and so had dragged himself to me, this man I'd loved as a fish loves the water, as a bird loves space, as the living love the earth. I opened my mouth, but a strange heaviness was on my tongue, and seeing that I went on making my paper cones and filling them with peanuts, that I continued my little routine as if only a warm breeze had blown over the hedge, Elie leaned forward and called through the laurels, 'So that's how it is, is it, Telumee?' And hearing him ask me for a word, just a word of comfort to help him bear the weight of the earth he already felt pressing down on him, I became once more, for an instant, the little girl with wild hair and tight smooth skin that I used to be, and I saw before me the Elie of the old days, the Elie who used to say to me under the flame tree at school, his khaki shorts flapping around his big knock-knees: 'Telumee, if I lose my way in the forest, don't forget that you're the only woman I shall ever love.'

I was choked with tears. An inexplicable shame filled me. All I could say, with a lump in my throat, was:

'Yes. It's very sad – but that's how it is.'

Those few words I couldn't give are the only thing I regret in my whole life.

Today, as I listen to his knell, my 'That's how it is' becomes the sound of the bell and lashes my heart. A liquid light comes down from the sky in waves, spreading out over the earth in layers, like slats in the shutters of a cabin. Through these strange blinds I watch the funeral procession go by. The last rays of the sun fall softly on the coffin, lighting up the dark clothes, caressing the peaceful faces of the little group that follows. There is nothing superfluous or ugly. In this light the smallest pebble, the tiniest leaf in the wind seem to be playing their own tune, behaving with deep wisdom. Though I hardly know why, I am filled with a kind of joy, and I see my own death in an unaccustomed manner, without confusion or sadness. I think of Queen Without a Name, who used to say long ago with a smile: 'Life is a sea without a port and without a lighthouse, and men are ships without a destination.' And she would always be breathless as she said this, as if dazzled by the splendour of human uncertainty. I wonder if people can bear this uncertainty, the sparkling brightness of death. But despite their frivolity about death, and whatever they do, in whatever direction they bustle, whether they chop or cut, sweat in the canefields, hold firm or abandon, or are lost in the night of the senses, there is still a sort of air, a panache, about them. They come and go, make and unmake, in the heart of uncertainty, and out of it all comes their splendour. That is why it seems to me God ought to be jealous even of one like Angel Medard.

I have moved my cabin to the east and to the west; east winds and north winds have buffeted and soaked me; but I am still a woman standing on my own two legs, and I know a Negro is not a statue of salt to be dissolved by the rain. On Sundays, when I meet people from Dara, Fond-Zombi, Valbadiane, or La Folie, they congratulate me on my new well and my electricity. And then they talk – about the tarred road, the cars going over the Bridge of Beyond, and the posts with electric cables coming nearer and nearer, already halfway to La Roncière, in place of the wild tamarinds and balatas. And then I am filled with nostalgia, forget who I am, no longer recognize the age I used to live in. Perhaps it will be said it was barbarous, that age, even that it was accursed, and people will deny it. But how can I care about what will be said tomorrow, when I've become sap in the grass?

As I struggled others will struggle, and for a long time yet people will know the same sun and moon; they will look at the same stars, and, like us, see in them the eyes of the dead. I have already washed and ironed the clothes I want to feel on my corpse. Sun risen, sun set, the days slip past and the sand blown by the wind will engulf my boat. But I shall die here, where I am, standing in my little garden. What happiness!

Study Questions

Suggested exercises for students

1 Comments on *The Bridge of Beyond* for discussion:
   'Madame Schwarz-Bart makes pity for the poor seem impossibly smug.'
   'The entire Schwarz-Bart trilogy draws upon the West Indian tradition of black resistance.'
   'This is poverty gilded over by literature and veiled in exoticism.'
   'In its structure the novel suffers from aimlessness.'
   'By being too close to the landscape, Simone Schwarz-Bart has missed the people.'
   'At the level of style, it's a total success' (M. Condé)
2 Compare the portrait of Telumee's childhood with another West Indian novel of childhood, eg. Geoffrey Drayton's *Christopher*.
3 Compare *The Bridge of Beyond* with Joseph Zobel's *Black Shack Alley*:
   eg. attitudes to French education, choice of settings, use of narrator.
   Rewrite an episode of *Black Shack Alley* with M'man Tine telling the story.
4 Compare *The Bridge of Beyond* with Jacques Roumain's *Masters of the Dew*:
   eg. attitudes to social change, to religion and the supernatural, use of Creole language and culture.

Easier questions

5 Collect six proverbs from *The Bridge of Beyond* and study the versions in several Caribbean Creoles.
6 Chose a proverb from the book and write or retell a story to illustrate it.
7 Make your own family tree.
8 Ask your grandmother to teach you a song or a story.
9 Ask the oldest person you know about their childhood days:
   eg. their favourite foods, ways of cultivating, home remedies.